BREAKS LIKE FLINT

SIMON WHITFIELD

Breaks Like Flint by Simon Whitfield

First published in Great Britain in 2024 as eBook and paperback

Copyright © Simon Whitfield 2024

The moral right of Simon Whitfield to be identified as the author of this work has been asserted in accordance with the Copyright, Designs and Patents Act, 1988.

All rights reserved. No part of this publication may be reproduced or transmitted in any form or by any means, electronic, mechanical, photocopying, recording or otherwise, without the prior permission of both the copyright owner and the above publisher

Paperback ISBN 979-8-3208-0396-8

This book is a work of fiction. Names, characters, businesses, organisations, places and events are either the product of the author's imagination or are used fictitiously. Any resemblance to actual persons, living or dead, events or locales is entirely coincidental.

ACKNOWLEDGEMENTS

Firstly, I'd like to thank a couple of dead people. Raymond Chandler and Raoul Whitfield influenced the style for this novel, and I thoroughly enjoyed reading their books over the past few months.

I'm grateful to my family, my wife especially, for their support and encouragement.

There are others I could name, who read and provided amazing feedback to help me shape this story. You know who you are.

It would be remiss of me not to thank Flint. Yes, he's a character, but he sprung to life in my head one day and dictated the first chapter to me whilst I was driving through Suffolk. I had to pull over and start a voice recording so I didn't lose him!

Finally, thank you readers. I'm hopeful that you'll find something you enjoyed. Working full-time and writing is a tough combination, and it's rewarding to have anyone who isn't a friend and relative reach out and tell me that they enjoyed my story.

I hope you enjoy reading this as much as I enjoyed writing it.

Simon Whitfield

1. A HOT LEAD IN COLD STORAGE

The weather sold me a pack of lies. The November blue sky has no warmth. Wispy clouds turn on me. They grow bigger, angrier as I look up.

There's a chill in the wind. Tells me I should dry my tears before heading outside.

Maybe I deserve everything I get.

The coat's enough to keep the chill off me for the most part. Gonna get my money's worth out of it, even if I gave up on the hat.

The deceptive, cheery sky looms over huge, grey buildings. They're surrounded by strong metal fences. Barbed wire. The works.

In front of it all is one happy-looking one-storey building. Looks like the world's most ill-advised bungalow. It links to the maze behind. A visitor's entrance.

Looks like one of those over-the-top day care places with the bright colours inside.

I guess there are similarities between day care and prison. The biggest difference might be the length of the sentence.

There's some folks back at the office might have made some money off my back this morning. Some would have lost out. Guaranteed that a few of them thought that my first time in this joint, I'd be an inmate, not a visitor.

A man behind the reception desk looks far too happy to be here. Thin face. Intense eyes make his nose an understatement. Light stubble on his pointed chin. Some kinda khaki uniform that makes him look more like a park ranger. Spends his days chasing picnic-stealing bears through forests. Hair's so short it barely qualifies for the name. His temples are stretching upwards, taking out the few remaining hair follicles.

I sign in.

He directs me to a bank of lockers off to the left, round a corner. Gotta put my stuff in there. Can't take anything in with me.

The only thing I keep, beyond the clothes on my back, is the police ID, hanging around my neck on a breakaway lanyard.

I'm passed on to an overweight, short man with a chrome dome and a bad attitude. He's in a grey outfit. Police-like. Unflattering. He leads me the rest of the way.

I'm walking outside, across a courtyard, back in another building opposite.

I follow through some corridors and up a flight of stairs.

No small talk from this guy. Nothing medium-sized or larger, either.

Upstairs, there's a row of small rooms. Glass walls. Glass doors. A table and four chairs in each. Not much space for anything else.

I'm led to the one right in the middle. All the others are empty. No idea why we're using this one.

I take a seat. He closes and locks the door behind me. Stands there. Gets on the radio.

Another guard appears through the secure door opposite. A short, platinum-haired broad with a face that tells you there's no good in the world. She ushers in the prisoner. Closes the door. Locks it. Watches on.

Elias Wilkins looks on at me. A smirk on his slightly lopsided face. A couple of scars on his cheeks that I don't remember being there. But he's still got charm. Despite his disfigurement, his lack of two fully working arms. His current living arrangements aren't even making a dent. A swagger. An engaging, friendly quality.

"I didn't think you'd be so keen to see me," I say.

He gives me that James Bond smirk I remember. "Likewise."

"It ain't a social call, Elias. You know things."

He cocks his head a little. "What sorta things?"

"About the folks that hired you. I know the Heathrow stunt was your baby, but someone invested heavily in it."

He shakes his head. "My idea. All the way. Had to sell nearly everything to keep it going."

I lean back. Let out a sigh. "I thought you might wanna see if there were any angles to play to secure an earlier release."

He laughs. "Release? For what? I've got nothing left."

I stare at him. He almost believes what he's saying. Almost.

"My house and my bank accounts are proceeds of crime now. I've got less pounds than you've got pet sharks. What the hell would I do with freedom?"

I shrug. "Put that mind of yours to something constructive. Invest whatever money turns up when your stint's done."

A smile. Starts small on his face. Gets bigger. "You're talking like you know things."

I nod. "No recording devices in here. I can't even write anything down. No lawyers. No one's gonna make things worse for you."

He sits back. Folds his arms. "What's my incentive to talk?"

"A clear conscience," I say. "Plus, if your knowledge helps, I could put in a word. Move up some hearing or other."

"And I assume you're gonna forget about anything I've got cheesed away?"

I shrug. "Couldn't prove it one way or another."

He leans forward. Rests his wrists on the table. "Seems mighty friendly for a guy who's lost so much from what I did."

I shake my head and look at my feet. "There's a couple of folks I wish were still around. I guess I can blame you for it."

He nods. Nice and slow. Smiles a little.

"But there are people who mean a lot to me now. People I've got to try and save. Gotta mean more than those already turning into worm food."

He cranks his head to his left. Stares at a wall as bland as any you'll ever see. "Not got a lot to spill, to be honest."

I lean forward. "Keep being honest. Tell me what you know."

He takes a couple of deep breaths. Looks around. "I could feed you some yarn. Make you run around in circles. What would you do about it?"

I shrug again. "Nothing. That's the point. I can do something to make your life a little easier, or I can leave you to rot in here. Your choice."

Quiet.

It goes on too long as he thinks.

"None of this was personal to you. I didn't mean to take out your partner. Break up your marriage. No one was gonna get hurt with my original plan."

"Who changed it?"

"VIRTUS," he says.

It's the name I'm expecting to hear. Still know nothing about them.

"You checked my phone?" he asks.

I nod. "You found the app? The one they use to communicate?"

I nod like I know what he's on about. Let him carry on.

"Yeah, they pushed me. Fed me ideas. Said they'd only pay up if I did things their way."

I nod. "And they dropped you like a stone when you walked in here."

He nods. "That's what I've got to let you and everyone else think. I'm hoping they'll remember me when I'm cut loose."

"If I get my way," I say, "there ain't gonna be anyone left to do anything for you when you taste freedom again."

He smirks. "What if they've already set something up?"

I shrug. "Between you and them. I just wanna find them. Stop them ruining any more lives."

He laughs. "Come on! I had your partner killed. Your trainer too. Shot your wife in the foot. You're gonna help me? You're gonna let me walk outta here with more dough than you're gonna make in a decade?"

I give him a hard stare. "They've got my girl and my kid. I'd let anything go. I'd sign release papers, hand over a few grand myself, if I thought it would get them back."

"You think you're gonna guilt me into dropping a dime here?"

I nod. "You've got one move. You take it, or you don't. We find out someone set you up, pulled the strings, maybe even ordered some of those kills. We do that and you're gonna be outta here pretty quick."

He nods. "You get your family back. I get my payday and my freedom, and we stick it to the people who put me in the cooler?"

I nod. "What do you wanna know?"

"Tell me everything," I say. "From the beginning. If it's gonna get me some place, I'll stop you."

He nods. Looks down at the table. "Then I hope that chair's more comfortable than it looks. It's quite the story."

2. THIRD TIME'S A CHARM?

Big ideas come undone because of the smallest thing.

The major players in their organisation are seeing things his way.

Trusting an entire plan to one main guy? Lunacy.

It didn't work with Elias.

It sure as hell didn't get any better with Graham.

Sure, there was one common denominator in both of those. Enoch Flint. The scourge that can't seem to stay away. Attracted to VIRTUS projects like a moth to a lightbulb.

What are the chances of him being a spanner in the works a third time?

Got to turn the tables. Flip this whole thing on its head.

Instead of threatening Flint to back off, how about they make him the centre of everything?

Yes, he's gonna go nuts trying to save his family. He'll learn soon enough that it's not gonna work. Especially if he's the one put at the centre of this.

Yeah, there will be other pieces moving around the board. This time, they're gonna be small-time. Desperate, impressionable people. The kind with little-to-nothing to lose and something to gain.

They ain't gonna have all their eggs in one basket this time. Spread the load. How hard is it to put out ten small fires in different spots than to put out one big one?

But it's all pointed at this guy. The one who keeps showing

up. The one they've got on a short leash right now, but he could snap the thing and run off at any moment.

But even a loose cannon can be predictable. You push some of Flint's buttons, he's only gonna react one way.

There's a plan coming together.

Make Flint out to be the nut he is. He's not a hero. He's a man who stumbles blind into stuff. Needs a lot of digging out of holes. Gets people around him killed.

If they start the party without him, he's only gonna gatecrash it anyway. Might as well make him the guest of honour.

The disaster of a detective is flying right towards the eye of the storm.

The best thing about it all is that he's not got a clue what's ahead of him.

3. WHAT A LOAD OF APP

The much-discussed mid-life crisis.

I thought I'd already fought those demons. Or given in to them.

Turns out, they don't come at you all at once.

Got myself wondering how long I can do this and keep what little sanity I've got left.

I wake up. Flick's side of the bed is cold. Of course it is.

No noise from the boisterous kid down the hall. Not that I can hear, anyway.

A quiet, empty house. Even with me in it. I'm a shell of a guy in a shell of a place.

Gotta go through the motions. Get up. Get dressed. See if I can stomach breakfast today.

Head to work. It's the thing that gives me purpose. They're all on my side, for once. They're gonna help me get my family back.

I hunt through some digital archives. I find Elias Wilkins phone results. Nothing conclusive on there. A few messages that could mean different things to different people.

I look through a list of apps. Wish he'd given me the name of the one they used to contact him. Something about media management.

I need some geek to go through this. Someone who knows what the hell these installed apps are. Rule a few things out. For me, a phone's still for making calls. An idea foreign to those from Generation Z.

Maybe I'm going about this all wrong.

I pick up the phone and ask for Police Scotland. A couple of spots on hold, and I'm on with Detective Sergeant Fiona Inness. She ain't the top brass anymore. Didn't take them long to ship another DCI to the islands.

"You got the full forensics from Graham Craigie's phone yet?" I ask.

"You still looking for a link to the people who've got your family?" She replies with a question.

"Gotta look in every nook and cranny. No matter how many spiders I flush out. Got a phone here from an old suspect. I wanna compare the two. See what apps they've got in common."

"I'll send something over."

The whole personal tragedy thing sucks, but it's an angle that gets you sympathy and quick results.

It ain't long until I'm looking at two lists, side-by-side. Wilkins and Craigie. Two people taken on by this secret group. Two who had their plans blown up like a small detail in a photograph. Had them taken apart like they'd been built from kids' building blocks.

There's a whole heap of things they've got in common. A couple of the big social networks. Some TV catch-up stuff. Nothing on here that screams conspiracy. That yells out that they're some combo of hired goons and terrorists.

I turn to my left. Stop myself.

He ain't there anymore. Can't ask his opinion.

The chair still sits empty. They've not got around to filling it with anyone new. Not sure if it's a mark of respect or a chance to save a buck.

Could have used Jasper right about now. This was more his thing than mine.

Failing that, getting on the blower, and getting Liam to throw his oar in. That ain't happening either. One of the few I've worked with that ain't dust to dust nor ashes to ashes. He threw a grenade into his police career and high-tailed it to the private sector.

But we got a new analyst.

A pretty gal from Dubai, of all places. Nahid Shamoon. Early thirties. Big, dark eyes. A wide nose that sits well on her face. Infectious smile. Very long, black hair. Dresses in business suits that could've come from a catwalk show. I thought everyone with money from the Emirates could be related to a Crown Prince. I'm not about to ask such stupid questions. The jewellery, makeup and outfits could be left over from some sugar daddy relationship. Could even still be going on. I'm not gonna pry.

She sits in the same massive office Liam vacated in a hurry. Got just as many screens on the go.

I ask if she's got a few minutes to eyeball the phone results. She's happy to take a look. I remind her that it's to help find my missing partner and kid. She sighs and nods. She already knows chapter and verse about it. So does everyone else in the building.

I'm walking back into my office when my phone rings.

Maybe Nahid works as quick as Liam used to.

But it ain't her.

I answer it.

Walk to the office next door. Try to wave and get someone's attention. They're gonna want to know about this.

4. SOMETIMES DEAD DROPS KEEP FOLKS ALIVE

"Mr Flint, I believe you were expecting our call."

Got to be a fake voice. False accent. A prim, proper, calm male voice.

No one talks like the butler Jeeves anymore, whatever American TV would have you believe.

Only one person used the Queen's English. That was the Queen.

"Someone said you'd be getting in touch," I say.

TV's no doubt got you thinking of the kinda getup near me when I answer. Some tech guy takes my phone, does something with it, hands it back. I'm in a room with crazy flashing red lights. Someone listening in on some oversized headset. Someone's looking at a map on a computer screen, zooming in. Tracing the origin of the call.

Except real life ain't like that. Not in my world, anyway. Could be different in the high-level places. Maybe spies and terror police have all the toys. We don't. All I've seen anyone do with a call is stuff after it's over.

I'm in DS Dobson's office, right next to mine. DI Chamberlain walks in and sits down. They both stare at me. I put the call on speaker and hold it in front of me like some pastry I'm about to take a bite out of.

"I believe, Mr Flint, that we can make the current situation mutually beneficial. For you, but also for the organisation I represent."

I shake my head. "I ain't looking to benefit you or your

organisation. All I wanna do is get Flick and Toby back."

"That's why I'm calling."

I get up and pace the room. "Come on then. Let me have it. What is it I've gotta do?"

"Sir, I believe you may have made some incorrect assumptions. Are you of the belief that we would simply ask you to do one thing, and that your family would be free to go? You would be free, so to speak, and able to interfere further with our goals?"

"So tell me what I've got to do. Tell me I've got to leave you alone. Seems simple enough."

There's a polite laugh on the line. "I'm sure it appears simple to you. You see, we're a complex organisation. Some detailed plans have been laid waste by your meddling."

I clench a fist. "I was only doing my job. You must be able to understand that."

"Doing your job? How about when you were removed from the Heathrow investigation? Were you doing your job then? You were suspected of killing your wife. Your job was on hold. And yet, you persisted."

"I had to clear my name. I couldn't just stop-"

"And the same was true only a matter of days ago," the man says, interrupting. "You were hired to find a missing girl, and yet you stayed after the body had been found. Your client fired you, and you stayed."

"I had promised some people I'd help. I couldn't just cut and run."

"Even after little Toby disappeared, you stayed."

I'm squeezing the phone now at the mention of the kid. "I couldn't get out by then. I was locked in. Don't blame me because you hired some unreliable nutcase to do your bidding."

There's a pause for a second. Is that some kinda classical music playing in the background? Who is this guy? What's he gonna do when he gets off the phone? Sit in his parlour in a smoking jacket? sipping expensive brandy he pours from his crystal decanter? Roaring fire surrounded by some fancy marble mantle?

"Yes, we have indeed made mistakes, Mr Flint. So have you. I suggest you think carefully about the offer I am about to make."

I pace around a little more. Take a couple of deep breaths. The stuff that's supposed to calm you down. It ain't doing a thing for me.

"Firstly, a man will drop a package to you in the next few minutes. You see the construction work taking place outside your building?"

I look out the window. Nothing out the back. Must be the other side.

"Of course you can't. Not from your measly office. Apologies. It's outside the front of the SITU premises."

I stop looking out the window at nothing but a drab car park. "Okay."

"A somewhat dishevelled individual, who is, shall we say, between dwellings..."

Takes this guy forever to say anything. Wish I could listen to him double-speed. Might just about be tolerable.

"There is a temporary fence around that construction area. This homeless man will drop a supermarket carrier bag just inside it. You will need to collect it."

I shake my head. "You expect me to then take some unknown, suspicious package back into a police building? You think I'm stupid?"

"My thoughts about you are entirely my own," he says. "We expect, however, that you'll take whatever actions you see fit. You can rest assured that nothing in this package is designed to hurt you, nor anyone else."

"You expect me to trust you?"

"I expect you to do what I'm asking you to do, not out of trust, but out of necessity."

I can picture this guy. White privilege. Greying hair. Slim build except for the gut of the rich and well-fed. Thin face folks would pay to punch. An expression that's supposed to ooze class and patience. Instead, it screams overbearance and condescension. Hell, been on the phone with the guy for five minutes. Already, pretentious words are falling outta my subconscious. It's like blood from a new wound.

"This conversation has already gone on too long. I'm sure you'd agree."

Five seconds was too long.

"If you could please install the app named Extra Media Manager on your phone. It is free to obtain from app stores. Once you have the app, simply open it, and tap the play button three times within a second or two. Cheerio."

He hangs up on me.

I get to work finding the app. One of thousands of apps like it.

DI Chamberlain stands up. Looks at my phone screen. "This

the app that was on the other phones?"

I nod. "Pretty sure it was on both lists."

I tap the play button three times.

Sure enough, something happens.

A new screen appears over the old one. A chat window. Says messages are encrypted with a proprietary algorithm. Might as well be talking to me in Russian.

A first message appears.

> I see you have the app installed, Mr Flint.

I reply with one word.

> Yes.

I wait a few seconds while they type out a reply.

> We do not tend to talk long on the phone for obvious reasons. We had this app built, among others, to communicate with our people, and to track them. I'm sure you understand our precautions.

He ain't any more frugal with words on a chat.

> You must not open the package. Deliver it to the Belvedere Arms Hotel, which overlooks your harbour in Cookston. A man will be sitting in one of two armchairs in the lobby reading a newspaper. You will sit in the other one, place the package on the floor, and leave.

> 1900hrs tonight.

He didn't ask if I already had plans. I guess he somehow knows already.

The messages start to disappear, starting with the first.

I sum up so someone can write this stuff down.

DS Dobson chirps up. "Flint, are you really gonna drop off a package? Pick the thing up, drop it off, without knowing what you're delivering?"

I shrug.

"It could be anything. Drugs. Weapons."

I sigh and turn to face the window again. "You think that hasn't already crossed my mind?"

"You want to be strung up for getting stuck in the middle of some illegal trade?"

I shake my head. "I don't wanna do any of this, but what choice do I have?"

DI Chamberlain wades in. "Flint, you've got to pick up this package. You've got to drop something off at that hotel. We get that."

I stare at her. Let her get to her point. "Just include us. We've got a little time to come up with something."

I smile. Nod once. "Wasn't planning on taking this on alone."

5. WHATEVER IT FAKES

Get the package. Get forensics to check it out. Leave it intact and deliver it.

Doesn't seem like a tricky set of things on the to-do list. Not on the face of it, anyway.

Get the first part done. No problem. Less drama than a night at home with the kids.

I walk outside.

Six feet high temporary metal fencing is sitting up on those concrete feet. All the pieces held together with zip ties.

Throws my head right back to the cathedral. Not that zipping together waist-high barriers would've stopped anyone. Wouldn't have saved the life of the one police officer I could've called a friend. A better floor would've helped.

I see the shopping bag. It sits in a gap big enough to fit a kid's arm through. But a stroke of luck. These metal fence panels round in at the corners. Gives me enough room to get my hand in there and pull the bag free.

Only one thing inside the bag. Looks about the size and shape of a DVD boxset covered in brown paper. This is what I'm reduced to.

Can't imagine they'd go to this much trouble for something like that. If I'm wrong, these people have gotta start looking up delivery companies. There's a heap of them touting for package customers. Sure, some of their prices are sky-high, and others are a little worse. Even if with the chance you're taking on a driver. They could throw your package over a hedge and called it delivered.

I head back to the office. There's a note on my desk.

Go speak to forensics. Take the package.

I take a walk through the building. We've got a small forensics team, but they're well-stocked with gadgets.

Small's the word today. Only one guy there when I knock on the door.

Jayden's family has been in Hampshire for at least two generations before him. Doesn't stop him looking like he could've migrated from northern India last week. A cheery expression's written on his roundish, half beard-covered face. He's old enough to be knocking on the door of middle age. Young enough that I ain't got much common ground with the guy.

Never seen him without a smile.

Maybe he's single. Loves the life.

Maybe he's married to a perfect, patient wife.

Maybe it only takes a good lunch from the local bakery to put him on cloud nine.

Either way, he's happy to help. Overjoyed, even, at having something interesting to poke his nose into.

He sets the package on the table with blue gloved-hands. Examines the thing from every angle. Pulls out a ruler and measures it. Walks off into a back room.

He leaves me alone with the package, staring at me from the desk. Begging me to rip it open. To hell with their demands.

He returns with a heat gun. He gets to work on warming up the tape until he can peel it enough to open the thing.

He's taking it seam by seam, fold by fold. Reverse

engineering the wrapping. He's like a teenager who can't wait for Christmas. Has to go and ruin the surprise.

He's got the first part off. He's got tweezers on the go. Opens out each fold. Heats up another strip of tape. Peels it away. Does the same with another.

He's still got that smile on that face. It's lurking just beneath an intense look of concentration, but it's there.

I wanna shout at him. Hurry up.

Another couple of folds in the brown paper. Starting to think it's been wrapped up in layers for a kids' party game.

Seems like forever has passed since I picked up the package, but he's finally got the paper removed.

It's a wooden box. A thin, sliding plywood lid. The thing's the size of a teenager's jewellery box, but not as fancy.

I'm thinking Jayden's gonna stop there. Tell me to leave the room in case it's filled with some deadly powder that's gonna puff out when the lid slides back. It ain't huge, but it could be big enough to take the nose off my face if it's full of explosives.

I'm ready to back off. Go and at least put on a motorcycle helmet. Maybe go alert the bomb squad.

But he's not messing around. Before I can say not to open it, he's slid back the lid.

He looks at its contents for a second. He stares at me. I stare at him. We're doing a damn good job of imitating each other. Confused looks all round.

A small stack of pamphlets.

He sets the box off to the side a little and spreads out the pieces of printed, folded paper. A couple are political.

Advertising the virtues of some wannabe MP or council official. A couple are religious. Offers to send away for a free bible. My last suspect could've saved himself some grief (and a police interview) if he'd had one of these.

About the only kinda leaflet missing is some sort of takeaway service. One's about pet rescue. One's about raising funds for a blind organisation. They don't mean much of anything when you put them together.

"Is this some sort of prank?" Jayden asks with a smirk.

I shake my head. "My pranks are a little more obvious."

My mind goes back to old TV shows where a host would secretly swap out someone's car with one that looks identical. When the supposed owner comes back, he'd smash it with a wrecking ball, drop a piano on it, something crazy. If I'm getting into the prank game, I'm going big like that guy. This stuff's small potatoes.

We've gotta spend the next five minutes looking through them, shrugging at each other.

He lays them out. Unfolds them. Takes pictures of each side. Someone's gonna ask what was inside, and without the snaps, they're not gonna believe what we say.

Maybe we get the image technicians to cast an eye. See if there's some hidden message in these somewhere.

"I was asked by the boss to check it out. Maybe make a substitute, if it was something dangerous." He picks up the leaflets, pushes them into a pile again. Flicks through them like a guy at a strip club with a fat fist full of singles. But this ain't some seedy place and he ain't in the chips.

"Can't see anything dangerous about these," I say, "Unless you factor in the chance you just took of getting a paper cut."

He puts them back in the box. Shakes his head. "Don't joke about paper cuts. They can hurt like hell."

I look at his face. He's serious.

The thing about forensics, I guess, is they show up when the action's almost done. They're on the scene to look backwards and figure stuff out. A hell of a lot safer than figuring stuff out from the other end. Your biggest risk of injury in forensics is gonna come from not looking where you're going.

Same could be said of someone like me, I guess.

I walked blindly into something. Put myself in the pocket of this mystery organisation.

But why on earth am I dropping off a few old leaflets? Who wants these?

Jayden's done putting the package back together. Wraps the thing back up. Has to use new tape.

I'm no expert, but the thing looks untouched by the time he's done.

"I had some stuff ready in the back room to make a fake for you, but no one's gonna sign off on that." He hands the package back to me. "Go tell the Inspector about this. She's gonna get a kick out of it. Pretty sure she's not gonna stand in the way of you delivering a few pieces of paper."

I nod. Thank him for taking his life in his hands.

Maybe I'll catch up with this guy again some time. See what it is that's got him so happy.

Maybe it's fun little pranks like this. For all I know, this is a typical day for the guy.

But I've been here a few years. Never seen him before.

Some lingering thought tells me I ain't gonna see much of him, or anyone else in this building, if VIRTUS get their way.

6. I'LL HANDLE WHATEVER THEY LOBBY AT ME

Hotels ain't my scene.

I've stayed in enough of them down through the years. Can't say I've found one as welcoming as TV and magazine ads claim they're gonna be.

Usually some dead eyed unsympathetic gee on the front desk. You get their attention. Takes them a second to stick that polite grin back on. Pretend they give a damn, or even a part of one.

Whether you lay down scraps or decent dough doesn't make so much difference in places like this. Your stay is still only as good as the fellow guests.

Even expensive rooms might fall victim drunkards. The loud, singing, door-slamming types plague the hallway at all hours. An expensive door is just as likely to get some clueless fool showing up. They get their numbers mixed up. Try to join you for the night. A couple of hundred's never given me thicker walls to block out the overly amorous couple next door. You're still gonna hear the shout-everything-you-say types. Even though they could be a couple of rooms over.

No, my scene is more like the white night trap on the ground floor, off to the left of the lobby.

Still, the Cookston High Harbour Hotel is a step above the usual places I visit. I've been allowed to wallow near a cheap drink in worse. I've been kicked out of better.

Even so, the big glass wall that enshrouds the place. Add the flags of twenty random countries at the entrance. It all says something. Maybe it's 'we're trying too hard'.

Maybe it's a front to ward off folks like me. The kind who baulk at the drink prices and wonder out-loud how ice and water can ever cost so damn much.

I breeze on through their oversized double doors. The lobby is straight ahead. A dozen comfortable cream leather seats sit on a dark tiled floor. They're in bunches of two and three. Gathered around thick, once-bright rugs. It's all sandwiched by ugly, bland paintings.

There's a faint perfume to the air. I can't place it.

Music's coming from a load of hidden speakers. Bach's Brandenburg Concerto Number Three. Fancy music for fancy digs.

I know I don't look the classical music type. Can't say I started out that way. But troubles come along and stick in your head. It's nice to at least hear some peaceful music alongside. Gotta close my eyes every now and then. Wish the world away. Deep breaths, and just listening to soothing melodies. Push the world outta my head for as long as possible before it finds a way to force itself back in.

A long, L-shaped reception desk to the right. Four people stand behind it. They're hoping to God I'm an Uber driver.

In my long coat, carrier bag in my left hand, I could be anything. Could be lost and looking for directions. Could be meeting a friend who's on their list. My duff duds could be a red herring. Could be one of those secret shoppers. Show up, wait for the staff to turn up their noses. Refuse me all kindsa stuff. Then I get to rub their noses in my wealth. Then tell them they're fired before gliding towards the nearest exit.

Makes me smirk. If only.

Relief fills their faces when I don't head towards the desks.

I head for one armchair, facing away from the door. It's stuck behind a squared pillar.

The guy sat in it might look conspicuous if we were twenty or more years ago. He's maybe mid-to-late twenties. Wearing an instantly forgettable suit. Holding a broadsheet newspaper out and actually reading it. Most folks get their news from their small-screened devices these days. Maybe he's old-fashioned. Somehow born later than I was, and came out like a forty-year-old.

My footsteps echo off the tiled surfaces. I step on the rug and it's like my feet have gone radio silent. I take a load off in a seat to the left of the other guy's, pointed at ninety degrees to encourage polite conversation. I put the bag down between the chairs.

The guy sniffs. Keeps reading.

A couple of seconds later, he looks left. Looks down. Sniffs again.

It's the most pointless of dead drops.

If I'd have just left the thing alone, not looked inside, I wouldn't have felt as self-conscious as I feel right now.

The newspaper guy sniffs again. If only the broadsheet was made of tissue paper.

I glance around the room. Pretend to admire the artwork on the walls.

"This it?" He says. Sniffs again. "You the guy?"

I shrug. "I guess I'm a little more presentable than the homeless guy who left this outside my workplace."

He looks at me. All serious. Almost angry.

He looks back at the newspaper. Sniffs again. "Maybe go get yourself a drink from the bar. Drink a little of it before heading back out. Give yourself a little time, so you don't look so obvious."

Advice on blending in? From this guy? The one who's sniffing every few seconds? The only one I've seen reading a big newspaper in public in the last five years?

I nod and go to stand up. "You want anything while I'm heading over?"

A shake of the head. Another sniff.

I wanna ask if he wants a pack of pocket tissues. Nasal spray. Anything.

I'm anything but upset to leave the bag and the news-obsessed guy with the blocked sinuses.

I head to the bar. I ain't even glancing back.

I get the smallest of gin and tonics. It's gonna cost as much as a large one in the places I'd pick.

A few sips when it finally arrives. Okay, but not worth what I paid.

I turn around for a second. The man's gone. So is the package.

I cast my eyes over the sea of partly filled bottles along the wall the other side of the bar. Nothing much to see.

I look around the smattering of small tables and hard wooden chairs. Only one other guy, the other side. Could be a pint of lemonade. No one but me's hitting the hard stuff just yet.

Windows stop this part looking too gloomy. Big, floor-to-ceiling ones. A near-perfect view out over Skeleton Quay. It's chalky, finger-like protrusions have occasional bobbing pleasure vessels in between.

To the left a few buildings is the park. The one where Jasper found me to share some bad news. The one Toby was playing in, until he wasn't.

I could keep drinking here, but the stuff in my kitchen at home's a great deal cheaper. It's only a ten minute walk away.

I drain the glass and put it back on the counter.

I get up and head for the door.

No one cares I'm there.

No one's gonna start asking about the two men who met in the lobby. The package that changed hands.

What the hell was the deal with the package anyway?

Why jump through these hoops for some pointless pieces of paper?

How is any of this gonna help get Flick and Toby back?

I clear the car park and walk along the streets in the darkness. I take the long way around, avoiding cutting through the park. Not a spot I find too relaxing anymore.

Like so many places around here, it's like a guy poking me in the ribs, asking me if I remember this and that. Most of it bad. Most of it probably my fault in one way or another.

7. ONE LAST CHANCE

The cold, empty house is still as cold and empty when I get back.

No miraculous freeing and delivery of partner and son just yet.

How long do I need to wait?

I've never done the bidding of a secret organisation before. Could be they take a while to sort out delivery. Don't have any clue if they work like Amazon, or more like the Royal Mail on a bad day.

I head to my study. The one place here I can stand being without the other two.

I buy a drink from the bottle in my desk drawer. I stop. Put the bottle away. Look around.

Nothing's changed.

I reach for the bottle again. Some kinda swirling oblivion is better than a grim reality.

I twist the top loose from the bottle, but I don't get any further than smelling the contents.

A message arrives on my phone.

Here we go.

I'm about to see what happens next.

I pick the thing up.

Gotta remember what the folks at work wanted me to do. I swipe down from the top. Hunt around. Find the screen recording option and set it going.

Open the app. Do the secret opening thing with the play button.

First message shows up.

> You didn't follow our instructions.

I frown and I tap out a reply with my stubborn fingers.

> Yes I did. I dropped the package off at the hotel for that guy.

I wait a few seconds. Another one arrives.

> You didn't follow ALL of my instructions.

Shows they're still typing. Maybe the booze has already hit hard, but I can't seem to figure if I'm talking to one person or a host of them. The follow-up message arrives.

> You opened the package inside the police station. You checked the contents and resealed it.

I guess I need to tread carefully. I type out a reply.

> How do you know the guy who put it there didn't open it up?

I get sent two photos of the package, sealed up exactly as I got it.

Another message being typed.

> It was sealed up with different tape. Shows up differently under our test light.

I've had enough of this. I've jumped through enough of their damn hoops already. My thumbs rush around putting my anger into words.

> What's the big deal? It was only pointless leaflets. Had to make sure I wasn't taking a bomb into the station. Had to check I wasn't making myself an accessory in some crime.

A quicker reply this time.

> You had your reasons, but you didn't follow instructions.

I reply again.

> What now?

Another quick reply.

> We will discuss and get back to you.

The conversation ends. All messages disappear a few seconds later.

I stop the recording.

I get on the blower to Inspector Chamberlain.

"They're saying I didn't follow their instructions. They know we opened the package. Sealed it again."

She swears. "Not sure the difference it makes," she says. "Wasn't anything valuable, but it must've been a test."

"See if I'd do what they wanted, no questions asked?"

"I guess so."

Quiet for a moment.

"What next?" she asks.

I shrug. "They're discussing what to do next. Might've screwed up."

"Flint," she says, "They want people on the inside of different places. It's valuable to groups like this. Someone they can use to cover their tracks. They're not gonna cut you loose because of one slight failure."

I let out a sigh. "I hope you're right."

She tells me to get some sleep. Let her know what happens if they come back soon.

The phone's not been on the desk for more than a minute before another message comes in.

I start another recording. Open the app. Tap the play button. Another message is waiting.

> One more chance, Mr Flint.

That's it? What does that mean?

> Something is going to happen around you. The way you respond will tell us whether you're serious about seeing your family again.

That doesn't clear up anything.

No more messages.

The ones that were sent vanish again.

I stare at my phone.

Don't know how long I'm doing it for.

I messed this up.

I had one good chance. I had to listen to the boss. Do what they said. Might as well have loaded a gun for Flick and Toby when I let the guy in forensics open it up.

But I can't see a situation where I'd have done a dead drop any other way. No chance I was doing it without knowing what I was dropping. I'm too curious. Not trusting enough.

And why the hell would I trust these people?

What have they done but make my life a misery for the past few months?

They've taken people from me. So many people I care about. Most ain't coming back.

Why should I do anything they want?

But the answer's there on my wall.

A photo of the three of us. Not often you see that kinda smile on my face.

I reach for the bottle again.

I ain't got any answers to my own questions.

This bottle's not gonna magic up any solutions.

But the solution inside's gonna make it all seem like it doesn't matter for a while.

With each gulp of the harsh amber liquid, I'm getting farther and farther from useful. A hell of a way to get back to caring.

I'm gonna feel rough in the morning. Make my outsides match my insides.

Maybe if I drink enough, I won't wake up.

I wonder what kinda conversation VIRTUS will have then.

8. FANCY A BREAK (IN)?

The computer screens might as well be melting my eyeballs right outta my head.

The guy next to me's just made himself a drink with the cheapest of cheap teabags. He's moving that spoon around, again and again. Messing with the cloudy brown stuff like he can somehow make it taste less like dirt with sugar mixed in.

Every sound the spoon makes against the side of the mug's like an alarm going off. He takes the spoon out. Puts it down on the desk in such a way that he might as well have fired a shotgun.

I ain't no use to anyone. Not here, not now. Maybe never.

Why did I come back?

Why am I working on this? Why do we help out the local police when they're swamped and we're a little dried up? It ain't what I signed up for.

Some fraud. Some guy in Cookston. Taken for a ride by landscape gardeners. Turned out they know more about fleecing than fence repairs. A few grand later, the grifters have done more ripping off than ripping up turf. He gets the police over. They've left a big hole. Some bags of aggregate and cement mix. Got no clue what they were doing.

The old geezer had no idea either. Watched them get this stuff. Hang around for a couple of days. Say they needed more money for supplies. Took his money and drove away.

It's as simple as following the money. Checking the phone numbers, car plates. They've got a website. An email address. Not that any of that costs more than a couple of cups of coffee.

Sometimes less. Still, they've gotta be registered somewhere.

I get as far as looking that up. Some address in the Isle of Man. Website bought from another IP address in southern Spain.

I do some digging. Get the details of some VPN company. Need to get in touch. See what they can tell me, assuming they wanna tell me anything at all, other than where to go with my request.

It's as much as I manage before I wanna go to the kitchen.

I get up. Make the short walk. Stick my head in the sink and turn on the water. Couldn't give a damn if it falls in my mouth or flows over the rest of my head like a rock in a river. Can't say I give two hoots whether it stops me breathing for long enough to cause a problem.

Wouldn't just be a problem for me, though. Wouldn't look good on the top brass if they find me drowned in the kitchen sink.

I turn off the water. I gulped down quite a bit. Not that I'm any better for it.

It takes maybe twenty of the paper towels from the dispenser to dry me off again.

I finish dabbing my face nearly dry when someone calls my name.

I turn around too quick. Feels like I turned right into a two tonne truck.

Some white, green-gilled officer I don't know is walking down the corridor towards me. Short, fuzzy blond hair. Keen expression. Weird jutting out angles to that face and jaw that tell me he was never gonna be a model. Got me wondering what this guy's first choice of career would've been before he landed here.

"Flint, we've had something come from the control room."

I sigh. "What's wrong now? Someone stolen my car? Rammed it in to a Tesco?"

He looks at me like he doesn't see the funny side. Maybe he's not wired that way. "There's been a break-in"

Not exactly news. There's gotta be a handful of break-ins in most towns this size every day. Not sure why it's news to us, or to me.

"The address... It's your house."

***

The police say they wanna know how it feels to be a victim of crime. We can better help the folks who need us if we know what it's like being on the other side.

They say stuff like that. They can't mean it. The only way to know what it feels like to be a victim of crime is to *be* a victim of crime.

Let me tell you, it ain't a walk in the park.

Not when you've got family kidnapped and held hostage.

Not when you've gotta do some suspicious package drop-off.

Not when you're still at their mercy.

And definitely not when they break into your home.

The half-glass side door to my office ain't half glass anymore. Might not be enough of the thing to call it a door, either. It doesn't take a detective to see how they got in.

We've got detectives though. Three of them.

My office has had its contents chucked in a blender, turned on with no lid. About the only things still in place are the desk and the sofa.

I haven't been keeping anything locked away in my desk. If I had, they'd have crowbarred their way in, just like they did with the filing cabinet. It's nothing now but a chunk of bent-out-of-shape metal in the corner. If they'd have asked, I'd have told them it wasn't worth the effort. Pretty much just got a few household bills in it so far.

Now I've gotta find somewhere else to put them. Unless the thief's taken them in some desperate grab my personal details.

I didn't think I had enough stuff in here to make this much mess. The floor and sofa and desk are covered. Paper, charging cables and pens. Anything any normal folks would have in their office. It's right there, on show for every police officer who wanders in. They even found a pair of socks from somewhere and left them on the sofa.

It's only been a few weeks since I got around to putting things up on the walls in here. A few years in the police has given me a wealth of pointless certificates. Some for qualifying, finishing courses, commendations you don't feel you deserve. I'd bought some frames. Wrecked my fingers opening them up at the back. Put the better-looking certificates and qualifications in them. Got them all lined up, nice and neat.

Now, the frames are on the floor. The glass from each of them is shattered. The certificates have been ripped out. Some even ripped up. I ain't clever enough to hide stuff in the back of a picture frame. Another thing I could've told my intruder if they'd have asked.

"Anything taken?" DS Debs Dobson asks. She's standing there, overweight, longish mouse brown hair. An expression too cheery for the situation. Could be her rounded face always has that jolly look. I could see how that might be a blessing and a curse. Right now, it's not feeling like a good thing.

I shake my head. "Not a lot here to take."

She nods. Looks around. Was gonna say something. Changed her mind.

She turns around. Looks at the splintered, shattered door. "Some blood on some of the broken glass. Doesn't look like the work of some criminal genius."

I raise an eyebrow. "Maybe it's just a coincidence then. When people have family kidnapped, maybe somehow they're an easy target for burglaries."

She puts on an exaggerated puzzled look. Shrugs. "Let's see what forensics turn up."

She turns to walk out. "Maybe we should get out of the way. Stop contaminating the crime scene. You know."

I nod. That's it. My home's a crime scene. It's happened again.

At least this time, I ain't the suspect. Working a full day in a police station's a pretty good alibi. Not that I'd have come home, broken stuff and ransacked my own house anyway. If I did, I'd happily have them take me away. Find me a nice cell this time. The kind with cushions on the walls. Some orderly handing out anti-psychosis pills like they're Skittles.

I could get myself a slice of a life like that. Painting time. Exercise. Wandering around in a bathrobe. Manic talking to fellow patients about mind control, alien invasions, and conspiracy theories.

There ain't many differences between folks like me and the gees in a nuthouse. I guess they've just got a label on what's up with them. The rest of us wander round, free, trying to guess what's wrong with us.

Can't really say why they called me home for this. Was it so I could look at a bunch of broken stuff and say I used to own it when it meant something?

All I can do is sit in my office. Get up and make a round of drinks when needed. Have someone I know take my statement.

They might call this a coincidence until they know any better. I already do.

I failed VIRTUS. They're sending a message. Might have even left something behind for me.

I pull out my phone and I load the app. I do the usual stuff. No messages. Not one.

If this is linked, if it's something to do with them, wouldn't they tell me what it is they wanted me to do?

I'm about to give up and put my phone away.

The thing vibrates in my hand.

A new message.

> You did not follow instructions last time.
>
> If you want to see your partner and son again, I trust you'll follow them now.

They're typing out the next message.

Things went wrong with the last package. The break-in shouldn't have happened.

There's one common thread.

I type out a few nervous words.

> I understand. Tell me what you want me to do.

A reply.

> Identify the man who broke into your house.

Three more words in a new message.

> Kill that man.

9. SOME NO GOOD BUM

I'm done staring at the screen.

I forgot to set the screen recording going first. I swipe down and do it now before the messages disappear. I think I caught them.

It's all gone blank, like my mind.

Kill the person who broke into my house? Why? Talk about being disproportionate.

Still, they play with the lives of others like they're pieces in an abandoned chess game. Move them wherever the hell they like. It ain't gonna matter to anyone.

My arms, my feet, my head even, don't feel like they belong to me. Not fully. Part possessed with numbness. Worry.

It wouldn't be surprising if the far wall disappeared. Got lifted out of the way. Revealed some posh audience. The kind who've paid the kinda large you put down when you rent a fancy apartment, all for a taste of opening night.

I'm the stooge on stage. The one dumped in a situation. Problem is, I don't know my lines.

That moment's the one chosen by Jayden to enter stage right.

"You've got one of those video doorbells?" he asks.

I stare at him. No words to chuck back in his direction. Nothing but a dumb, blank look. A fly could've flown in the gaping hole that's my mouth and I wouldn't notice. Hell, a caterpillar could crawl in, build a cocoon, and leave a butterfly and it'd have no effect on me right now.

"Flint?" DS Dobson this time. "You okay?"

I turn away. Shake my head. "DI Chamberlain here?" I ask.

She shakes her head. "Want me to call her?"

I nod.

Jayden's request has made it through my mind fog. I nod. "Yeah, the video doorbell."

I open the app. Rewind a little. Back to 09:50. I hadn't long left the place empty.

Someone approaches. A little short. Maybe five and a half feet. Black. Short hair that's got a natural frizz to it if he lets it grow longer than a couple of centimetres. Light beard. Wide nose. Small hoops in both pierced ears. Sunglasses. A long, green raincoat. Scruffy dark brown trousers that don't fit right. Walks right up and smashes something through the window. Must've been too caught up in my hangover to even pay attention to the phone alerts.

"That's him," I say. "The intruder."

I leave off the part where I'm supposed to find him and kill him.

Jayden has a look. Puts on a puzzled face. Nods. Grateful that stuff like this makes his life a little less impossible.

DS Dobson's ready to hand me her phone.

I hand mine on to Jayden. "See if you wanna send that video to your email."

He nods and takes the phone. Leaves the room for a moment.

"Okay, Flint. What's going on?" Holly's on the line.

"Another request. From them."

There's a shuffle. She's sitting up in her chair for this.

"They know who broke in here. Same guy that dropped off the package to me."

"They want something from him?" she asks.

I shake my head a little. "Not exactly. More like they want nothing more from him. Not even taking in oxygen."

"Sorry. Say that again."

"They want me to kill him."

Silence.

More silence.

Enough to fill any size hall, for any amount of time.

"You record the messages as we discussed?"

"Yes. I think I got them."

"Good. Send them to me. We'll talk it over here. See what we can come up with."

She ends the call. Promises to get back to me.

She's off to have one hell of a conversation.

I'm stuck here with an impossible task.

How do you kill a man?

How can you bring yourself to take a life when it's the last thing you wanna do?

And how do you leave a house full of police officers to do it?

No good came from that damn package.

One thing's for sure, though. VIRTUS aren't messing

around.

***

"Didn't take long for an ID," Jayden says. He walks back into the room. "Pretty well known. The digital forensics guy knows him by sight."

I look up at that face. The smile's come back.

"Leo Ryan."

I've heard the name. My messed-up head can't place it.

"Leo?" DS Dobson chirps up. "The homeless guy? Usually spends his time in a dirty tent near the town centre. He's got a few small crimes to his name. He's not done anything like this before, though."

I shrug. "First time for everything."

As true for me as for anyone else. First time deliberately killing someone. I've found it hard enough living with the guilt I've already packed on my back. It's bad enough when you get people accidentally killed. When you do it on purpose? That's gotta haunt you.

Maybe not everyone. Maybe VIRTUS are so accustomed to blowing people away that it all feels like a game of Grand Theft Auto. Not to me, though.

Jayden hands my phone back with a thank you.

He won't be thanking me if I do what I've got to do. I'll no doubt be creating further work for him.

How do I weigh this kinda thing up? Flick and Toby for the homeless Leo. Two lives for one. Can simple maths make this easier?

Can I fool them? Couldn't I just get the man to lie down?

Maybe get him drunk enough to pass out. Some fake blood around him. Send a snap on their app?

Not gonna work.

I get a new message.

> You know your target by now. Send a photo of the body in the tent.
>
> Bring evidence to the hotel for twelve. Blood, a finger, your choice.

My phone rings.

I jump about a mile in the air.

A deep breath. I tap to answer it.

"Flint? We've got an idea. Might not be a good one, but it's a jumping off point."

"Let's hear it," I say.

She gives me the same bad idea I had a few moments ago.

"Not gonna fly," I say. "They want physical evidence."

Quiet again. "How are they gonna know it's from him?" She finally asks.

I shrug. "I didn't ask. Suppose they might have a way of testing the stuff."

She sighs. "I would doubt it. I think they just want some token you've done it. What have you got to do with it?"

"Hand it over. Back at the hotel. Twelve today."

Quiet for a beat.

"Hand the phone on to Jayden please."

I walk back into the office. Hand it over. "DI Chamberlain

wants a word."

He starts with a ma'am. Soon finds himself sitting in my office chair. Looks like his luck just ran out and took his life savings with it.

A short conversation.

"I understand," he says. Hangs up.

He gets up. Closes the door.

He looks at me. "This is new territory. Always had to investigate crime scenes. Never once got to invent one."

I give DS Dobson the gist of the request.

There's a weak, sad smile. He's keeping his eyes fixed on me like I'm under house arrest, but I might bolt for the door. "Any ideas where we start?"

I shake my head. "Not a clue."

Quiet while we both think. Take this in.

"I've got one," DS Dobson says.

We take it in turns to stare at each other.

"How good's your acting?" she asks.

10. DON'T BOTTLE IT

It's an idea, I'll give her that.

Maybe the best one we're gonna get.

She's on the phone, looking for some vital part of this new plan.

I need a backup in case her guy doesn't come through with the goods.

I head to the kitchen. Find a small jar, complete with its lid. One Flick's gonna clean out, ready to throw in the recycling waste. Could turn out to be useful. I turn it over. Look at the label. Pasta sauce. Something red inside's not gonna cause too many to ask too many questions.

I give the thing a rinse. Looks clean enough to me.

I head back through to the office. Our little command base for planning a fake murder.

DS Dobson's written out a list.

> Find Leo Ryan
>
> Give him money. He'll get himself drunk.
>
> Forensics to search/sort out tent & stage scene.
>
> Arrest Flint.
>
> Find a body.

I look at my watch. "Ten o'clock, nearly. That's a lot to do in a couple of hours."

She nods. "I'm starting with the final bit. Jayden's about to head back, find some old blood samples. I'm about to call the local cops, the morgue, anyone who might have a fresh body."

I wince and let it fall away again. "Never thought a day working for the police would turn out like this."

She stands up to leave. "Just be grateful there's not some national emergency right now. If there was, you'd be on your own with this."

Jayden grins. He gets up too. "Might stay that way today, as long as no one says the Q word."

We both nod like it's a serious comment. Police can be a superstitious lot. Avoid certain words. Wearing specific things. Sticking to routines. Like any of it makes a damn bit of difference. I guess they like to feel that in a job where chaos reigns, they've got a handle on some part of their life.

I walk them to the door.

One's gonna find some blood to misappropriate.

One's gonna find a dead body to cut bits off.

It's great what colleagues will do for one of their own.

***

DI Holly Chamberlain's got a team ready.

In fact, they're already wandering, looking for Leo Ryan.

On dry days, when the town centre is busy, he ain't hard to find. He'll be sitting in some alcove, a bag open in front of him, trying to look feeble. Hoping for change and any other cash donations that could come his way.

They find him in a covered shopping area. Huddled in a corner between a Superdrug and a card shop. Looking pretty miserable. That is, until some random people make his day.

A few pound coins go into the bag. Even a couple of five pound notes. One tenner. He's made more already today than he's got in the past week.

Experience tells Leo that he needs to hang around while the going's good. Resist the urge to gather it up and spend the dough straight away. No matter how hungry he is. No matter how thirsty. No matter if it's been a good few hours since the last throat-scratcher.

You don't give up a good spot. Not when people are throwing berries and cabbage at you. Don't wanna hand it to a rival. Have them jump in your grave and take what should've been yours.

What's funny is that this spot's not been this profitable before. Otherwise one of the die-hards would've got there before he'd even crawled out of his sleeping bag.

He's in the chips and he's gonna make the most of it. At least, he thinks he does. The dough starts to dry up. Nearly half ten. Gets a little quieter. The early bird shoppers have nabbed their worms and they're off. The lunchtime crowd ain't making a move down here just yet. Nothing but a few pence in the past half-hour. There ain't the footfall to change that any time soon.

The time's right to get out of there. Find somewhere to get a sandwich and a hot drink. Who's he kidding? He's off to the off license. Buy some cheap booze. That'll warm him up from the inside. Food won't matter so much when it takes effect.

You could count the seconds before he was sucking the end of a tall plastic bottle. The cheap cider's made from potatoes and turnips. Doesn't matter. Not to him. The end result's the same.

Get back to the tent. Get sloshed. Put this miserable life to bed for a few hours. Go hunting for some hot food when he's up and about again.

The hooch is already getting into his bloodstream. He sways and stumbles down the side street. The stuff's cheap but effective. He knew it would be.

Must be effective. He's seeing two tents instead of one.

People next to one of them.

There are actually two tents here. Someone's set up right next door. Same colour. Same type. Which one's his?

He props himself up on a wall. Looks at one tent, and then the other.

Someone walks up.

What are they gonna do? Help him out? Take his money? Take the mostly-empty bottle he's holding?

No chance. They're not his friend. They're gonna take something. He's not got much to take. He's gonna defend it.

He pushes himself off the wall and nearly falls the other way.

Says something. No idea what he's even trying to say.

The guy gets a little closer. He looks angry.

Take him by surprise. Get him before he gets you.

He swings a fist. Misses.

He's on the ground already. How did that happen?

No one's beating him up. No one's checking his pockets.

One man, and now another one with him. Both looking down, staring.

He's hit his head. Something hurts pretty bad.

If these guys aren't here to rob him, maybe they know a little first aid. Get him patched up.

Get him sleeping off his war wound.

A tent unzips.

Someone's dragging him. Can't even fight against it now. Even if he had a good reason.

Now they're picking him up. Carrying him.

He'll be back in his sleeping bag shortly.

He'll sleep this off.

Should've gone for food first before hitting the drink. The stuff wouldn't have gone to his head half as quickly.

Now he's at the mercy of whoever these people are.

He's gotta hope they don't want to hurt him.

He could wake up in a dumpster with nothing again.

Nothing he can do about it now.

Just lie here. Hope for the best when he opens his eyes again.

***

I get to the side street.

Both tents look pretty much the same, inside and out.

One major difference. One's got a passed out drunk guy inside. The other's empty.

I stand back. Next to Holly. Point at both of them.

"What's the plan?" I ask.

"We moved him to our copied tent. Same stuff inside. Looks

pretty convincing to me."

"Why the second tent?" I ask.

She looks at me like she's my old English teacher and I forgot my homework for the tenth lesson in a row. "We can't go messing up his tent. Had to create a copy. We can do what we like with it then."

"And what is it we'd like to do?"

A couple of paper-suited guys come along with red liquid, paint brushes and a spray bottle. They crouch down beside the copy tent. Take it in turns to fling and spray the stuff around.

"We making it look like he's the victim in a slasher movie?"

She shrugs. "Things get messy pretty quickly when you use a knife in a small space."

Jayden walks up. Hands me my jar. Half full, but it ain't tomato sauce.

"We got a little lucky," he says.

I look down like it's a ticking bomb. "Please explain how,"

He smirks. "The guy fell over by himself before any of our lot got near him. Hit his head. He'll be fine, but he opened up his forehead. We managed to collect some of his actual blood. We've left the wound open. Got a doctor standing by. We'll patch him up, get him medically assessed when we're done."

I nod towards the jar. "There's more than a little blood in here."

He nods. "Had some old samples in the lab, marked for destruction. I chucked them in there first."

He reaches into a pocket. Pulls out a plastic sandwich bag, but it ain't got sandwiches in it. Hands it to me.

"Seems he got brave and pulled his own tooth recently. It's decayed, but it's another thing you can hand over."

I look closer at the tooth. Looks fresh.

"I dipped the ends in the blood," he says. Looks proud of himself. Like someone's gonna award him with a blue ribboned rosette for best in show.

I nod. "Thank you."

I look back at Holly. "We think some blood and a tooth is gonna fool these people?"

She shakes her head. "We're working with what we've got for now. DS Dobson's been on the blower to the local cops. Might then try the morgue. We're hoping for an unclaimed body."

I raise an eyebrow. "What are you planning on doing to it?"

She shrugs. "Nothing too drastic. A thumb, a toe, something like that."

I stare at the forensics people chucking the fake blood around. One stops and pours out a little at the tent entrance.

They back off. Nod. Turn to us. Thumbs up.

The scene is set.

Time for me to get out my phone. Snap a few photos. Send them to VIRTUS.

I take a few. Different angles. Showing a heavily bloodied face. An open sliced wound on his neck. Gashes on his arms and plenty of little cuts to his hands. They've been busy. Done one hell of a good job.

My stomach's not too keen on lunch by the time I get out of there.

I hand the phone to Holly. She swipes through the photos and nods her approval. So does Jayden.

Seems if you wanna make a convincing murder scene, the police are pretty good at it. I guess when you've seen enough, knocking up some fake blood and wounds isn't too hard.

Holly gets on her radio. Shakes her head at me. "No fresh bodies," she says.

Looks like I'm heading to the hotel with nothing but a few photos, a jar of mixed up blood and an old tooth.

Could be enough all together.

It'd fool me.

I've got the walk over there to come up with a convincing story of how this went down.

Something close to the truth would work.

With any luck, this'll get me clear of them.

But my sinking heart's not convinced I'm gonna see Flick and Toby again soon. Even if they believe the evidence and every word that comes outta my mouth.

***

Back at the Cookston High Harbour Hotel.

Same meeting place.

Same seat.

Same guy. Still sniffing. Different newspaper.

My watch ticks over to twelve as I sit down. Take the cheap backpack off my right shoulder. I set it down by the man's feet.

"Anything exciting going on?" I ask.

He's puzzled. I nod towards the newspaper.

He shakes his head. "Nothing that's not happened a hundred times before. I'm more interested in this morning's news right now."

I nod. "You'll be sad to hear that Leo Ryan is dead."

His eyes dart towards me, and then back to the broadsheet.

"Had a disagreement with someone while drunk. Big, ugly knife fight in his tent."

He glances over again, expressionless.

"Got you an early Christmas gift," I say. "It's in the bag."

He folds the newspaper closed. Folds it in half. Does it all like he ain't in a hurry. Like he's never been in a hurry his entire life, and he's not gonna start now.

He sets the thing down on a small table to his right. Leans down. Picks up the bag. Rests it on his lap. Unzips it.

"Found out a couple of things," I say. "Getting that particular jar of pasta sauce ain't a walk in the park."

He lifts the jar towards the top of the bag, but not all the way out. Gives me a suspicious eye and then puts in down again.

"You seen my photos from this morning? Sent them in a chat conversation."

He nods. Sniffs. Sniffs again. He hadn't done that for a minute. Now he's catching up.

"You look further down, there's a bag. Something wrapped in tissue inside. Seems the poor guy had been suffering with a cavity or two. Until today, that is."

He nods. smirks. Lifts the bag near the top. Stares at it. Sniffs. Puts it down again.

He zips up the bag with a nod. Puts it back on the floor.

"What now?" I ask.

He picks up the newspaper. Tucks it under his arm. Stands up and picks up the bag. "You're gonna order yourself another drink. I'm gonna go speak to someone."

He turns and heads straight for the exit.

But there's maybe six cops blocking his way.

Three could've come from anywhere. Tall, built like trains. DS Dobson I recognise. Two others looks vaguely familiar. One's a blonde woman. Thin, but with muscle tone that shows through the gear she's wearing. One's a short guy. Glasses. Wide face. Angry expression.

He stops. Stares at them.

They head straight past him. Got their eyes fixed on one guy in that joint. Me.

They make a beeline.

My sniffing acquaintance is still standing by the door. He's watching them walk across. Looking at me, open-mouthed. Could be shocked. Maybe it gives him some brief relief from trying to use that useless nose of his.

"Enoch Flint?" asks the short guy with the wide, angry face.

I nod, getting to my feet. "Yes."

"Mr Flint, you're under arrest for the murder of Leo Ryan."

Two others are closing in. Flanking the guy.

"You do not have to say anything, but it may harm your

defence-"

The two on the sides are about to grab me. Might not harm my defence, but I might harm them.

"-if you do not say, when questioned, something you later rely on in court."

He finally got to the end.

Sniffy's still by the door. Watching. Looking around.

Others are watching too. Tuts. Shakes of the head. Some looking utterly gobsmacked. Some curious.

They grab my arms. I jerk them back.

I step back, set myself.

They come at me.

The first one to grab an arm's to my left. I lean in to their grab. Swing a punch at their throat. Bullseye. They back off, gasping for breath.

Now it's the turn of the guy on my right. I jerk my arm back and then swing an elbow at him. Land a quick punch. I get my right arm around the guy's neck.

But it's as far as I get with my struggle. The three others pile on. They wrestle me to the ground. Pin me on my front. Get the cuffs on me.

The guy who muttered the arrest wording's still standing there. Looks like he's gone outside to find someone's stolen his car.

"I didn't do anything!" I shout out.

The man by the door's gone. Wants to make a getaway before someone links the two of us.

"I didn't even know Leo Ryan!"

I'm fighting against the officers holding me. They drag me up to my feet. Lead me out the door. Stick me in the back of a waiting cop car.

The short man gets in the driver seat. DS Dobson gets in the passenger side.

"Was there any need for the rough tactics?" I ask.

She turns round. Smiles at me. "Had to make it look convincing. Bravo on the fightback, by the way."

The car starts up.

"We'll get back to the station," she says. "Wait a few minutes."

She looks at me in the rear-view. "If you behave, I might even take the cuffs off."

I look out the window, shaking my head. "You're liking this a little too much, aren't you?"

She shakes her head. "Don't get me smiling and laughing, Flint. We've still got to make this look real."

I nod. "Understood."

It ain't easy sitting in the back seat of a car with these bracelets on. Got a little more sympathy for those I've arrested.

Not too much. Most of them deserved to be uncomfortable. Most deserved a hell of a lot worse.

Gotta wonder what the past couple of minutes have done for my long-term career prospects.

To be honest, I think I harmed them in a bunch of different ways myself years ago. A fake arrest ain't gonna be what keeps me from being anyone's boss.

Couldn't really give a damn, anyway.

VIRTUS are gonna think one of two things.

They might believe I did what they asked. They don't know Leo's sitting in a cell on some jumped up drunk and disorderly charge.

They might think I've got a foot out the door. That I ain't gonna be of any use to them. That Flick and Toby are now expendable.

They've got to let them go now.

I've done everything they've asked.

Trouble is, when you start getting into bed with criminals, there's no telling how the night's gonna end.

11. FOOL ME ONCE

He sits there on a bench, in the cold rain, over the road from SITU HQ.

For once, the sniffing makes sense.

Gotta be around four o'clock. He's gonna see something that confirms his suspicions.

Enoch Flint, awake, almost happy, but free as a bird, walks out the door.

So much for the arrest.

The police showed up at the hotel. It was enough to put his heart in his shoes.

But they blanked him. Still no idea who he is. Who he works for. How much power he wields on a daily basis.

No, they walked straight on past. Collared Flint instead.

Hours had come and gone. Not a word from the guy. Had he dropped a dime on him? Had he somehow turned the situation on its head?

No he hadn't.

Didn't take a genius to see the flaw in their plan. He shows up with some blood and a tooth. Doesn't mean a guy's dead. Could mean no more than a trip to a bad dentist.

He knows Flint's car. Sees it still in the car park outside the station. All he had to do was watch it. See if anyone came for it.

The meddling man's now unlocking the can and climbing in. He thinks he's fooled VIRTUS. He ain't got enough wool to pull over their eyes.

He gets off the bench. Turns for the high street. He's seen enough.

Flint's useless to them. Won't do a damn thing they ask. Won't follow any instruction. He ain't gonna inform, plant evidence, sabotage an investigation.

All the guy can make himself is a spanner in the cogs. Nothing more.

Got him wondering what happened to Leo. If he ain't lying on a cold slab, where is he?

He looks down each side street and alley as he walks. Should be able to see the man. Might be able to smell him first. Even with his nose.

But there's a smell of something else. Bleach. One back alley wreaks of it.

He turns and walks down. It's the signature smell of a cover-up. Fits in well with what the fuzz have been up to.

Sure enough, Leo's tent is around the corner. The paving around it's spotless. Still smells. Enough to sting the nostrils. Enough to even clear his head for a moment.

Someone's moving inside the filthy yellow tent. Muttering something about pigs and wasted time and money.

Here he is. Alive and well. No blood. No stilled heart.

Flint's a fool. How long did he think his deception was gonna last?

Not long enough.

He could jump in a taxi. Head to Flint's place. Make him pay.

But that ain't the way VIRTUS would want things done.

Sure, Flint ain't any use to them in one way. Might be very useful in another.

They couldn't take down an airport.

They couldn't ruin a community.

They might be able to turn this failing cop into something.

Reputations rise and fall. There's an obvious one waiting for a full-on nosedive.

It involves Flint.

It starts with Leo.

He walks over to the tent. Reaches for his wallet. Pulls out a tenner. That'll get the homeless man's attention. Distract him from what's in his other hand.

He crouches down. Unzips the tent.

The dark eyes of Leo Ryan are wide like dinner plates. He stare back at him.

They ain't gonna do much more staring. Not with any thinking going on behind them, anyway.

Get a good night's sleep, Flint, he thinks.

Might be your last chance for a while.

12. I LIKE THE SMELL OF WARRANTS IN THE MORNING

Faking a murder and staging an arrest can take it outta you.

I ain't slept so well in months.

My head hit the pillow at ten. Stayed there.

But it's off again now.

Some loud noise has seen to that.

My cloudy brain's not figured out what it was.

Then it happens again. A rhythmic thud against the front door.

Not a gentle knock, like a guy with a parcel. The beating heel of a hand that demands the door opens or it's gonna come through it.

I shout something about waiting.

Head's still spinning a little as I chuck on a t-shirt and trousers.

It ain't letting up as I shuffle through the mess on the floors. I still haven't had the energy to pick stuff up since the police left.

Thudding at the door again.

"Alright!" I shout. "I'm coming!"

I get there. Turn a latch and a key. Open the thing.

An army of police officers. None of them look familiar. Must be the local fuzz.

"Mr Flint, can we come in?" It's a tall guy. Black hair. So

black it's like the vacuum of space. Neat, like it's been painted on. Thin glasses. Whole head's like an inverted triangle with some edges that ain't been knocked off.

I give them a frown. "The place had eyes over it all yesterday. Nothing doing. Anyway, you already know the guy that broke in."

He's got a sad look. Shakes his head. "This isn't about that. May we come inside and talk about it?"

I know what that means. They're not getting in the door. They're gonna have to sit out in their cars and call in a warrant when the courts open.

If they arrest me inside my home, they can search the place, no questions asked. If I make them arrest me outside, it makes their life harder. I ain't about to do things the easy way.

I step outside. Pull the door closed behind me. "What's this about?"

He steps back. "Leo Ryan was found dead in his tent."

No idea whether to laugh at that or shake my head. "You sure it's not what went down yesterday?"

He looks confused.

I'm not gonna say another word. Let them do the talking.

"I'm not talking about yesterday. I'm talking about this morning."

I've got nothing for them but blank looks. They've got nothing for me but angry ones.

"Mr Flint, I'm arresting you on suspicion of the murder of Leo Ryan..."

I wanna shout out about how ridiculous this is. How they've

got wires crossed. How they should know something about who I am.

I wanna cry out. Ask the heavens why I keep getting arrested for murders I didn't do.

He gets to the end of his caution. I ain't paying attention. It's not like I need to hear the words.

At least they're not getting out the bracelets. Cops know the drill. If your suspect behaves, they get a little more wiggle room.

I'm led to the back of a marked car again.

Spent too long in the back of these things.

Wish I knew why it's me that's always stuck in these situations.

Someday my luck's got to turn around.

But someone, somewhere's getting all the good luck that's deserting me.

Maybe every time I get arrested, some other gee wins the lottery. Gets given a car. Gets told they're having the baby they've always wanted.

Must be enough good luck circling this planet of ours.

Always seems to avoid me, though.

Wish I knew why.

***

Been here before. Could even be the same cell.

They all look the same anyway. Same royal blue vinyl coated mattress. Could double up as a crash pad.

Schools up and down the land are using something about the same thickness. Some illusion of safety in their sports halls.

Someone, some years ago, made a pretty penny from peddling them. Mats that are less than an inch thick. Like they'd be the miracle cure for kids who fell when rope climbing. Maybe ankle biters across the land had fallen from climbing equipment. Hit a hard wooden floor. Broken something. Some teacher cries out, "If only we had a few millimetres of inadequate foam to break their fall."

Maybe they ain't used in educational establishments anymore. Even kids must have rights. But they're still used here. As someone's idea of a suitable sleeping surface. Whoever that someone is, they're wrong. I bet they're not using one on their bed at home, are they?

I've maybe still got a couple of hours of sleep to get me over last night's drinking. It ain't gonna happen in here.

Even if I were in fancy digs, there's too much rattling round my head.

What happened to Leo?

Did we overdo the staged murder yesterday, somehow make it a real thing?

Did the guy have some problem that wasn't picked up in custody? Somehow let out to die alone?

How could that be my fault? The whole thing was set up by senior officers. If anyone's gonna take the rap for this, shouldn't it be them? Are they in neighbouring cells, awaiting their own lawyers? Somehow I doubt it.

There's something else going on here. There are some blanks I need filling in.

Police have a duty of care. Leo spent a chunk of yesterday in one of these sparse rooms. He was released without charge. Taken home to his tent. That kinda thing doesn't happen if you're unconscious.

No, something happened afterwards. While I was drowning my evening in cheap booze, I was being set up for Leo's death.

I might as well have done it. A part of me wanted to. A little bit of me wants to burn to the ground anything that VIRTUS ever touches. Gather up the ashes. Burn them again.

But I didn't do it.

What does it matter when there's evidence against me? Must be, otherwise I'd still be in my own bed.

I gotta wait for a duty solicitor to show up. They'll sit down. Get told something or nothing at all. Then we chew the fat for a couple of minutes about the stiff. Only hours ago he was walking around, maybe spending some more of his recently acquired dough.

Problem with all this is I've been here before. Yeah, they found out they were wrong, but even a false arrest leaves a mark. People still think you must've done something to end up in custody. Folks don't get the arm put on them for minding their own business and being good little citizens.

I'd already had my three strikes. I was out the door and looking for a new life when VIRTUS forced my hand. More than once I've had one foot out the door. Now, I'm grabbing on to the doorframe with my fingernails. If I'm gonna find Flick and Toby, I need this job.

But I'll already be suspended. Already tarnished by another accusation. Doesn't matter if it's unfounded.

Unfortunately, my usual alibi is locked away somewhere. Held captive by this mystery organisation. Only Flick could've told them where I was. But I don't know where she is. No girlfriend, no alibi, no chance.

The police are coming round to the idea that they're better off without me by now.

VIRTUS are gonna think I'm as useful as a blind train driver.

Flick and Toby? What do they think of me? I let them down. Abandoned them. Again. There's gotta be at least a passing thought that their life's better when I ain't in it.

Gotta admit, it's looking a lot like the world's against me. There's nothing left for me but to rot in a cell. When I get back to thinking this way, the magnetic lock clunks. The door swings open.

Time for the interview.

Let's see why they think I killed the guy.

Let's see if my free lawyer is worth any more to me than the fee I'm paying him.

Let's see if I've got even the slightest chance of getting out of here. I could carry on with my miserable, doomed existence.

13. THE VIDEO'S GOT TO BE PHONEY

My free solicitor ain't worth what I'm paying.

Sits there, studious in his dirty grey suit. Long, greasy, greying hair. Thin face like he last ate when I was working my last case. Maybe he doesn't get a gig like this very often. Looking on with beady, sunken eyes. Not a sound from lips as thin as razor wire. He just stares as the detective throws every new bit of evidence down on the fixed table in the interview room.

There's more stuff on that table than there should be. None of it makes sense. None of it surely real.

But they have it. Makes me look bad. Would make any attempted explanation as weak as diet hot chocolate.

All my legal representative said was to say nothing. Confirm my name at the start. Chuck in my favourite two words in response to everything else. Can't do that. I know what it feels like on the other side. Doesn't mean I'm gonna give this detective anything useful though.

An overweight detective is sitting there. Looks like someone dragged him out of the seventies and dusted him down. Thinning hair on his scalp. Makes me look like I've got the hair of a male model in their twenties. Angry face. Looks like the kinda guy that might advise the TV people on Line of Duty. One things for sure. He ain't getting on the other side of the camera.

"So Mr Flint," he says. Looks down at the paper sprawled over the desk. "You're telling me you didn't send *any* of these messages?"

He looks up again. Stares at me like I'm in the way of a

perfectly good view of the opposite wall.

I shake my head. "Didn't even know he had a phone. You gonna check mine?"

He rolls his eyes. "What's that gonna show me? How good you are at covering your tracks?"

I stare at him. "It's gonna show you that a police officer is being set up."

He purses his lips. Looks down. "We've got twenty messages from you. Different times. All showing as being from your phone number. Over a two hour period. A hell of an effort in setting up."

I nod. "It takes a hell of a set up when someone's innocent."

He pulls out a laptop he had stashed on his side of the desk. "We're gonna check your phone. We're gonna take a long, hard look. Recover deleted messages, the works."

He lifts the lid on a device that could be older than my second-hand car. Stares at a blank screen. "We're gonna confirm everything with your network provider. See who sent what, where and when."

I nod. He gonna start that right now? With that thing? He's gonna have to wake up the hamster in there first.

"But I think I know how that's all gonna go," he says.

The laptop's awake now. He types in a password. Messes with the touchpad. Looks all confused at the keyboard before he finds the buttons he's looking for. Spins the thing round for me and my pathetic personal legal advisor to see.

A video starts playing. Loud enough to make my lawyer jump.

Leo's recording a selfie video. He's running. Still recording like it's important that he says what he wants to say.

"He's after me."

There's a slur to his words. Drunk again.

"Enoch Flint's chasing me. I think he's gonna hurt me."

I scowl at the screen. Glance over at my lawyer. He looks like his wife just left him.

The video ends. Another one starts. Same style as before. Leo's out of breath.

"He got me, but I got away. He's coming after me again. I broke into... his house... and I'm sorry... but he doesn't need... to kill me!"

The video stops again. I sense there's one more.

Another clip starts.

"He's here again. I can't get away. He's too fast... too strong... and all I can do... is hide. I just need to..."

A load of noise and some random shots of the ground, of his feet, of the side of his head. A close-up of some long grass, all blurred. The phone ain't moving anymore.

Some screams. My name's mixed up in them. Some screams of terror. The kind you only get from someone doomed to stop sucking in air any second.

A heavy clunking sound.

Silence.

A couple of footsteps.

The phone's picked up. Turned over.

The next bit makes no sense.

It's my face looking into the phone.

The video ends.

The laptop spins around again. The lid closes.

My solicitor puts his notebook on the edge of the table. Leans back like he's just folded on his last hand of a poker night. Like all the chips have been played, but none of them made it his way.

The detective looks at me. "Anything to say?"

I've got nothing.

I could protest my innocence. Say it must've been a lookalike. An imposter or something. It's all gonna sound pretty hollow.

Can't even muster up the words to say it ain't me in that video. Who's gonna believe that? Not the Crown Prosecution Service. Not a judge. Certainly not a jury.

"You've seen the text messages, the videos, and the forensic evidence we have. Mr Flint, we have enough and to spare to charge you with murder."

I've got no words.

My pointless solicitor's looking at his watch. Hoping to catch the next train. Hoping beyond all hope that he's never gonna see me again.

I'm the legal representation case no one wants. I'm the lose-lose. The fly in the Martini of a decent court record. I'm the guy that people look at in the newspapers and on TV and they say, "Of course he did it."

"Mr Flint," says the detective. I'd almost forgotten he was here. Too busy watching my life spiral like the swirl of a freshly flushed toilet bowl. "You are accused of the murder of Leo Ryan. Do you have anything to say in your defence? Now would be a good time to say something."

I shake my head. "I know how it looks, but I didn't do it."

He nods. Doesn't believe a word of it. Why would he?

If the shoe was on the other foot, I'd throw the book at him. Hell, I'd throw the whole library until something stuck.

No one's got anything more to say. Not after the videos that spoke a million false words. The kinda words that get a man convicted. That deny appeals. That crop up again when parole is denied, again and again.

I'm off to the big house, and I ain't getting out, except for my few days in court.

I'm a copper on the inside. Gonna be dead within a year.

I sat in this chair, wondering what they had on me.

Now I wish I'd never sat down. Wish I'd been anywhere last night that gave me an alibi.

Now all I'm doing is coming up with ways to defend myself from my fellow criminals.

Can't think of a damn thing.

Can't concentrate on a single word.

Flick and Toby are doomed. I can't save them now. Can't even save myself.

I'm led back to my cell.

They'll call me out in under an hour, guaranteed. The same detective's gonna read a charge sheet to me. Can't see any other outcome.

DC Flint. Often on the wrong side of the rules. Occasionally found out. Disciplined to within an inch of his police career.

Resigned once. Dragged back in. For all the good it did.

Now I'm out of the police for good. No one gets slapped with a murder charge and carries on in the job.

I've got to get used to life in prison.

For once, it's for something I didn't do.

14. EVIDENCE IS TENT-AMOUNT

It ain't the charge sheet like I thought.

Spent a little longer in the cell, too. Almost enough to fall asleep on that bed. Another three hours and I'd have dosed off.

I'm back in the same interview room.

Same detective.

Same lawyer. Earning his money today. Assuming any lawyer who sits there stunned ever truly earns their fee.

"We have preliminary results back from forensics," he says.

Where's this going? Someone else's fingerprints? DNA that's not a match to me?

There's no gleam of hope in those eyes of his.

"First of all, what else can you tell me about your movements yesterday evening."

I shrug. "You know what I was doing. Sitting at home. Drinking. Alone, on account of my family being kidnapped."

He nods. A hint of sympathy in there somewhere.

"Tell me about your association with Leo Ryan," he says.

I shake my head. "Didn't know anything about the guy before a couple of days ago."

"When you learned he'd broken into your house?"

I let out a sigh. "He wasn't the only one. You'll recall the people who took Flick got there first. Made a better job of it."

"But you thought you'd make an example of him for targeting you again, didn't you?"

The questions are harsher now. Trying to really push my buttons.

I shake my head. "No."

"You were happy to let someone break in, take what they liked and *not* want any kind of revenge?"

I look over at my lawyer. A waste of a good chair.

My fists are clenching so hard they'd stand a good chance of smashing rocks. "By the time he broke in, anything meaningful had been taken. I had no need for revenge."

"How about the request for VIRTUS to kill him in order to free your family? Aren't they as you say, the only things meaningful in your home? Surely you'd have done anything to get them back?"

I shake my head and laugh. "We staged the death of Leo. Last I heard, it had worked."

He leans forward. Opens the folder in front of him. "What about the latest message on your phone? They knew it hadn't worked. They asked you to try again."

I frown. "No such message was on my phone when I looked."

He points at the paper. "Unread, in their app."

I sit back and stare at him. "If it was unread, how could I have seen it and done what they wanted?"

He looks around the room for a beat. The solicitor is planning his next family vacation in his head or something. He certainly ain't trying to help me.

He moves to the next few sheets of paper in the file. "Did you touch Leo Ryan during the events of staging his murder, earlier yesterday?"

Finally, a sensible question. I nod. "I think so, yes."

He looks at me. "You're sure of that?"

I shrug. "A lot happened in a short space of time. I was there while things were going on with the fake tent. I'm sure I ended touching a few things."

He smirks at me. "I've got statements from forensics at SITU that you weren't ever close to him when he was passed out."

This ain't going anywhere good.

"And I know for a fact that you haven't arrested him or been near him before. You said yourself that you'd never heard of him until recently."

Well done Flint, you've talked yourself into a hole. Nice job.

"Have you ever been to Woodland Green?"

I nod. "It's a spot north of town. A good patch for dog walkers, folks with kids. There's a play park."

"You ever take Toby there?"

I nod. "Sometimes."

"You been there since it last rained?"

No clue if I have.

"Any explanation why your DNA was mixed with Leo Ryan's blood at Woodland Green? You know, the spot you like to visit?"

No point in having this lawyer. I could have Perry Mason in his heyday and I'd still be going down.

"It last rained, for the record, the night before last. You been there in the past forty eight hours?"

I'm hunting through my memories. Last night was a drunken blur of laying around at home. The day was spent in chaos. Working. Setting up a murder. Being fake arrested. The night before? Another night alone at home.

I shake my head. "Haven't been near there for at least a few days. Maybe weeks."

Damn it, why couldn't I have been there yesterday?

Why couldn't I have been with someone, anyone last night?

He sighs. "Forensics tell me your DNA wouldn't have survived there after a couple of falls of rain."

The longer these interviews go on, the lesser my chance of finding any kinda defence at all.

"You say that false tent was erected next to Leo's one," the detective says. He's got another set of nails to hammer into my career coffin. "Did you go inside the original one?"

I shake my head. "I don't think so."

He shuffles through his papers. Finds a new sheet. "Then why is your DNA also inside that tent? Is that where the chase started? You tried to take him out there?"

I sit back. "You got any CCTV of the area? Should show that I wasn't near him last night."

He smiles. "You know the quality of the cameras in this town. We can see someone of your height and build in dark clothing. A hood obscuring his face."

Can't catch a break with anything.

"Plenty of people my size," I say.

He shakes his head. "Not many with your fingerprints or DNA. Not many with your exact face, I'll wager. Tell me Flint, honestly, why did you kill Leo Ryan?"

I plant my hands carefully on the table. "I did not kill Leo Ryan. I did not go to his tent. I did not chase him. I did not kill him. It was not me on that video. I know this sounds crazy. I know you're gonna think I'm cuckoo. That I'm away with the fairies. Truth is, some powerful people are wrecking my life, and you're falling in to their trap."

He shakes his head. "We follow the evidence, Mr Flint."

I stare him down. "You're following a false trail of evidence because that's where they want you. Something bad might happen if you're taken in by this."

He shakes his head like he's shaking off a stubborn wasp. "Something bad's already happened, Mr Flint. Murder. I'm here to make sure you can't do any more damage."

15. SOME WORDS ARE NEGATIVELY CHARGED

"Mr Flint, it's been a long day," says the detective. No kidding. By the look of him, he ran a half marathon in a suit while I was in my cell. He's next to me. The guard's in front, opening another massive door. The kind you might break through if you had diamond-tipped power tools and a spare eight hours.

Now, I'm being walked out to the custody desks. Still wearing my slip-on shoes. No need to take them away when they've not got laces. You've gotta be pretty dedicated to hang yourself with things like that.

My stompers are making a squeaking noise underfoot. It's the hard, grey industrial type flooring. Looks like it maybe used to be made of single-colour Lego bricks before every bump got worn down to a nub.

I'm a lamb to the slaughter. Innocent for once. Paying for someone else's choices. Heaven knows enough people have paid for mine over the years.

"I gave you every chance to be honest with us," he says. "but what you've said doesn't fit with the evidence."

I'm ushered into a little weird-shaped booth section. The whole custody desk is a horseshoe, split up with curved partitions out front. Could be, it's supposed to look like a flower in bloom from above. Not that anyone's gonna see it from up there.

Could fit six Custody Sergeants in different bits. Each dealing with their own suspect. Every one with their own unique brand of stern expression. I'm in the one on the far left. A guy with grey hair. Looks like he's blaming me for it. His widening face is at odds with the narrow features in the middle. Lips so tightly pressed together I'm thinking they could've been superglued.

The rest of the place is empty. Could be coincidence. Could be by design. Don't let too many see the ex-policeman getting charged.

The detective's stood opposite me. Looks at a screen that's been turned in his direction. He starts reading aloud. Tells me that on a specific date in a time range of a few hours, I killed Leo Ryan in a premeditated attack. That I'm charged with first degree murder.

I'm to be remanded until my next court appearance. That means I ain't getting outta here. No bail. No phone call. Nothing but a close-up view of a grim prison cell.

He's still talking. They threw some other charges in there. I stopped listening.

I've got maybe a couple of hours left here. I'm gonna get moved to something more permanent. Some place a little louder. Could be the place I visited Elias. We might even be neighbours. What a turn up that would be. A killer and a thief, stuck with the cop that caught him.

But no, they wouldn't do that. They still find a place for ex-police where they can be safe? Gotta hope so. Anything else is a ticket to be the guest of honour in someone's beat-down. Maybe worse. They stick a copper in with the riff-raff, may as well measure him for his coffin as part of the physical exam.

There's no doubt who's behind my set-up. VIRTUS didn't like what I did. Couldn't stand that I lied to them. Didn't do what they asked. Again.

At least they're making me pay, and not Flick and Toby. At

least I hope there's only one edge to this particular sword.

I messed things up for them. I refused to put it right. I lied to them. Why wouldn't they mess up my life? But I've gotta say, they've done one hell of a good job at the stitch-up.

If I ever get out of this, I've gotta find the people who put me here. Gotta let them know that while I hate them, I respect their efforts.

The trouble is, I ain't getting out of this. Not today. Not tomorrow. Not for at least twenty years with good behaviour.

As for Flick and Toby? I've got no clue what's gonna happen with them. Not a damn thing I can do for them anymore.

If VIRTUS can at least decide there's no value in holding them hostage, they might let them go.

If that's what happens, I can live with life behind bars. Can't let another couple of people get their lives ruined because they dared to get near me.

But what if they do something else?

What if my family become part of the clean-up? Another mess to sweep under a very large and lumpy carpet. What do they do when people and things ain't so useful anymore?

A casual observer's gonna see my clenched fists. My gritted teeth. My angry, subtle shakes of the head. They're gonna think I'm angry at the police. Maybe angry with myself.

For once, I'm not angry. Anxious. Unsure of the future.

Mine's pretty set in stone. No doubt about that.

But there's more than just me stuck in this spin cycle. I might be the red sock in a batch of white laundry, but what happens when you stop it and cast the offending item away?

Do you try to recover the rest of the batch? Do you live with everything looking pink? Do you chuck the lot away and start again?

VIRTUS can get to me inside if they want. They can get me a message too. Let me know that I'll meet up with Flick and Toby again in whatever blackness follows this life.

If I'm lucky, they're gonna tell me that all's forgiven. That they're gonna cut them loose. Give them a shot at a life without me.

Problem is, I ain't lucky.

16. NOTHING GOES WITH FLINT LIKE LAM

Not much time has ticked by. The charge sheet's become an invisible audio clip. Runs through my head like a voicemail I can't delete.

My stuff's put in a bag awaiting transfer. At least I'm not stuffed in clear plastic for the journey.

Seems I'm not even getting slapped with cuffs. Not yet, anyway. Something about respecting that I was once a law man. If I behave, the bracelets stay off.

Looks like I'm moving to big-boy prison on a quiet day. No minibus. No complimentary shuttle service. No random bounty hunters looking for a quick few bucks, even. Got my own ride to the cooler.

They walk me down the side. Through more big doors. A property room off to the left. To the right's a covered walkway. A ramp that leads down in zig-zags. Down, down, and further down. A symbol of a prisoner's life choices, I guess. Wonder if they thought about that when they built the place.

I get back to the covered car ports. Big roller doors at either end only open when some guy upstairs gives the okay. I've gotta look to the big man upstairs for some help now. Pray for a miracle. Hope I ain't praying to the God of the Old Testament with all that wrath and smiting. Had enough of that kinda reaction.

Maybe my divine intervention's gonna come any second. Seems to be running late. The only thing sitting in a bay at the bottom of the ramp is a marked police car.

It's the usual drill. One officer opens a back door. Left-hand-side of the car. Leaves me standing there while they check the seats. Make sure there ain't any sharps and weapons stuffed in any gaps. He then stands up. Beckons me closer. Invites me to take a seat. Someone puts their hand on my head. Pushes me clear of hitting it on the door frame. Makes me think of the Old Testament again. Blessings and anointing of the kings of Israel.

The most I could be blessed with is a smooth ride and an understanding driver.

My seatbelt's put on for me. It's like I forgot how to do it myself.

The door slams shut. Gotta get used to doors slamming in my face.

I ain't even looking ahead when the loud rumble of the roller doors start.

Light sneaks in. Floods in a moment later.

Bright sunlight.

Make the most of these moments. Take them in.

Most of the sunlight I see for the next few years is gonnna be through toughened glass or fences.

The car's put in gear. Pulls away.

We've gotta wait for the world's slowest moving gate to slide open. If that thing closes at the same speed, someone's gonna make a break for freedom through it sooner or later.

I lift up my head. There's not two officers in front of me, like I'm expecting. No one sat in front at all. Just one other person in the car, behind the wheel. I see the side of her head. It's a head I recognise.

"I know it's not exactly a Limo, Flint, and I'm not any kind of a chauffeur, but are you gonna wear that face the whole way?"

Inspector Holly Chamberlain's behind the wheel. No idea how she got this gig. No clue why she's gone out of her way to make this happen.

I'd like to think the woman's got a plan for getting me outta this, but I don't wanna think anything too hopeful.

Be the pessimist. Expect the worst. It's for the best, really.

***

"Seems you've been busy since we last spoke," she says as she drives clear of the custody building.

I nod. "It's pretty exhausting being stitched up for murder."

She's got her rear-view mirror angled so she can watch me. Her eyes, a little magnified, are staring back at me through it.

She shrugs a little. "All I know is the guy was very much alive yesterday when we were done with him."

Some more of the world goes by the window. Could look a little different when I next see it.

I look in the mirror. "I didn't do it, Holly. You know that, don't you?"

There's a slight nod. "What I know doesn't hold up well to the facts, so I'm told."

We both quit speaking. Nothing but the engine and the dull drone of tyres on the road.

"We've got a long journey," she says. "Want to tell me what happened? No lawyers. No one but a friend with a listening ear. Not even any recording devices in the car."

I nod. "It ain't a long story. You know most of it. I hit the hay last night after the set-up yesterday. VIRTUS must've known I was pulling the wool over their eyes. They've dropped me right in it."

She looks at me in the mirror. "Why would they do that?"

I look down at my feet. "I guess I wasn't playing their game. They got tired of me."

"What about Flick and Toby?" she asks. Her eyes are a little wider.

I shrug. Got a tear in each eye. "Can't do a damn thing to help them now, can I?"

Quiet again.

"Flint," she says in a lighter voice, "truth outs in the end. You know that."

I laugh. "Try telling that to the guys that get out of prison twenty years late! The evidence finally turns up. Some lives are ruined while people wait for the truth."

"If what you've been saying about VIRTUS is right," she says, "we can't ignore it. They're gonna get more powerful. Cause more problems for more people."

I nod.

"You got in their way a couple of times before," she says, looking at me again. "You think you could do it again?"

Another laugh. I didn't plan this one. Just kinda happened. "If I could somehow get set free. Gotta get my job back. Get hold of a ton of resources. I get all that? Yeah, maybe."

Another round of silence. Gonna be a few of those. We ain't gonna keep up the chat for the next hour or more.

"I just wanna get my family back," I say. "That's all I want."

She nods.

"I guess taking down VIRTUS could be thrown into the mix, but if I could get away... I'll find them. Save them. Then I'll turn myself in again."

"You're a good man, Flint," she says. I see a smile in her eyes. "Underneath it all, you're not too bad."

What's she trying to do? Cheer me up? It ain't gonna work. If this conversation was at a bar and we each had a drink in-hand, maybe I'd leave warm-hearted. But not here. Not the back seat of a police can. Not when the destination is detention for a couple of decades.

"If you had one more day of freedom," she says, "What would you do, right now?"

I shake my head. Stare out the window. "Can't do much with a day. Couldn't even tell you where Flick and Toby are. Not even sure they're still alive."

"What if I kept digging? Could find something. Could you follow it up without making a scene?"

I smile. "What if I had a solid gold private jet and a gun that fired untraceable bullets. We can all play this game but it ain't gonna produce a winner."

We stop at a red light. She looks back at me. "I'm serious, Flint. If you got free, right now, you got somewhere to go? Somewhere the police won't find you?"

I give her my best frown. "I can hide, but what's that gonna do?"

She shrugs. Turns around. Starts again when the light turns green. "Could buy yourself some time until I can figure out this thing with VIRTUS."

"On your own? In your spare time?"

She laughs. "What spare time?"

I nod. "Exactly."

She shakes her head a little. "I've got contacts. People who I can get doing more digging than I can do. Poke around. Find out some stuff."

I look around the car. "So, what? You're just gonna pull to the curb and let me out? Have a nice life Flint. See ya when I see ya?"

A vigorous shake of the head this time. "I can't let you go," she says. "It's career suicide and a criminal charge to boot."

"As nice as it is to live in this little fantasy you're cooking up-"

"But if something were to happen, Flint..." she looks in the mirror again. "Say, you're not in cuffs and you catch me off-guard. We misjudged the threat you might pose to me. It becomes a stupid mistake. A risk I shouldn't have taken."

I shake my head. Look at my feet again. "I'm not putting you in that kinda position."

More silence.

"You know," she's sounding all casual again. "There's a village a mile or so ahead. No CCTV at all. No radio coverage. Phone signal's spotty."

I think I know what she's getting at.

"Picture some kid hitting our car with some false plates. Some cheap Ford Fiesta. I'm gonna have nothing I can do. Even less if they keep on driving."

I raise an eyebrow. "You already set something up?"

She shakes her head. "Flint, I've got no idea what you're talking about. I'm just driving you to prison. All the while our microphoneless front and rear dashcams are capturing the journey. Your personal effects are still in a bag back in property. You're not getting your phone. Sometimes, though, folks leave something in the glove box. Could get people some place if they break free."

I'm shaking my head. "This is madness."

She nods. "I agree, but all the sane options have gone."

"Why would you do all this?" I ask.

"Because I also want to stop VIRTUS, and I think you're key to making that happen."

"Can I object to this plan?" I ask.

She shakes her head. "Not if you've got any sense. Feel free to object if you like the taste of prison food, and knowing you could've saved Flick and Toby."

I let out a huge sigh. "I guess I'm in."

She nods once. "Good. Now, you might want to hold on to something. This can be a hazardous patch of road."

***

A traffic collision ain't usually a good thing.

Maybe, when that idiot who's been tailgating you for miles ends up wrapped around a tree. Most of the time, though, it ain't something to celebrate.

Hit-and-runs aren't the kinda thing that'd get you to invite friends over and open up a bottle of something.

But today is different.

Right now, this moment's the exception.

If I could, I'd have a street party set up and waiting. Brass band. Streamers. Banners. The works. Celebrate how I got out from under the law to start something useful.

I watch the whole thing happen.

A light blue Ford Fiesta. Hasn't seen a wash, let alone attention and maintenance in two decades. It's on the wrong side of the road. Foot down. Speeding towards us.

Inspector Holly Chamberlain's looking back at me. She's pressed back into her seat.

I'm pressing hard with extended arms into the seat in front. Braced for impact.

She blasts her horn. The car's still heading straight for us.

She slams her foot on the brake. Tyres squeal. The back end acts like it's hit a patch of snake oil.

The blue car's still coming.

Holly's got no choice but to steer off the road.

Problem is, only half the car follows her.

The front passenger side wheel hits the grass of the verge. There's no time for the rest of the car to join it.

The blue car slams into the driver side.

We're knocked farther off the road than maybe Holly expected.

The tyres have no traction and we're heading towards a big tree and a tall fence.

The whole car's complaining as it comes to a halt just before another big collision.

Nothing's moving, but it feels like everything is.

There's a groan from Holly.

She turns her head. Looks back at me. "This better be worth it," she manages to croak out.

I'm out of my seat. The car's pretty smashed up on the other side. Small pieces of glass everywhere. Air bags have made a hell of a mess.

"Don't worry about me," Holly says in a sleepy kinda voice. "Get the things and get away. Now."

I'm squeezing through the gap until I'm in the passenger seat. Can't help thinking this process might've been a little easier if she'd have used a police van instead.

I open the glove box. A big padded envelope has been stuffed inside.

I take it out. Open it up.

Cash. A couple of hundred.

A burner phone. Charger included.

A slip of note paper with a phone number scribbled on it in a hurry. Maybe Holly got a burner phone herself to keep tabs.

"We had some phones stashed away a while ago." She starts rubbing her neck and then her head. "Bought with cash. Same with the SIMs. No need to register them to use them. No one's gonna figure out who got them, or when."

I take the stuff. Open the passenger door. Turn back to check on Holly.

"I'll be okay," she says. "But maybe you need to do one more thing."

"You want me to call a tow?"

She shakes her head with a smile. Winces. "You've got to hit me."

I'm stepping out. Backing away. I shake my head. "I ain't going that far."

She sighs. "Flint, it's gotta be believable. No one knows about the stuff in the glove box. No one knows anything about this. They're gonna think I couldn't stop you from getting out from the back seat?"

I move a little closer. Goes against my nature. Never hit a woman. Now doesn't seem like a good time to start rewriting the rules. Especially not with fists instead of clear heads.

She points at her left cheek. "Hit me on this side. Might already have a bruise coming from the collision on the other."

I nod. Swing a fist. Pull back.

I barely make contact. I shake my head.

"Flint!" She stares at me. "You've got to hit me. Hard! Now!"

I scrunch up my face. Pull back my fist. Try again.

A harder hit this time. Much harder.

"Good!" She shouts with her mouth covered. "Now get the hell away from here!"

I turn and hightail it away. Leave the car door open for effect.

I head for the nearby woods for cover. Gotta keep moving. Get away from roads and towns. Place where people might see me.

Can't help but think about Holly as I run over uneven ground. Who sets something like this up? Who lets a prisoner go free? Who's willing to crash a car, take a hit to the face and risk their career on me?

There have been times I've misjudged Inspector Holly Chamberlain. She ain't your typical boss. She believes in her people, even when they stop believing in themselves.

But I can't keep wondering if she's okay. Someone's gonna call the police. Get her the help she needs. Get her back to Cookston.

Me? All I need to think about is staying out of sight. Stay hidden for long enough to come up with a plan.

Nowhere to stay.

Some money, but not enough.

No weapons.

Just a burner mobile phone.

I've got to figure out how to take down VIRTUS. Got to save Flick and Toby. Got to do it alone. Got to avoid the police.

Pretty straightforward, I'd say. A nice, easy weekday afternoon.

Except for one more thing.

Someone's shouting at me from a distance. Chasing me.

The near-impossible tasks just keep piling up.

17. WHO DO YOU CALL WHEN THE POLICE ARE AFTER YOU?

The light's going.

The sun doesn't care that I don't have a clue where I am. Doesn't care that I need to see. Need to find my way out. It's time it was going to bed, and there ain't a thing I can do to change its mind.

What else can I do? Sit here in this dark, wooded area (maybe the tenth one today) and complain? Complain that the giant ball of cold fusion millions of miles away doesn't give a damn about me? In truth, I know it ain't the sun's fault. It ain't even the earth's fault for turning.

There's no one and nothing to blame for this mess other than me.

I listened when my boss had other ideas.

I went along with crazy plan after crazy plan instead of just doing what I was told.

For all I know, Flick and Toby are already dead. Could be that all this is meaningless.

It's colder out here than I would like. The damp cold that seeps into your bones the longer you're out in it. Still, could be worse. I could be on the lam on Orkney. Colder weather. Less hiding places.

But I get to thinking about the good news as I walk into a clearing.

No boy in blue has laid eyes on me yet. No one's got me in cuffs. Should be grateful for that.

Still no clue what to do next though.

I've got a couple of hundred in cash. Where can I spend it? Somewhere without CCTV? How many places are there now that fall into that category?

Maybe I could buy myself a disguise. Hair dye. Change how I look in any way I can.

But people can tell a fake. Their eyes pick up the signs. Report it to the brain. These folks think its intuition. It's not. They've seen something off. Different colour eyebrows. The wrong skin tone for the hair. A shifty look in their eyes. Something. They just don't know what they've seen to put them on edge. Maybe they'll never figure out what it is they've seen.

Either way, hiding ain't easy.

There's a village ahead. Gotta hope it's far enough off grid. That they've not all got video doorbells. Night vision cameras stuck to their walls.

I've got to get a little closer. Creep around. Find somewhere to sleep. Find clothes that don't have blood on them. I thought I got away without any scrapes from the crash. Turns out, I was wrong.

I'm on a half dirt, half gravel pathway. Leads right towards the cluster of buildings and streetlights ahead.

I trudge along.

What's Holly thinking? What can I do on my own?

What can any man do when they're on the run?

I'll get through the night somewhere. Give her a call in the morning on that strange number. This isn't a task I can get done alone.

Getting closer to a rear garden of a good-sized house. No lights on inside. No dog out back.

It's a fence I can hop with ease. Some cuts and bruises try to tell me otherwise, but I've got to ignore them. Like I've got to ignore everything else wrong with this situation.

Would a prison cell be any worse than this? Really?

Sure, the beds aren't great. Yeah, there's a chance of getting a little beaten up. But at least there *is* a bed. And food. You get that too.

What have I got? Injuries I can't treat. Could be leaving a nice trail of blood, for all I know. Gonna wake up in some dumpster with a sniffer dog licking my face.

It all sounds crazy, but the helicopters, the dogs, firearms, the lot will be out to find me. I'm charged with murder. I assaulted a police officer and escaped custody. A couple more of the big things and I'm gonna top the Most Wanted list. At least I would if that wasn't made up by news agencies to make something out of nothing.

I walk to the back of the house.

Not a sound. No sign of movement.

But then it all happens at once.

Something moves. A dog barks. A damn big dog. A light comes on. Shines in my face. A scream, muffled by double glazing.

I turn and run back the way I came.

A door's opening.

The dog barks are louder. It's on its way across the big garden and it wants my nuts as a snack.

I manage to scale the fence. Just.

The dog's teeth catch the edge of my right shoe. It's got enough of a grip that it takes it from me. I ain't going back for it.

I jump down the other side and sprint away on one shoe and hurting legs.

This might not be the village for me. Not right now.

I have a grimace-like smile on my tired face.

That stunt's jumped me up a few places on that imaginary list.

***

There's a blissful little moment of sleep, right at the end. You start to come around. The peace of your night's rest hasn't yet melted away. Not yet cooled by frosty reality. Ready to confront you when you open your eyes.

These few seconds are gonna be my only moment of peace for a few hours.

It comes flooding back.

The arrest. The charge. The breaking free. The big dog stealing my shoe.

I had to scram from that place. Word gets around pretty quick in these rural spots when someone spies you on their property. Wasn't gonna end up in some old lady's place. Getting sprayed with some mace she keeps handy for emergencies.

I gave the next village a miss too. No clue how far word of mouth gets, or how fast it gets there. Could be wherever I was gonna stop, some folks would already be waiting for me. Gossip over phones and the Internet moves faster than a guy on the lam with one shoe.

My weary eyes take in my surroundings in the vague light of some point too early in the morning.

A curved and badly damaged, water-stained ceiling. Parts of it could fall on me at any moment. I can make out chunks of rotten plywood. Insulation that could be as old as I am. A skylight that's so sun-scorched that it hasn't let much light in over maybe the past decade.

The smell hits me. Like wet dog.

More like a wet dog slept in a sewage pipe and then had a lie down on this shabby lump of light brown carpet.

Back a few years ago, a family of four went on vacations in this thing. Hard to imagine it now. One kid over where the floor's rotten. Another by the broken plastic window. Parents on the other side. Now, there are bare twelve volt wires, threatening some pathetic level of shock. But only if someone's stupid enough to hook up a battery.

There's no bathroom in here anymore. No kitchen. Nothing but a few chunks of twisted metal on the walls, showing what was once here.

A torn apart, open space is all that's left. Holes in the floor. A broken door lock. Holes in the roof. No idea why someone kept this thing. Couldn't even be worth anything as scrap.

At some point, someone's gonna know I'm in here. They're gonna peer in around one of those horrendous makeshift curtains. Past that dark brown floral pattern that died years ago and should stay buried. They'll see some vagabond sleeping rough. Someone who used to be someone. Someone who used to have a family. Used to be loved. Used to not be wanted for murder and escaping police custody.

There's a hint of animal waste in the air. To be expected on a farm. Never known one to smell any different.

Sounds of cows in the distance. Some other animal I can't place a little closer to me.

I've got to get up, get moving before it's feeding time.

I sit up on the old, flea-ridden carpet and the fleece blanket that was left in here to rot. I look around to gather my things.

But I've not got any things. Just the phone and the cash in my pocket.

Don't know what I'm gonna do today.

Just get up and keep walking and running.

Stay away from the law a little longer.

Try to find some clean clothes. Call that phone number.

Find my way back to some place I know. Maybe head back towards Cookston. It's stupid enough that the police might not expect me there.

I need some decent shelter. I need someone on my side.

I get up and head out the door. No one around. Nothing but barns and outbuildings that defy physics by staying standing.

I creep out and make a clean getaway. No one's ever gonna know I was there. Not unless those pesky wounds opened up again.

I got myself too wrapped up in the modern world before yesterday. We've all done it.

How many folks these days know their own phone number?

How many know their partner's? What percentage of people could be chucked in some random field and have any clue which way was north? How to get home?

Damn satellite navigation and its ease. No more homing instinct. It got chucked on the same pile as manually washing clothes and figuring out Morse Code.

Gotta keep moving until I find a place I recognise. See if I can make some kinda progress in a day that's just beginning.

For all I care, the day can go the same way as the car crank and the typewriter. Who needs it?

***

"A sighting last night in Vale's Keep," the tall, bespectacled, spotty officer is out of breath as he charges in. Looks as welcome as a Black Sabbath singer at a Christian bake sale. "A village a few miles from the crash."

He brushes some imaginary hair away from his upper forehead and waits. No clue what he's waiting for. He's like a dog expecting a 'good boy' and a pat on the head.

The Superintendent stares at him. Those bushy grey-black eyebrows. Cold blue eyes stand out on the roundish, wrinkled face. No words are necessary.

He's interrupting. He's backing away. Nearly touching the door. "Thought you'd like to know."

He nods. It's so slight it might only be picked up by an expert in micro expressions. "Thank you PC Yardly."

He grins like an idiot and flees the room like he's in danger of being tasered.

He can get back to what he was doing. Looking for holes. Loose threads. The one thing that doesn't make sense about all this.

He does his best, of course, to remain courteous. Professional. Treat DI Chamberlain with respect. Pretend to be a little more human and caring. Understanding, even. She'll go over the details of this story and something won't add up. He can feel it.

Trouble is, there's nothing else, other than facts that back up her crazy story.

"Why were you heading to the prison again?" he asks her.

She removes the ice pack from the side of her face and glares at him. She talks through a busted lip. "I told you. An inmate had information on one of my old cases. Figured I'd take Flint over while I was already going that way."

He nods. "A two birds, one stone kind of thing?"

She nods. Looks like it made her dizzy.

"He a friend of yours?" He tries to come across carefree, but it's too high-pitched. Sounds forced. Never mind.

She shakes her head. Half smiles. About all she can manage with her face like that. "Never seen him outside of work, so nothing more than a colleague."

This is a waste of time. The evidence from the dashcam agrees with everything she says. They still haven't found the other car. It's like it vanished. Plates were fake. They know that much. Some stolen piece of junk, no doubt. Probably never gonna find the guy with the scraggly hair behind the wheel.

"Any idea where he might've gone?"

She raises the eyebrow on the good side of her face. "You think I keep tabs on all the sergeants and detectives under me? Why would I know anything about the guy?"

He shrugs. "Just asking the usual sorts of questions."

No, her supervisor was suspicious, but those suspicions aren't checking out. She's looking pretty clean for now.

"Thank you, Inspector," he says. He pushes his chair back a little and starts to get up. "I hope your injuries heal quickly, and that we find the man who did this before too much longer."

She smiles. Seems genuine. That can be faked. He should know. "I hope so too, sir."

18. A LONG WAY DOWN, BUT A SHORTCUT TO FREEDOM

Life hasn't got half so many ups and downs as the land around Cookston.

One moment you're driving at the base of a valley. The next, you're over a hill. Then you find yourself peering down a hundred feet or more at some river below you.

Why anyone chose to settle in a place with pretty much no flat land is a mystery to me. Maybe they liked the look of chalky, grey cliffs being pounded by waves when the wind picked up.

It all looks okay to me at the moment. Found my way to some spot within maybe five miles of home.

I'm on one of those bridges. High above rocks and water.

People were pretty determined to settle near here. They flattened land to build a couple of houses. They built these bridges. That can't have been easy. Somewhere along the way, some workman must've asked questions. Is it was worth the risk of plunging to your death? Are the travellers gonna thank you? Chances are, they'll save a half hour. Not having to go the land-based route. Not even give the builders a second thought.

Still, if they hadn't built this bridge, I'd have to find somewhere else to stand and stare down.

Day light's nearly gone. The lower part of the sky's lit up in orange and pink. The bit above my head's mostly resigned to a deep, greyish dark blue.

The bridge has one lane each direction. A pavement either side. A railing up to nearly my chest.

I'm stood in the middle. Right where the ground and the water's as far away as it's getting. Would be quite the fall. A hell of a bungee jump if you're into that kinda thing.

I'm only interested in the kind of drop where you don't come back up.

Another day wasted.

Still no clue what to do.

No closer to bringing down VIRTUS. No closer to even knowing another damn thing about them.

They've got my family. They might think I'm stuck inside. Maybe they know by now that I'm not. They think they've got leverage to make me do what they want.

I think I've got a way out. It starts with a fall for maybe three seconds. Ends with a thump at the bottom.

VIRTUS have no need to keep hold of Flick and Toby when I'm gone. What are their chances of getting outta there? Have they got as much of a chance if I throw myself over? That gonna get better or worse if I go charging through the door, guns a blazing?

But I ain't gonna go filling henchmen with daylight and saving the day like some movie hero. Not now. Not when I'm on the run. Can't even buy new clothes. Can't dare to show my face anywhere.

No, their best chance of surviving comes when I'm done doing the same.

The light's a little dimmer still.

It's a good final sunset, at least. Couldn't wish for a better one.

The kind that deserves music and celebration. The kind that stirs up beautiful music from nowhere that runs around your head until it's tired. For me, right now, it's Rachmaninoff's Piano Concerto Number Two. Quite the piece of music to sing in your head when you're all by yourself.

No one's here to see this but me.

It's for the best. No witnesses. No one to traumatise when I climb up that pole and get over the barrier.

I'll stand here. Watch a little longer. Wait until the light's gone.

Then I'll get on with putting my own lights out.

So long world. Goodbye to the places and the people who knew me enough to judge me and not enough to help me.

The sunset's close to being done for the day. It's getting pretty damn cold. No wonder I'm the only one dumb enough to be out here.

I put my hands on the railing. Stare at them. Stare past them at the water below. Looks black now. Time to fling myself down to its inky, rocky depths. VIRTUS can congratulate themselves on another life taken, albeit indirectly. My exhausted brain can find no better way of getting Flick and Toby out of this mess.

My hands grip the railing tight.

They're glowing a little.

What's wrong with me? What crazy stuff's my imagination throwing out in my final moments?

But they're definitely glowing. Getting brighter. The glow's travelling up my arms.

Then I hear it.

The car to my right.

Not some kinda divine intervention. I ain't getting my Its-A-Wonderful-Life moment. Maybe the angels have all got their wings and they don't give a damn.

I'll wait for the car to breeze on past.

Except it doesn't.

It slows down. Stops not far from me.

Don't they know they can't stop on a bridge like this?

A door opens. "Flint!"

It's a voice I recognise.

A voice I can't seem to stop hearing. One that belongs to someone who just will not let me die in peace.

19. HOW NOT TO TALK SOMEONE DOWN

"It ain't worth it," she says. "You've got the whole worst part of your life ahead of you."

I'm staring down at the near-black canyon. I shout back at her. "That supposed to help?"

She closes the car door and walks closer. "You get to put on weight. More weight. Try fad diets that don't work. Get more and more health problems. Then there's the whole mid-life crisis thing, but you're pretty much there by now."

I look in her direction. Can't think of a thing to say.

She's a little closer. She sighs. "I didn't put my neck on the line so you could wield an axe at it."

"From where I was, you got yourself a good cover story," I say. "I bet you aren't even getting a warning."

She lets out a laugh that dies as quickly as it was born. "Wonder what would they'd do if it was you behind the wheel instead of me."

I look at her. She's an arm's length away now. "You trying to cheer me up? I've gotta say, so far, you're not doing a sterling job."

She just stands next to me. Peers over the edge. "How far down do you think?"

I shrug. "Far enough."

She turns away. "Personally, I don't think you can say you've come far enough yet, Flint."

Silence for a moment. It ain't long before we're both watching the last of the sun sink below the horizon.

"How'd you find me anyway?" I ask.

"You missed the keyring-type thing in that cash envelope?"

I pull it out. Flick through it. There's some thin piece of plastic in there.

"A GPS tracker. Links to my phone."

I laugh. "The police all over are working up a sweat hunting me down. All that time, you've had the answer to all their questions right in your pocket?"

I look down. Shake my head.

She shrugs. "They never asked if I was tracking you."

"What would you have said if they did?"

"I'd have started talking about anything else. My injuries. Lady problems. Anything to cut that session short."

"You just abandoned me." I turn. She ain't looking pleased with what I'm saying. "Gave me cash I can't spend without being spotted, and nothing but a note. I spent last night in a broken-down caravan."

She shakes her head. Sighs again. "You missed a few clues, didn't you? For a detective, you're not that observant."

I look up at that big post next to me. "I can still scale this thing, you know. Throw myself down there. What's there to live for? More insults?"

"Near the crash site, did you see the newsagents?"

I shake my head. "Small shop right by the road. A place like that, it's a convenience store. A great place for food. Mobile phone top-ups. Maybe even a new T-shirt."

"What's your point?"

She stares at me like I'm the dumbest fugitive in the history of fugitives. "They don't have CCTV. One dummy camera. You'd have got in there, bought some stuff, and come out with everything you needed."

I look at my feet. "Didn't feel like pointing that place out?"

She laughs. "I was a little busy being punched in the face."

The sun's fully set now. I don't know what we're both staring out at.

"You at least call that number on the slip of paper?"

I look at her. "Thought it was to get hold of you. You're standing right here."

She squeezes the handrail. She's angry now. Frustration's boiling over at my lack of any sense. "You know, Flint, it might be better if you *did* die."

I look at her. Mouth hanging open. I've got no words.

"I thought drastic action wasn't going to help you, but it just might." She's got a funny look in her eyes.

I look down into the canyon. "Anyone ever told you how amazing you are at talking down a potential suicide?"

She lets go of the handrail. Turns away. Paces around. Back and forth. Like she does when she's got an idea.

She turns to look at me. "What would they do if you weren't a threat anymore?"

"Maybe release Flick and Toby. Maybe just kill them." It pains me to even let those words spill from my lips.

She nods. "Another couple of bodies to deal with? It's the messy option. What's the clean option?"

I shrug. "Draw a line under everything Flint and move on."

She nods again.

I look right at her. "You're saying I should..."

I nod towards the huge drop.

"Hell, no!" Her eyes widen as she talks. "I don't think we want you to *really* be dead."

I ain't got a clue what she's getting at. Maybe she doesn't get let out at night for a reason. No idea where she even calls home. Her apartment complex might share a pool with the local nuthouse.

She walks off. Raises her phone to her ear.

It's getting too cold for standing outside and waiting for an Inspector to finish a phone call. People have perished in less time.

I move around a little. Jog about. Stamp my feet. Rub my hands together. A quick death from a fall is better than a slow death from pneumonia and frostbite.

She's off the phone. She heads back over to me.

"Flint, I've got you a place to stay. A step up from a caravan."

I frown at her. "The catch?"

That fury is still in her somewhere. It's lurking inside those eyes. "I called the number *you* should've called."

I stare at her like that didn't answer my question.

"A safe house."

I don't think I look any less confused.

"Safe from what?"

20. SAFE AS HOUSES?

Someone says the words 'safe house' to you, you're gonna have certain expectations.

Me? They started with something safe, and ended with something with four walls and a roof.

I'm driven a few miles along the coast. There are more static caravan parks than you can shake a stick at. All got beautiful coastal views. Some facilities. Brats who run around someone else's holiday home at night kicking up a fuss.

I give Holly a sideways look when she pulls into one of them. And not one of the good-looking ones.

"Are you kidding?" I say.

A micro shake of the head. "Middle of nowhere. Out of the way. Constant stream of people coming and going. Makes sense when you think about it."

Yeah, she's pointed out the positives. What about the other side of that coin? Plenty of space for hiding underneath. Pretty much no insulation. Thin walls. Easily broken windows. Isolation ain't great when someone's after you. Just consult every horror movie script ever written.

"You say the words safe and house, I'm gonna expect certain things. This place has got more of an insecure shipping container vibe."

She gives me that look that's supposed to shut down my complaints. She's put effort into helping me. I guess I've gotta keep this trap of mine snapped shut and be a little grateful.

At least she stops by one of the nicer units. Looks to be a

double-width. Big enough for a family of six with a dog. Enough room to spare for a tiny fridge and a TV the size of a calculator. It's got a balcony and decking at one end. A pitched roof. Looks almost like an old lady's bungalow.

The grass between each caravan's been cut in the past couple of days. No one's gonna give up their time to follow behind with a rake, it seems. The cuttings are left in clumps everywhere. Longer grass hides under the edges of each metal box on stilts. Seems they don't bother with a strimmer either.

A red Audi is already parked in the blue-grey gravel spot to the left of the caravan. Some woman standing next to it. Height somewhere between five-six and five-seven. Greasy-looking brown hair, held back with a some kinda hairband or ribbon. A shade of lipstick that matches the car. Eyes that match the gravel. They look nervous. A face that looks rounder on the left side than it does on the right.

She puts on a smile. Looks as nervous as the eyes. My mere presence doesn't usually instil so much fear. Maybe this is what a couple of days on the run does for people. Could be a normal reaction to someone who's cracked out of custody.

"You Flint?" she asks.

I nod. Maybe she doesn't watch the news. I've gotta assume I've been all over it for the past few hours. Maybe I'm wrong. Maybe prison breaks happen all the time. Police might just not tell people. They don't want the mobs with torches and pitchforks. Anger spirals when vigilantes go looking for an escaped inmate.

She holds out a timid right hand. I shake it. It's got all the inherent strength of a wilted lettuce leaf. "Agent Demi Wheeler," she says. Looks in my eyes for a second and then looks away like it was a bad idea.

I cast a look at Holly. I turn my attention back to the woman in front of me. "Agent? Agent of what?"

It's her turn to look at Holly. There's a 'you haven't told him?' kinda look on her face.

Holly takes a step closer to us. Speaks in a quiet voice. "Security Services. She's an old friend. A former colleague, in fact."

Agent Wheeler looks over both shoulders. Looks back at me and Holly. "Shall we take this conversation inside?"

Maybe she ain't nervous of me. Maybe she just ain't a fan of being outdoors.

She walks up the two metal steps to an opaque glass and PVC door. Pushes the handle down like it's a hand lever on an oil rig. She's inside. Holly follows.

I step up once. The little set of two metal steps isn't as strong as it likes to think it is. The thing creaks and bends. If I stand still and jump a little, I'll be back on the ground pretty quick.

I hurry up the other step and inside. The caravan doesn't feel sturdy, but it's better than the steps leading up to it.

To my left is the living area. Two large white fabric couches face each other. A small flat-screened TV, the cheap kind, sits in the corner. Far left and tucked away, like no one even remembers it's there. A big, beige rug and a dark wood and glass coffee table sit between the sofas.

A breakfast bar divides the area from the kitchen, dead ahead of me. I think it's bigger than my own. Full-sized brushed steel appliances. Even a washer/dryer. Beech coloured units will hold the usual supplies for family dinners.

A work surface that's light grey with flecks of a hundred

different colours. Looks like someone threw paint around. Added some tiny plastic shards from kids' toys. Kept going until enough stuck to the surface to make an acceptable pattern. Looks like the kinda work surface someone chooses when they don't know what to choose.

The floor throughout is a grey, wood-effect laminate. Three, maybe even four bedrooms and a couple of bathrooms to the right.

As far as caravans go, this one's okay. Ask me if I wanna vacation in one and it's still an emphatic no. The best caravan might still not stack up to an average hotel. Not to me, anyway. Ask me which caravan I'd prefer to stay in, you might as well ask which room in Hell I wanna reserve for when I get there.

I'm led down the hall to a large room. Twin beds.

"Pick one," Agent Wheeler says. "I'll take the other."

I look at her. "We've got a few rooms and we're sharing one?"

She nods. Deadly serious. A much sterner, more confident figure inside than she was a minute ago in the fresh air. "I'm not taking my eyes off you for a moment. It's the only way I could get this job off the ground."

I sit on the bed farthest from the door, to the left. I face the two women. "What job is that, then?"

She gives Holly that look again. Unspoken words to the tune of 'you mean you didn't tell him that either?'

Holly rolls her eyes. "There wasn't time to go into any details."

The agent looks out the window, above the bed she's left with. Shakes her head a little. "With your help, Flint, we want to take down VIRTUS."

I lean back until my head touches the wall. I look up at the ceiling trying hard not to look cheap, but failing. "How am I supposed to do that?"

"Flint," says Holly. I look at her. She's giving me the headmistress look again. "I took a hell of a risk getting you here. Doing what I've done the last couple of days. Play nice, would you?"

She turns to leave.

"You're not hanging around?" I ask.

She shakes her head. Keeps on walking for the door. "Got a day job, Flint. This is all above my head now. Good luck."

We head back out to the living area. She sits on one of the white sofas. I sit on the other.

"You can sit back. Relax," she says. "I'm the one with work to do for now."

I shuffle forward. Hunch over a little. "What do you mean?"

She sits all the way back. Lets out a sigh. "I've got to sort out the mess you've made. Got to talk to some people at work. See if we can make you vanish."

I frown. "Is that really necessary?"

She nods. A grim expression on her face. "MI5 can't make all your baggage disappear. We can make you look like you've disappeared, though. Best thing. Get out of the way for a few days."

Gotta wonder what kind of level this woman's at in that organisation. They employ thousands of people at MI5. Some are agents. Some are computer nerds. She called herself an agent when we shook hands. Do they all do that, or is she more than she seems?

"What about taking down VIRTUS? Saving my family?" I ask.

She looks at me deadpan. "Let's take this one task at a time. With any luck, my ideas will buy us a little more time to do both."

I nod. Can't say I agree. I'm in a hurry. She seems keen to take things at a leisurely pace.

I know which method I'd pick if I was calling the shots.

21. IN TOO DEEPFAKE

The first night in a new bed usually means a bad night's sleep.

This place worked out better than the last caravan. I slept like a rock, even with the strange woman in the same room.

Strange is the word. Wonder if anyone's told her she talks in her sleep. She doesn't toss and turn when she can't sleep, either. She full-on thrashes around. Must've been times I thought she was fighting an ant infestation. Or she was being attacked by some land-based shark that had sneaked in through the window.

But despite the weird night, she's up before the sun. I hear something cooking in a frying pan. The smell reaches me. Eggs. Bacon. I smile. She can stay.

I throw on some clothes. Go to make sure she's cooking breakfast for two. I get to the kitchen. I walk into a cloud of that greasy, salty, meaty bacon smell. Looks like there's too much in a couple of pans for just her.

She shouts out. Far too joyful. "Good morning!".

I nod and smile back. "I guess we'll see if the morning's a good one. But bacon at least improves it a little."

She points a spatula at the TV in the corner of the living area. Didn't even notice it was on. "Improved might be a better way of putting it. It's a low jumping off point."

I turn around and I see it. My name in big letters. Some breaking news story. My picture. Maybe something about my escape from the police. How I'm a danger to society and I must be caught. Except this looks a little different.

I turn up the volume so I can hear it over the sizzling stuff in the pans.

"Enoch Flint, still at large after escaping from police custody, is in the public eye again today."

A poor quality video flashes up on the screen. Some woman I've never met. She's got a cutesy girl-next-door vibe. Mouse brown hair at least to her shoulders. A perfect row of teeth. A decent looking gal. Even through that sad expression.

"I've held back on sharing this because I didn't want to hurt Evie," she says to the camera, "but I can't keep it a secret anymore."

She gonna admit she's got a thing for fugitives? Can't think of what else she's got to do with anything. And why's she talking about my ex-wife?

Plenty of other Evies out there. She could be talking about anyone. Except my gut seems to know straight away. She's only talking about one person.

"Evie Flint was one of my best friends until her husband, Enoch, stopped me from speaking to her. She was cut off. Isolated. I wanted to help her but I didn't know how. I mean, he was a police officer."

This girl lives in some alternate reality or something. I knew Evie's friends. Never met this woman. Haven't seen her in any photos. I didn't interfere with the woman's social life one bit. In fact, I can't say I was often a part of it in the later years.

"Not only did he keep her shut away at home, but he abused her. She sent me the pictures. A video of one night when he was angry."

Gotta say, it's starting to feel like I've not woken up yet, and this is some weird dream. Seems there's a numbness sneaking up my legs. I watch this much longer and I'm gonna feel like some floating apparition.

"Keep watching!" the agent-turned-fry-cook shouts from the kitchen. "There's more!"

They cut to another video. Evie looking upset. Looks like she's recording it on her own phone as she's running. "He needs to keep away from me. I can't take this anymore."

The phone moves. Her face disappears. Loud crashes. Maybe furniture being tossed. A window being broken. The phone falls to the floor. Still recording. Points straight up at the ceiling. "No, Flint. Leave me alone!"

Evie comes into view from the left. Another person from the right. Puts their hands around her throat. I've got to look back at Agent Demi Wheeler. She's got a resigned, serious look on her face as she nods.

I'm back to looking at the TV. Whatever this is, wherever this came from, it's crazy. There I am, strangling my ex-wife on video. The thing is, it never happened. None of it.

They start showing photos of bruises. Black eyes. Swollen faces. That's not something that ever happened to her. Not when I was with her.

"Where'd they get all this from?" I ask.

Demi wanders over with two plates of food. "I can take a guess. Seen this kind of thing before."

"What kind of thing? Flat-out lies? Character assassination?"

She nods. Sits down. "You eating, or are you not in the mood?"

I shake my head. "Lost my appetite."

She shrugs. "I'll leave it here in case you change your mind."

I start pacing the floor. Fists clenched. How could someone do this to me? Why would they feel the need? I'm an ex-cop, already on the run. Already with a screwed up life. My life's burning down, and they're trying to bulldoze the wreckage before I'm even out of the way.

The TV's still going. "Miss Molly Andrews brought this to our attention yesterday," says a newsreader. A grey-haired, serious fellow. Thin face. The thickest eyebrows I've ever seen. "Early this morning, she was found dead in her home. A note was left. It reads in part, 'I can't bear to live with the guilt. I allowed another monster in a police uniform to destroy more lives. I'm sorry to the people I have let down.'"

He looks straight down the camera. "Miss Molly Andrews, viewers. Aged thirty two. She won't see thirty three."

The TV turns off. I look back at Demi. Remote in-hand. "That's enough of that," she says.

"Well, what else do they say?" I ask.

She shrugs. "Couldn't find Evie to corroborate. Seems like she's vanished. They start wondering if you've done anything to her. They're taking all this at face value. They're using you to paint a grim picture of the police in the entire country."

I look at the TV. Back at her. "You're not worried?"

She smiles. "Worried about what? That you're some nutcase abuser of women?"

I've got nothing to say to that. I let her keep going.

She points at the dead TV. "I can spot a deepfake at a distance."

I frown at her as I sit down on the other sofa. "Deepfake?"

She nods. "Someone takes your face, puts it on someone else's body. Some people might set up and record the video with similar-looking people. Edit you onto the guy afterwards. You seen those TV ads where they do it? You get someone like Albert Einstein talking about an electric car. Winston Churchill praising a green energy supplier."

I nod.

So does she. "Same deal. You look closely, you can pick it apart."

I shake my head now. "Can't see them pulling their own headline story apart, can you?"

She looks down at the floor. "The sad thing is, news feeds off news. There's no stopping it online these days. Even a completely fake story is believed by a third of people online, even after it's been proven to be false."

I'm wearing some kinda sarcastic smile. "So to everyone out there, I'm a murdering wife-beater. Someone on the run, who should've never been allowed near a police uniform."

She looks at me. A sad look in her eyes. Could be sympathy. Could be nothing but pity. "I'm afraid so."

I get up and pace around some more. "VIRTUS have done a real number on me, haven't they?"

She nods. "But today, we start turning things around so they're facing the right way again."

"How do we do that?" I ask.

She gets up. Walks to the bedroom. Returns in a minute with an open laptop. "I've got some people I can get in on this. We've got a plan coming together."

I walk closer. "Will it get me my girlfriend back? My son?

My life?"

She shrugs. "We'll have to do our best and see what happens."

22. TIME TO PICK A SUICIDE

There are some things I don't like. They're the same kinda things most folks consider to be basic manners.

Please and thank you means something. An apology really can go a hell of a long way. I ain't saying we men have gotta hold car doors open for the ladies. Just that the world's a better place when people treat everyone else like people.

What got me thinking this way?

Maybe my head's in a funny place on account of being on the run.

Maybe I just don't feel safe in this safe house.

Whatever's going on, my stomach has stopped leaping around inside me. I can manage my bacon and eggs.

Still warm. Didn't leave it too long. The bacon's crispy, chewy, but not hard enough for making road signs outta it yet. Not even tough enough for a Lady Gaga outfit.

I'm working my way through it when she walks back in the room.

She's been gone for ten minutes. On the phone to some more staff at the security services. Took me longer than it should've done yesterday to process this as being MI5. My brain's not what it was. Not with so much unresolved stuff rattling around in it.

"We've got a solution," she says. Gotta say she's looking mighty pleased with herself.

I'm still looking down at my plate. "A solution to what?"

"You know. Your predicament."

I look up at her. "Does the solution involve an official pardon? Would be handy as I've not done any of the stuff people think I've done."

She shakes her head. "Things are too big to do that right now. We've got to work with what we've got."

I scoop some egg onto my fork. "How do you suggest we do that?"

I pop the egg onto my mouth. Start chewing.

"We figure the best course of action is to kill you."

My mouth fails open. Can't stop staring at this clear lunatic. This sounds like a joke. Problem is, she ain't looking like she's joking. In fact, she looks like she's just put the last piece down of a ten thousand piece Jigsaw puzzle.

I ain't the type to chew with my mouth open. No one ever wants to see your half masticated morsels. It's not a pretty sight. I'm usually pretty good with stuff like that.

Today, though, with that news, it's like my lower jaw wants to try out life as a doormat.

It's a much longer silence than I want. Longer than makes any sense at all. Maybe it just feels like it.

Still no smile. No laughter. No pointing a mocking finger.

She's serious.

I try to swallow the food in my mouth, but since I started chewing it's become sawdust and nails.

"VIRTUS, and the general public would both be appeased by your death. Wouldn't you agree?"

I raise an eyebrow. Stare at her. Nod a little.

Can't help but think the world might be a better place without me.

But if that's the case, why'd my Inspector stop me jumping off that bridge? Why talk me down from suicide, just to have me zotzed some other way?

"So we've got work to do with a new identity. Birth certificate, passport, believable personal history, driving license, the works."

My throat's expanding out a little. This isn't as bad as it seemed a minute ago. I swallow the eggs.

I say, "You mean to make it *look* like I've died!"

She frowns at me. "Wasn't that clear? I'm sure I said..."

She stops. Searches her memory of the conversation. Shakes her head. "Never mind."

"It's gonna speed up decision time for Flick and Toby," I say.

She nods. "If they were going to let them go, they'll do it. If they were never going to let them go, well..."

It all goes quiet again.

"Can't we get Inspector Chamberlain to contact them? She could use my phone. Say they want to negotiate their release or something."

She looks away. Deep in thought. Trying to find the holes in my suggestion. She turns around. Heads back for the bedroom.

"I'll be back in a few minutes," she says.

The food on the plate's more palatable now. Maybe I'll set myself a challenge. See if I can clear the plate before she comes back with any other digestion-interfering news.

VIRTUS have got me where they want me. The thing is, I've never been great at staying where people wanted me.

***

We've got three of us sitting round the table in this double-width static caravan now.

Holly's back. The day job's on hold. Maybe she's been seconded onto this whole operation. I didn't ask.

"We've got to give this careful thought," Demi says.

Holly nods. "Can't have some daft story people won't believe. Nothing that's supposed to leave a body we don't have."

I smile. "Rules out getting shot and stabbed, I guess."

Holly rolls her eyes. Looks at me. "How many people do you think have topped themselves by shoving a knife through their own chest?"

I shrug. "Does it have to be a suicide?"

Holly shrugs. "Makes things a little neater, doesn't it?"

"What about suicide by cop?" Demi asks.

A shaker of the head from Holly before she even fished speaking. "We're not turning him into some anti-establishment martyr."

Demi nods with a frown. Looks a little exaggerated for my taste.

I show the ceiling my palms from a distance. "Why not go with my original idea, before you brought me out here?"

Demi looks at Holly out of the side of her eyes.

Holly glares at me. Wants me to shut up.

"Just chuck me off a bridge," I say. "A good chance of the

body being washed out to sea. Simple."

Demi frowns. "What do you mean your original idea?"

She has no idea what I was thinking of doing.

I shrug again. "I had a thought. If I jumped off that high bridge near Cookston, things might improve. There might be more chance of VIRTUS letting my family go if I'm out of the picture."

She frowns. Looks at something that ain't quite me. Keeps staring.

An eery silence.

I look at Holly. She looks at me.

Please, someone say something.

I get up and start pacing the floor. "All I wanted, all I could do, was to try to get them to release Flick and Toby."

Holly nods. Looks at Demi. "Now he's got your resources, he's singing a different tune."

It's like Demi's not listening. Like someone froze her and didn't tell us. She's off in some other world. Maybe wondering if her life's worth all that much.

Her gaze darts away. It's like she's back from the body snatchers. She looks right at me. "You sure you're mentally strong enough for all this? If things get a bit much, are we gonna find you up there again?"

I shake my head. "You telling me everyone hasn't thought about that at some point? I ain't any less stable than anyone else."

She looks down. Shakes her head. Not another word. What's going on in that head of hers? What's happened to her to make a conversation on suicide put her in some far away land?

Holly nods. "I could get on board with the bridge idea. Leak to the news outlets. Flint's no longer a problem."

A problem's all I ever seem to be. I try to stop screwing up my face. Not sure I manage it.

She continues. "Once it's recorded, once the media are reporting your... untimely demise... I should be able to get hold of your phone."

I'm still putting foot to floor, trying to wear a pathway in the cheap carpet. "I've got higher priorities than my old phone," I say.

Holly looks at me like I'm an idiot. There's something about that look from folks that makes me feel like I'm home. "It's so I can communicate with VIRTUS. Tell them you're dead. Negotiate for the release of Flick and Toby."

I shake my head and point at her. "They'll rope you into something. Get you doing some shady deals instead of me."

She cocks her head. "It's possible. How else do we find out more about them? What do *you* suggest we try if we're gonna stop them?"

There's a whole lot of figure-this-out-as-you-go-along coming out of this gum-flapping session. I ain't the least bit convinced we're gonna get anywhere.

I shake my head. Still wander around the place. "You think any of this is gonna work?"

Holly's looking at me. She's got an out-of-her-depth look on that mug of hers.

Demi keeps retreating to that place in her head that's so much more interesting than being here.

I kinda wish I had somewhere to retreat to. Instead, I'm stuck here. Got to pretend I no longer exist as anything other than a floating corpse, lost at sea.

***

How do you come back from being dead?

That's the question that keeps forcing its way to the front of my mind.

Even if we can get Flick and Toby home safe, what then?

Am I supposed to head home? Breeze through the door like I'm on some lame sitcom, say, "Honey, I'm home, and you wouldn't believe the day I've had!"

I don't think so. Things ain't gonna come out of the wash all pristine like that.

Folks don't show up alive again and get to pick up where they left off.

No one's putting the pieces of my life back together, whatever they tell me.

What are the police gonna do when things sort themselves out? They gonna release some statement about me?

Sorry, but we were wrong about a couple of things.

No, Flint didn't abuse his ex-wife.

No, he didn't kill that homeless man.

No, he ain't even dead. Didn't jump off that bridge like we told you.

Actually, he's very much alive. He's living in Norfolk under the name of Nigel. He now teaches pottery classes to old age pensioners.

I don't think so.

But this question's getting in the way. Can't concentrate. Can't figure out what to do next. Can't see holes in even wild ideas.

I've been chewed up and spit out by the monsters in my life, and only a couple of them are my typical demons.

They're getting me my new identity. Not something I can cast off. The glue sets pretty hard on that kinda life-change.

The name Enoch Flint ain't gonna be any use to me anymore. All it's ever gonna do from now on is shut down opportunity and invite a heap of awkward questions.

The rumours, the false accusations all go away when people think I'm a goner. Problem is, they take my real name and my career with them.

So long Enoch Flint. You were an ordinary cop, made for a different time. Your results led to spectacular success or triumphant failure.

Gotta wonder what the future holds for me, whatever they call me now.

23. THESE PHONES HAD BETTER BE SMART

I'm about done mourning my own death when Holly gets a message. Something interesting from digital forensics.

She gets on the blower to Nahid Shamoon, our analyst. Puts the call on speaker. Lays the phone down on the table like it's a newborn being put down for a nap.

"I've got the phone results from Elias Wilkins from Heathrow. Also got Graham Craigie's from Orkney. Looking at them side-by-side."

Holly nods. "Anything notable found on them?"

"Both have got the same strange app on them we know about," Nahid says. "Extra Media Manager."

I wanna talk but Holly glares at me. "Flint had the same app on his phone," she says. "He recorded some video. Opened it up and tapped the play button three times. It became some sort of encrypted messaging app."

Silence for a moment while Nahid takes that in. "Yes, that makes sense. Each instance of the app has different content. Messages encoded using some proprietary algorithm."

Each of those words are English. I know they are. Used some of them myself in different conversations. Problem for me is that this time, they're stuck together in some strange order. It ain't understandable by mere mortals.

"Give me a little longer," Nahid says. "If I dig into this a little, I might be able to find a little more. Who made it. The company that put it on the app store. That kind of thing."

Holly nods. "Thank you. Could you send me a quick report

with the details of the two apps?"

Nahid agrees and ends the call.

"I'll forward the report on," she says, looking at Demi. "See if any of your team can do anything else to find out who's behind it."

She nods. "Should give us a lead."

I nod a little. "Let's hope so."

***

Demi's gone for a few minutes.

She said a few minutes. More like a couple of hours.

She comes back waving a USB stick at me.

Might as well have had something written on the outside in black marker. NEW IDENTITY: JUST ADD PERSON.

I pick it up. Put it in the laptop. Random files. I open a picture. It's a passport. The page with all the personal details. So strange to see my photo next to some other name.

I screw up my face a little. "Peter Hart?" I ask.

Demi nods. "That's who you are now, temporarily. Digitally, anyway. Until we put the work into something more permanent."

I click through a few more files. "So what happened to Enoch Flint in the end?"

She drops a newspaper down on the table. I'm right there. Front page.

Disgraced Detective Dead - Suicide Suspected.

An article that says what I expect. The ex-cop was accused of various things. Was on the run. Police were closing in. He chose to jump off a bridge and end it all. Body's believed to have been washed out to sea.

I keep looking through the documents. Fake birth certificate. Makes me a couple of years older. Thanks for that.

"I thought you might like the name," she says. "It's not Flint, but it all means a kind of hard stone."

I look at her.

She's got some pleading look in her eye and her lips stretched into a weak smile. "Close as I could get, don't you think?"

I poke out a bottom lip and nod my approval. I liked my old name. then again, I liked my old life, looking back.

"All documents are on the relevant systems. Some minor changes from the last guy that used it and you're good to go."

"The last guy?" I ask. "What happened to him?"

She scrunches up one half of her face. "I don't think I can tell you that," she says.

Well, that's got me feeling calm and relaxed. There were better ways of avoiding answering.

She hands me a box I didn't see her holding. A new smart phone. Still in the box. I pull it out.

She nods. "All set up and ready for you to use on a temporary basis. You've got to be sensible, though. Our encryption and VPN and all that stuff can't protect you online. Not if you log into old email or send messages to people as Enoch."

I look at her like she hasn't said the most obvious, dumb thing anyone's ever said to me. I guess someone's figured me to be just as stupid before. I've met quite a few people.

I take a closer look at the phone's box. The tape's been cut. Already opened. Their tech people, as promised, have messed around and done their thing with this.

She leans over the laptop. Opens one document. "Details of email and social media accounts we've set up and developed for the name. Passwords are all there too."

I nod. Thank her for the effort.

She shrugs. "We've got a few of these false identities sitting around. We add someone's photo to some documents, and it comes alive, all of a sudden."

I turn the phone on. I wait. I wait a little longer. Spinning cogs and animated padlocks show on the screen. Seems forever until the thing's ready to do something.

"What about my old phone?" I ask.

She looks towards the door. "Holly's got it. She'll be getting in touch with VIRTUS. Telling them you're dead. No longer a threat. That kind of thing. See if she can secure the release of your family."

I'm staring at the phone. Got no clue if I even wanna use the thing. Who would I contact, and why? "And if that works?"

There's a look on Demi's face like she wasn't expecting that question. Like the idea had never crossed her mind.

"You work with us to take down VIRTUS," she says, "and when we're done, we should be able to give you your old life back. Well, as much as we can."

"Just one more question," I say.

She looks at me.

"How am I gonna be useful to VIRTUS as... Peter Hart?"

She smiles. "We'll get to that. With your help, obviously."

I ain't convinced by any part of this plan.

Why would VIRTUS let my family go? Why would they start up again with a stranger to attempt another round of chaos?

All I can think about now is Holly's conversation with them. Pleading for release of two hostages. If that goes well, I couldn't give a damn how the rest of it goes.

If it all goes badly, then Enoch Flint might turn out to not be as dead as some people think he is.

***

She opens up the app. Taps three times on the play button, just as Flint had done on every screen recording.

She starts out simple enough.

> This is Detective Inspector Holly Chamberlain.
>
> Using the phone of Enoch Flint because it's the only way to contact you.

She waits.

> Hello D.I Chamberlain.

A polite reply. Didn't give anything away. Time to get straight to the point.

> You will be aware that DC Flint has died. We would like to discuss the release of his family, Felicity and Toby Parsons.

More waiting.

Even more.

She might as well go make a drink and come back to this.

> A very clever move, D.I Chamberlain. We require evidence

of the death of Enoch Flint. Can you provide this?

She thinks back to their previous attempt at deceit. The blood. That didn't end well, but she's got no idea what gave the game away.

Another message arrives.

> Evidence required needs to be definitive proof. Something he could not live without. Blood or a finger insufficient.

Oh dear. This isn't going the way she had hoped at all.

She tries again.

> The body was washed out to sea. What are we supposed to do?

She waits. Not long this time.

> Tell the truth.

Do they know? Are they guessing? They must be guessing. How could they know when only three people in the world know he's still alive?

> If you can provide one of Enoch Flint's vital organs, you will secure the release of his family.

Well, there goes that idea.

That is, unless she can find something to trade.

She picks up her phone. Calls a number from her recent history. Let's see what she can drum up to substitute.

Unless...

She ends the call before it connects. Makes another call instead.

This is a much better idea. No messing around. No dancing to someone else's tune.

Why didn't she think of doing this before?

24. AUTOPSY TURVY

Demi's been in the bedroom with her laptop.

She wanders back into the living area. Something's got her interested.

"An email send on by Holly," she says. "Autopsy results from Leo Ryan. She's busy doing... something else."

She knows what that something is. She ain't telling me.

She puts the computer on the table. Pulls out a chair and plonks herself in it. I get up and sit beside her. She opens up the attachment.

Cause of death asphyxiation. Quite a clean method of killing that's difficult to trace back to a killer. Not surprising.

Identifying marks and tattoos. I'm half hoping there's something random here, like my last big investigation. Nothing doing. One old tattoo on his neck. Nothing we didn't already know.

This guy didn't have much of a medical history. No doctor we could ask about him. No NHS records except for a couple of emergency room trips due to alcohol poisoning.

We keep reading.

I keep getting to the bottom of the screen and waiting for Demi to get there too. I'd look across, see her mouthing some words with her lips, and then eventually scroll down.

Some stuff we already knew about Leo's in the report. A bunch of stuff no one needs to know about anyone's in there too.

There's stuff about scar tissue. Hardened arteries. Blackened internal organs. Severely damaged throat, and not just from the strangulation.

It's all consistent with some diagnosis the guy should've had at least a few months ago. Seems no one told him. Lung cancer. Final stages.

He must've been coughing up blood and who knows what else. Must've had pain and problems elsewhere as the cancer spread. It's a wonder the guy was able to even stand up towards the end.

Whoever took this guy's life may not have known that there wasn't much left to take. He was gonna be dead within weeks or months.

Could Leo have known?

Would it have made any difference if he did?

It ain't a question I'm ever gonna get answered.

I've asked a few of them lately.

Just as Demi reaches the end of the document, I look at her. I'm gonna say something.

Some noise from the computer. A notification in the bottom right.

Another email forwarded on from Holly.

Another autopsy. This one's of Graham Craigie, Orkney's worst ever serial killer.

Time to see if this one tells us anything interesting.

***

A heart in a box.

That's what this all comes down to. It ain't even anything to do with Valentine's Day.

Maybe they'll know it's not Flint. Maybe they'll have no idea.

Doesn't matter. It's a prop anyway. A thing to draw them out of the shadows. Force someone to show themselves.

Holly had expected a meet-up at the same hotel. Same sniffing guy. Maybe even the same newspaper.

Not this time.

The message was clear.

> The top of the Sands Road car park. Place the box in the centre. Stay nearby and await further instruction.

She looks around. About the worst place to choose. Certainly the worst car park for miles around. Six levels of concrete misery, swirling up to a view of a few ugly buildings around it. Some sections with stucco on the outside. Sea pebbles scattered around. The ones that are still there, anyway.

Word is, this place is about to be condemned. One look around and you'll think the demolition crew are already here, getting a jump on the job.

They still have their handful of loyal customers. People who park there, day after day. We're all creatures of habit. It's easier to stick to what we've always done. Doesn't matter if our choices put us in some crumbling mess.

Holly's holding the thick cardboard box by the holes for handles on each side. Flint's phone is resting on top.

She's gotta keep paying attention to that, and to the radio earpiece. Flint's phone will have further messages about the package drop-off. The rest of her team will get her through the radio. Keep checking in. Letting her know if anything changes.

Exits will be blocked off. Entrances monitored. People standing by at every point you can get in and leave this deathtrap.

Add to that the GPS tracker she's had implanted inside the heart. If Nahid's watching on the laptop at ground level, she can keep a track of it. Whatever happens, they'll find something useful.

The VIRTUS representative will show. Collect the package. They'll stop them before they can leave. Even if he gets away, they can see where he goes. Then, they'll find out more about this organisation and its plans to cause disruption. At worst, do a hostage exchange. This guy for Flint's partner and kid.

She gets to what she thinks is the middle of the top floor of the car park. Puts the box down.

No one else is in view. Three cars are parked up here. As far away from each other as they could have managed without driving off the roof. All empty. Checked a couple of minutes ago.

She takes one step back from the box. Looks around. Still no one.

Thick clouds sit above her. A thin fog at ground level, but it's a little thicker up here. A cold day for standing in a higher spot in the open air. Could rain soon. Could even snow, if you believe the local weather.

Holly's getting a little twitchy. No one's entered the car park. No one's left. Is she gonna get a message to leave the thing here and walk away?

Flint's phone buzzes. Another message. About time.

> We are collecting the package. You will need to follow the next message exactly if you hope to secure the freedom of

our hostages.

She gets on the radio. "Ready everyone. Keep an eye out. Things could start moving quickly."

There's some weird feedback on the radio. A constant light buzzing.

It's getting louder.

She takes out her earpiece for a moment. She can still hear it. The noise isn't coming from the radio.

The buzzing's louder still. It's coming from somewhere above her.

Flint's phone goes again.

Attach the box using the zip ties on the bottom. Then stand clear.

The buzzing's really loud now.

An item about the size of a rucksack appears in mid-air. The thing looks like a UFO from a third-rate Sci-Fi movie. Just needs the flashing coloured lights. Add in the sound of something like an organ or panpipes being played.

The thing hovers above like a bee and gently lowers until it lands next to the box.

Holly walks over. Sure enough, some open zip ties are there.

She pauses.

This thing's gonna fly off and they'll be no closer to finding out anything.

Thank God for the GPS chip.

She gets out her phone. Snaps pictures of the drone. Looks for a serial number. A model. Anything. No identifying marks of any kind. Damn.

She gets on her radio. "Got to attach the box to a drone. What can we do about that?"

Silence.

"Anyone?"

More silence.

Finally, Nahid chimes in. "It could be controlled from somewhere close by. Sometimes these things have a short range. If we follow the GPS, we could see where it stops."

She nods. "Keep watching on that screen. I want updates every few seconds. The rest of you, clear out and see if you can find anyone who might be flying a drone!"

She types out a message in reply.

> How about you collect the box personally?

A response is being typed. Then it appears.

> Attach the box to the drone with the supplied zip ties. Failure to do so will halt negotiations for the release of Felicity and Toby.

She sends out one more message over the radio. "I've got to attach this thing and watch it fly off. Anyone got eyes on this thing? At least to see which direction it goes?"

She waits longer than she'd like for a reply. "Ma'am, PC Erikson. I'm in a car on the ground. I'll do my best to follow it."

This is it. The best they can do.

The plan's half in ruins because of some daft little lump of plastic and spinning propellers. Still, it's only *half* in ruins. The backup's gonna save the day.

She attaches the box. Maybe there'll be another chance to

nab someone from VIRTUS. Maybe they're round the corner and about to get jumped by some of her officers.

She stands back. Sends another message.

>Done.

The reply comes quickly.

>Stand well back.

She takes a couple of steps back.

Another message.

>Further back than that.

She spins around. Looks everywhere. Still no sign of anyone. How are they watching?

She does as she's told.

The drone lifts up. Hovers about a foot off the floor. Goes up a little further.

Then in a couple of seconds, the thing shoots straight up in the air.

It fades from view as the clouds and the fog swallow it.

The buzzing gets quieter.

The drone's going. Not even a clue as to the direction.

Quieter still, and then it's gone.

Time to try the radio again. "Anyone see where the drone went?"

A whole lot of negatives in reply.

"What about the GPS signal?"

"We've got it, ma'am," says Nahid. "It's gone a few hundred yards and stopped again. Northern end of the high street."

"Heading there now," says PC Erikson. He's keen on finding the drone, and probably for some official recognition.

"Update me as soon as you know more," Holly says. "We can't let this thing get away."

"It looks like the roof of that closed department store. There's access from the back alley if you head up the fire exit stairs. They go all the way up."

Only a few seconds until PC Erikson sounds out of breath on the radio. "I'm heading up the stairs now."

We've got him. Finally.

"Wait!" shouts Nahid. "The drone's moving again!"

"Keep heading to the roof, Erikson. You should still see whoever's up there."

The few seconds between updates is maddening. If only she could see what's going on.

"I'm on the roof." PC Erikson again. "There's no one here. I haven't passed anyone on the stairs."

"Nahid, an update on the drone's location please." Holly's got a sense things are slipping from her clutches again.

"It's heading for the quay," Nahid says. "It's moving pretty fast."

Holly's about to order someone out there.

"It's cleared the quay, and it's heading out over the river."

Brilliant. This is gonna end up out of their county any minute. That's when things get complicated really quickly.

"It's still moving," Nahid says. She's getting a little exasperated. "Right out to sea... and it's stopped."

"Stopped?" Holly says.

"I'm only getting a last position now. No live updates."

"What does that mean, Nahid?"

"Either the battery's given up, or the drone's been deliberately crashed into the sea."

Holly lets out a frustrated sigh. "Anything from the department store?"

"Nothing, ma'am," says PC Erikson. "No signs of anyone that I can see, inside or out."

Brilliant.

Well, that was a waste of a particularly dull morning.

Still no closer to VIRTUS. Still no idea who's working for them. Not so much as a clue.

Okay, they've got a drone. Or at least, they *had* a drone until they plunged it into the sea. Someone might be able to tell her the make and model. See how many have been sold recently. It's not gonna get them any closer. Not the way these people work.

Those people at MI5 who laughed when she asked about air support are gonna look pretty stupid now.

25. OH NO! POOR LEMMINGS!

Graham Craigie's file says something similar. Sure, he died of a very specific type of trauma-related injury, but he was done for, either way.

Brain tumour. Inoperable. Maybe only a few weeks, a couple of months left.

Two people. Both with terminal illness. Coincidence?

What about Elias? He seemed healthy enough. Seems to want to keep on living. Was he targeted purely because he had lived and breathed revenge for about twenty years?

Maybe.

Three people. Desperate in their own way. Two of them probably wanting to go out with a bang. Get VIRTUS to pay off some relative when they've gone.

I'm starting to build up a picture of how these folks operate. You can only get people to do what you want when you get something out of it. When you're at your lowest ebb, and some group comes calling. They promise money, treatment, whatever, you go along with it. When things turn a little sour, you carry on. You justify each deviation from the original plan. Before you know it, they've got you trapped. No way out.

"Desperation," Demi says, out of nowhere. "One hell of a motivation."

It's like she's thinking the same thing as me. Can't say I'm ever a fan of someone else saying what I'm thinking.

I look at her and nod. "Couldn't get more desperate than the three lackies we know about."

She looks away nods. "Like poor little lemmings."

I look back at her with a frown.

"You know lemmings?" She says.

I nod whilst maintaining eye contact. "I've heard of them."

She gets a little animated. Starts gesturing with her arms and hands as she talks. "They've got this in-built thing about jumping off high places."

My frown deepens a little. "I don't think that's strictly true."

She nods. Wide eyes. Enthusiastic. "It is. Saw a documentary about it. You ever play those Lemmings computer games? You had to stop them falling off the edge of things and then you had to help them get home."

I shake my head. "Never played the game. Heard about it. You know why they stopped making them?"

She shrugs. "Loss of market share?"

I tilt my head. "Maybe. Could have something to do with the *truth* about lemmings."

She stares at me like I'm about to break the news about Santa. Shatter some illusion she's held on to for way too long.

"That documentary," I say, "who made it?"

She shrugs. "No idea."

"An old thing? Black and white?"

She thinks hard. Tries to remember. "Might have been. I'm not sure."

I get up and pace around a little. "You hear of the controversy around that old film? Some old Disney nature thing?"

She shakes her head. Looks like she doesn't wanna hear what I'm about to spill.

"They made it up," I say.

Her eyes are wider. She shakes her head. "No they didn't."

Flat-out denial.

I shake my head and sit on the couch with a smile on my face. "I ain't yanking any chains. The guys who filmed it strapped cameras to the front of their cars. Hurtled towards the helpless creatures on a cliff until they had nowhere to go."

She's still shaking her head. I can't believe that she can't believe me.

How can a grown woman think animals breed just to all go throw themselves off cliffs where most of them die?

I'm starting to wonder about the MI5 entrance exams. If she can pass them, there might be hope for someone like me. Maybe even the guy who collects trolleys at Wal-Mart.

I do a reassuring small nod with wider eyes. "They edited the whole thing to make their migration look like a mass suicide."

Looks like her face has deflated. She opens up her laptop and taps away. Frowns. "You're right," she finally says.

I know I'm right. That ain't news to me.

"Makes you wonder what else you can trust from Disney."

I button my lip. I wanna point out that little mermaids don't exist. There ain't such a thing as a talking mouse. Animals, whatever Disney have tried to get us to think otherwise, don't think, act and talk like humans.

I'm half expecting her to ask me if Rapunzel's real when she next opens her mouth.

"Those poor people," she finally says. She's looking out a window.

I go and take a look. No one there. She's not flapping her gums about someone on the other side of the thin glass.

"Exploited. Pushed towards things because of sheer desperation. Because their life felt like it meant nothing."

I nod. I don't feel quite so sorry for Elias, and I wasn't too keen on the others, but I get where she's coming from.

Take people with needs, deficiencies. People who are desperate to live or to leave something behind for family or friends. Get the most down-and-out folks people can dream up. Strap a bomb to them and send them to some crowded area. A promise of eternal glory works for some. Money for loved ones works for others. If none of that works, ease them in gradually. Trap them. Then you can rely on good old-fashioned blackmail to get the job done.

I came into today hating everything I knew about VIRTUS. My motivation was nothing more than seeing my family again.

Now I wanna bring these people down. Really make them pay.

Once Flick and Toby are safely out of the way.

26. LIST YOUR VIRTUS

Modus Operandi.

A Latin phrase. One a hell of a lot of people have devoted a lot of hours, days, weeks and even years to. Police often refer to an MO like it means something. Sometimes it does. Sometimes it means as much as a serial abuser's latest apology.

The theory goes like this. You figure out how someone works, it's a kinda shortcut to figuring out who they are. They commit their crimes in a specific area? What are the travel links like? Is it most likely they live round there somewhere?

Crimes committed in a hurry? Someone ain't keen on being caught. Elaborate crime scenes? They're toying with the law. It's a game to them.

You do all that stuff right, you might be turning from a side road onto easy street. You could predict future events. Find out where they're gonna hit next and how. It's all nice, in theory.

Trainee cops have it drilled into them. Jumping to conclusions can result in disaster. But they start talking about MO. That's at least a close relative of forming incomplete opinions.

People know how the police think. Someone who's even watched every detective TV show going, they're gonna have some idea. It ain't hard, from there, to bamboozle the boy in blue. Don't stick to one way of doing things. Mix things up. Avoid a pattern of committing crime.

They say that's easier said than done. Some folks have been desperate for their spree to be random. Trouble is, a lot of them never quite pull it off. They try so hard to be unpredictable. But you put all your efforts into that, you just change from one pattern to another. Even when nature looks like it's in chaos, there's some secret order to things.

So what has all this got to do with me?

We know a little about how VIRTUS work. Target the ill and destitute. There's a few of those around, especially living on the streets.

Okay, it ain't a long list to point to an MO, but it's something.

I can cling on to that. Do some digging online. Use my new persona.

Hunt around on old newsgroups. Forums. Places people virtually gather. Maybe even hit up the dark web. See if I can find anyone else who's desperate and willing. Find out about those who might've been used by VIRTUS in the past.

Trouble is, I've got a sneaking feeling their flagship venture was Heathrow. I might just end up tapping into stuff I don't wanna be near. Streams of a thousand other organised crime organisations.

Time to see what I can dig up.

What the hell else am I gonna do while hiding away in this overgrown tin can?

27. YOU LIKE CATS?

You ever see a TV show or a movie with someone stuck inside, going stir-crazy?

Funny to watch. Not so funny when that's your here-and-now.

Feels like days since I had anything like a taste of freedom.

In fact, prison would've given me more freedom than this place. At least I wouldn't be officially dead. I could've befriended some huge guy. Tattoos on his face and neck. No hair. Few teeth. A face like he chews bricks like a kid chews on jelly beans. Known by a name like Big Jimmy. Made him laugh. Made some promises about how I could help him when I crushed out. No one would mess with me if I had a friend like Big Jimmy. I could wander around the yard. I could pick my jobs. I could have the run of the place.

Okay, my luck ain't like that. The straight is I'd probably be dead or in the infirmary by now if I was in the cooler. Big Jimmy the most likely candidate for putting me there.

I've had next to no luck in finding any possible VIRTUS candidates online. I suppose if the information was out there, some MI5 intel folks would've found it by now.

There's gotta be somewhere I ain't looking. Somewhere that'll give us a better idea of their hired-under-duress types.

Demi's still wandering around the place. She looks as bored as I feel. Security detail ain't a thrilling card to draw from a pack.

She walks over to me. Has her phone out. "Wanna see something funny?"

She sits beside me on the sofa and points the screen, now rotated sideways, at me.

A video starts up. Some TV advertisement from maybe fifteen years ago. Some new brand of cat food. Must be made by a company on a budget, looking at the quality of the ad. Some tinny, naff jingle is playing on a loop in the background. I feel like I've heard it before somewhere.

All natural pet food, apparently. Makes a difference for some reason. What do they put in the other stuff? A woman puts some gunk in a bowl and puts it on the floor. A cat wanders over and looks vaguely interested. A bad cut and the feline's stuffing their face with the meaty chunks.

The camera cuts away to someone who looks a little familiar. A woman with long, dark hair. Beaming smile that's as genuine as a Chinese DVD bought from eBay.

"I've tried all sort of cat food, and I couldn't get my cat to eat any of it," she says.

Looks like this food didn't work at first. I'll overlook that for a second.

"But this new pet food does the trick."

She stoops down. Picks up the cat. The thing wants to be anywhere else but there, by the look on its face.

With both facing in the direction of the camera, she says, "Meow do you like that?"

A big logo for the pet food fills the screen. Fades to black. Done.

Was that it? That was supposed to cheer me up?

I look over. She's got a beaming smile a little like the gal in the video.

I shrug. "A little amusing. Not sure what I think about the pun at the end, though. Seemed a little obvious."

She still got a crazy grin on her face. Did I miss something?

"You notice anything unusual about the video?"

I wanna point out the bad cuts. The cheesy nature of the whole thing. Doesn't seem to be what she's looking for.

The smile goes. She rolls her eyes and stands up. "You're a detective, aren't you?"

Why do people keep saying that to me? Like being a detective means you've gotta spot every tiny detail about everything.

"What is it you think I should've noticed?" I ask.

She looks at me like we're an item and I forgot our anniversary.

She messes with the phone in her hand. Holds it towards me with the screen pointed at me. It's paused on the woman at the end. "Recognise her?"

I look a little closer. My observation skills are a little limited because of the tiny screen.

Finally figured out why she looks familiar. Add on a few years, a little weight around the face, take away the apparent joy, you're left with...

"Is this you?" I ask.

I look up. She's beaming again. Nods.

I hand the phone back with a little smile. "You were an actress?"

She nods like her head's gonna fall off.

But hang on. She showed me some naff cat commercial from years ago. That couldn't be the highlight. Was that the highlight?

"You get cast in anything I've seen?"

The smile fades. "It was a bad time for getting into the acting game," she says.

I nod like her excuse means something.

She turns away. Carries on explaining. "I got paid a little for it. Auditioned for other stuff. Never found the right roles, I guess."

I give her a sad nod. Not that she can see it when she's facing the other way. "Hard to get a regular gig, I've heard."

She nods. "Had to find a day job between auditions."

"The day job turned into a career?"

She turns around. Doesn't look like she's trying to cheer me up. If anything, she's dragging the mood further down. She nods.

"But it got you here," I say in a voice more cheerful than I feel like using.

A stern nod.

"The cool thing is, you can show that to people. Not everyone can say they've been on TV, let alone been paid to act."

A bit of a smile comes back. "I guess you're right."

She walks out of the room humming something.

It's the damn jingle from that advert. I knew I'd heard it before.

I could've got a Jack Bauer type of agent. No. Not me. I get the crazy cat lady. The failed actress. The woman who's stuck in her own past choices. Her regrets. Her missed opportunities. Someone so stuck in their own head ain't great at protecting the people around them.

I should know. I've played that gig more than once.

I wonder if Holly knows about Demi's history.

I wonder meow she feels about it.

28. CHAT ON THE NET, YOU CAN STILL GET SNAGGED

I'm back online. Not as myself, but I'm on.

It ain't something to celebrate.

There's probably more garbage uploaded to the Internet in a day than I can read or watch in a year. Keeps on happening. Day by day. Hour by hour. Now, the useful stuff is stuck somewhere in piles of trash.

How are you supposed to find the worthwhile bits in so much that's there to waste your time? How can you find useful instructional videos on YouTube? So many of their recommendations are pets doing the crazy things pets do. Newsflash! Pets are weird. They ain't human. They're not gonna act like one. Doesn't mean every little thing they do needs to be recorded. Doesn't need to be shoved into an already saturated 'funny' video arena.

If you took out the useless stuff, what would be left? Could it fit on a USB drive? Possibly.

But I'm deep-diving into the waste. That's my self-appointed task for today. Find something, anything, that points towards VIRTUS.

I've looked before, but I wasn't sure what I was looking for. This requires more than a quick Google and the following of half a dozen links.

Demi's been educating me on the Dark Web. Thought it was a new TV series involving Batman and spiders. She compared it to the chunk of an iceberg that sits underwater. I liken it to an overspilling landfill.

Forums. Newsgroups. People still use them, apparently. Chat forums. Discussion groups. Something called a Wiki.

Still not found anyone talking about VIRTUS. Gotta try harder.

I find a site that sells the kinda stuff you can't get on Amazon. Drugs. Cannabis starter kits. Firearms. Sexual services. You can even hire a hitman for three quarters of a Bitcoin, whatever that is. Seems like the wrong way to hire a guy like that, to me. So many possibilities for crossed wires.

They've got their own forum. People posting questions about untraceable ways to kill their spouse. How to order this stuff without it being delivered by a guy with a hat and a blue siren. Anyone got a good recipe for hash brownies?

It goes on and on. Let's see what I can come up with.

I get a 'burner' email address, now that I know what one is. It'll stay good as long as I keep the tab open. I sign up with the username 'MurderMan12673'. Not original here. No one cares.

I ask if anyone else has heard of VIRTUS. Anyone had any dealings with them? Do they keep their promises?

I hit post and wait to see if anyone replies.

I try another one. Anyone use the Extra Media Manager app? Who knows about the secret chat function?

Do the same with this one as I did with the last one.

Wait. Browse around in a couple more online dumpsters and wait a little more.

I keep looking. See what else they offer on this site. A sex doll made to look like a female of any age you request. If you're after something like that, you've gotta surely find a better place to blow your dough.

I check back on the email tab. A reply. Already.

Nope. SPAM. Asking if I want a date for tonight, cash up front.

I'm about to carry on surfing through the web's sewage-filled sea again. Another email arrives. Another reply.

> Yes, I've used the EMM app. I found it useful to talk to a specific group about a problem. DM me for more.

Didn't take long, as it turns out. Now to figure out what a DM might be.

***

Holly's in the EMM app at the same time I'm trying to talk to someone else about it.

She's still trying to secure the release of my family. The look on her face that's reflected back in the screen's enough to say it ain't going well.

> We have the sample you provided. We don't believe it's Enoch Flint.

She thinks. Sends a message back.

> You can believe whatever you like. I deal in facts. Not beliefs.

They're typing.

Still typing.

> Our forensic tests on the sample are inconclusive. One thing we do know is that the DNA sequence does not appear to match.

Damn. She's been made. What now?

> Don't you people know that DNA degrades very quickly upon decomposition? You're not gonna get an easy match to one of his hair fibres.

A bluff. Let's see what it does.

She waits maybe five minutes for a reply. Not sure she's done much breathing in that time.

> As much as I would like to discuss the veracity of that statement, I feel we need to refocus on the matter in hand.

She nods.

> I agree.

They don't take so long to reply now.

> How would you like to pay for the release of Felicity and Toby?

How does she reply to this? The UK have a long history of not negotiating with terrorists. Are these terrorists? Are their motives political or religious? Seems a narrow definition of a word that once meant 'to instil terror' but she ain't gonna change the tide on that.

> I need to take this higher. See what the Home Office say about paying a ransom. What are your demands?

A very quick response.

> Half a million each. Paid in Bitcoin. Promise to pay within the hour.

Holly needs longer than that.

> What if I can't secure the money in that time?

They're already working on a reply.

> 59 minutes. If you fail to promise to pay, we have nothing more to discuss. You'll get your answer on the twenty four hour news channels.

Oh no. What does that mean?

This is a hell of a lot bigger than her now. A full-blown UK-based hostage situation. This might take more than the Home

Secretary. This might need the eyeballs of the Prime Minister.

Start by contacting Demi. That'll be quicker than throwing this through the police's increasingly convoluted command structure.

She hopes Demi's got some handy shortcut. Some way of getting a cool million from British funds in just a few minutes.

If she hasn't, the news ain't gonna make pleasant watching for the next couple of days.

***

A DM ain't anything to do with an animated mouse with a hamster colleague, as it turns out.

Direct Message. It was right there, in front of my nose, big and obvious.

> What have you used EMM for?

A quick reply.

> VIRTUS took my child. I had to pay a ransom.

Sounds about right.

He types a reply.

> They have my family. Did they release your child after you paid?

A quick response.

> Yes.

Something sounds a little too straightforward about this.

> Have they left you alone ever since?

Another simple, quick reply.

> Yes.

I need more.

> Who did you meet with? Where? When?

A long wait as the reply is typed out.

> I didn't get his name. A local hotel lobby. About a year ago.

It's time to see what this person's about. Are they for real?

> What's your name?

Another wait.

> Can't tell you.
>
> In fact, I'm not telling you any more.

I get a message pop up. This user's blocked me. Can't say anything else to her.

Gotta do something pretty bad on this kinda service to be blocked. I could be the first to achieve it.

Either way, that conversation was no help to me at all.

I check the burner email inbox again.

Nothing but some junk about erectile dysfunction. Amazing how quickly those emails arrive when the address has only existed for about an hour.

***

Useless.

The Home Office. MI5. The lot. Utter waste of time.

It's been 58 minutes. Messages are passed up and down the chain.

They don't like the lack of assurance of release. Not even any proof of life.

Poor intel for securing a hostage release.

So they've done it before, when they've got some of those things? Something they no doubt keep quiet.

Of course governments pay out for hostages. If it wasn't a profitable line of business, people would've given it up a while ago. They'd focus on the trendy, profitable stuff like sextortion and ransomware.

But the folks in charge of the country ain't gonna do it this time. Not unless Holly can get back on that chat and get some more details. Get something to prove the hostages are really in their care. Prove they can release them, alive and well.

Back in the EMM app.

> I need proof of life.

A quick reply.

2 minutes to go.

> That's hardly an answer.

She types out something else.

> What about a place to meet up and exchange?

They're typing...

> Not until promise of payment. Payment then needs to be sent to a Bitcoin wallet we'll provide. Hostages will then be released. Details will follow.

Another quick message.

> One minute.

She can't feel her fingers. She types out one more desperate message.

> Can I get more time? The Home Office need proof before agreeing.

A reply almost instantly.

> You had enough time. One minute.

It's too late.

She can't even get through to anyone now to ask.

> With more time I could secure your payment.

One final message appears.

> You've wasted your hour. You should watch the news to see the consequences.

So this is it.

This is what failure feels like.

This empty feeling's all you're left with when you couldn't save someone.

How the hell are they gonna get Flint to help them now?

He's gonna know the negotiation hasn't gone well.

He might even know already, if he happens to be watching the news.

29. DON'T BE AN ARSON

Watching the TV news. All I can think is one thing. I don't have to worry about cleaning up anymore.

I'm seeing live camera footage from Cookston. A spot near the park. A place where, not too long ago, life was okay. A social media influencer and a police detective were scratching out a living. All while repairing a run-down sorta house.

It's a little more run-down now.

It's run down as far as a place can get. Or at least, it will be.

Right now, there are golden-red flames taller than me shooting out of the windows. The dark grey roof has been replaced with a pillar of smoke that seems to ascend forever.

The words at the bottom keep changing. Right now they have five words that are on point.

DISGRACED DETECTIVE'S HOUSE ON FIRE

Why do they have to keep describing me using those two words? Disgraced Detective. Sounds like a bad pulp story series. The only thing that's put me squarely in that category is a pack of lies.

I'm gonna get a call from Holly any moment. She'll tell me how she tried her best. How VIRTUS were being unreasonable. All the stuff I already know.

The one thing I really know about this group is that they like sending messages. Their own encrypted hidden chat app. They like other messages too. The not-so-subtle hints that there's worse to come if you don't comply.

The fire's got bad enough to tear the place down, piece by

piece. First to go is the roof over my new office. Goodbye green walls. Goodbye filing cabinet I didn't even get a chance to fill with crap. Goodbye fancy desk with the buttons underneath and the fancy recording system. All gone. My chances of a career as a private detective have also gone up in smoke. That is, if there was anything left after the last debacle.

The roof of the whole house isn't gonna stand up to much more. It's already looking a different shape.

A fire crew show up. Start chucking gallons of water per second at the problem. Pretty sure they're too late to do anything other than wet whatever's not already burning. They certainly aren't putting out flames like the kind they're seeing.

But why would VIRTUS attack an empty home? What could they gain from it? What message are they trying to send?

Holly calls.

"I tried my best, Flint."

"What happened?"

"I was given an hour to raise a million to pay a ransom. They didn't believe you were dead."

I'm watching the windows explode. They were only fitted a couple of weeks ago.

"I take it the Home Office weren't keen on laying out that kinda lettuce?"

"You'd take it right."

I nod. "They say anything about Flick and Toby when the deadline passed?"

Silence for a moment.

"They're not talking to me anymore. The app's gone dead."

Can't be good news.

A horrifying thought hits me.

"Holly, is this a message from VIRTUS, or is this their way of ending everything to do with me?"

"I don't follow."

"Could there be people inside? If so, you don't think they could be-"

"No, Flint! They can't be! I'll find out what I can from police and fire at the scene. I'll get back to you as soon as we know anything more."

The call ends.

The roof of the house caves in.

Nothing left but charred brick walls.

At this point, I've got no clue what else I've just lost.

***

Demi's wandering round like she's been let out of the loony bin for the afternoon.

She's humming. A nervous version of that damn cat jungle.

It's been close to an hour.

The flames are out. Smoke's still rising.

Might be that it's gonna be too soon to get inside. See who's there or who's not.

My phone rings.

I've got it and I'm hitting the call button before the first ring ends.

"Flint, I've got news from the fire crew."

It's Holly. Let's hope it ain't bad news.

"No bodies have been recovered," she says. "Looks like the place was empty. No sign of a young boy or an adult woman inside."

At last, something close to good news.

There's a change to the broadcast.

Seems no one knows what to make of all this. As far as the world knows, I chucked myself off a bridge a couple of days ago. Dead people don't usually come back to life just to burn their house down.

Someone's playing a game here. They're not letting anyone else in on where and when they're moving the pieces.

Demi's as clueless as both ends of the phone call.

"You got any ideas about who's behind this?" I ask.

Holly sighs. "Nothing yet. I think we're both thinking the same thing, though."

The TV news changes again.

Like the timing was practised, the word VIRTUS appears on the screen as Holly says it.

'VIRTUS' CLAIM RESPONSIBILITY

"Holly, I've gotta go watch the news. You might wanna see this too."

I hang up. Demi's turning the sound up.

Some average, young-to-middle-aged anchor. Sculpted brown hair has a new piece of paper in his hands.

"We burned down Enoch Flint's house," he reads aloud. A strong start. "The former detective did not commit suicide by jumping off a bridge. The police have been lying to you. We will do what we can to remove his hiding places."

I don't like where this is going.

Demi's got a look that sums up what's going on inside my head.

"We know the police have lied to the public a lot. Ask yourself whether you trust this organisation to protect and to serve you. They have so many secrets. What else are they hiding?"

Short and sweet. He's done already.

Clever. Use me as the poster boy for poor policing. Tar every officer with the same brush. Some of the newspapers will be all over this.

Demi's on her phone already. Demanding to speak with the producer of the news broadcast. How did they get this letter? When? Who delivered it? Could be about national security. To hell with protecting their sources.

I head to the poor excuse for a bathroom. Splash some water on my face.

I watch in the mirror as water drips from my nose. My chin. Eyebrows. Ears.

Enoch Flint.

Still very much alive.

Even though he's died once.

I've got a feeling the second time might stick.

***

I wanna go lie down in a dark room.

Got a lot to process.

The fire. The news statement.

What are VIRTUS trying to achieve?

You don't just set a house on fire to prove a point. Who knows? Maybe these guys do. Seems Heathrow and Kirkwall were warm-up acts. Are we about to see the main event?

My phone makes a noise it's not made before.

Incoming text message.

Unknown number.

> You played dead and lied to us. We've called your bluff.

A second message arrives.

> Your move.
>
> V

Spectacular. Seems they've managed to get through the allegedly impenetrable MI5 security. Got my number. My name makes not one jot of difference.

The message says other stuff that ain't typed out.

They found me once. They can find me again.

30. GOT MYSELF A HEMINGWAY OUTTA THIS

I'm done with the news. Again.

Sick of being called some no-good law-breaker.

A hell of a lot of folks have done a lot more for a lot less bad press.

But watching things unfold on that TV screen's never gonna improve my mood.

Demi's ditched me for a few minutes. Said there was something she needed to pick up. She got in a panic when I showed her the messages. There's no telling they know where to find me, or if it makes any damn difference to anything. I'll let her do the worrying.

For me, I can't help but wonder about Flick. About Toby. About Holly failing in securing their freedom. They're a slippery bunch.

But they're out in the public domain now. That statement to the news channel means something. They wanna step out of the shadows. Cause mayhem in increasingly public ways.

The brass who said I was talking crazy will have to eat their words. VIRTUS exists. I wasn't chasing ghosts.

With time on my hands, I hit up the dark web groups again. See what's going down. See if there's any reaction to the stuff broadcast over the airwaves.

Nearly all the recent posts are about the police. Can't trust them. Can't even reason with them without them wanting to stitch you up for something. Lies and cover-ups. So many have their own stories about corruption. Constables, Sergeants and

Inspectors doing the wrong things, but in the right ways. They know the law. They know how to get caught. They also know a thing or two about covering their tracks.

Each post starts with some wild accusation. Some fairy-tale of police invading homes, taking things that ain't theirs. I can see through a lot of it. Bad eggs throwing muck because they got caught. Police didn't ruin their lives. They did that themselves by choosing the wrong path some distance back.

But folks jump on these posts like kids on a bounce house. They chuck on comment after comment. You get a page or two in, they start talking about stopping the police. Getting revenge. Putting things right.

VIRTUS have got folks riled up, alright.

It'll be interesting to see where it heads.

I'm intrigued, but also more than a little concerned.

This kinda storm's been brewing about the boys in blue for a while.

I just wonder if the whole setup's gonna withstand what's coming their way.

***

Demi's back. She's wondering why I'm even reading this garbage.

Gotta wonder why most of the police's response to bad press is to bury your head in the sand until it goes away. Go quiet until stuff calms down. Until some other story crops up and grabs the public's attention.

"If you can tear yourself away from the laptop," she says, "I've got some stuff for you."

What's she got for me? Cool spy gadgets? My own gun? Doubt it.

It's only a manilla envelope. You ain't gonna fit many weapons in there.

She hands it to me. It's got a few words printed front and centre.

NEW IDENTITY DOCUMENTS

Not exactly a gift, but it could be worse.

I open it up. Tip its contents onto the table.

A passport. Driving license. Birth certificate. A lease agreement for a car. A couple of credit cards.

"It's as much as we could get together in a couple of days," she says. "Still got to sort out more long-term accommodation. Any preference on where?"

I shrug. "If it ain't home, I'm not so bothered where it is. Might change my tune if it can be somewhere warm and sunny."

I hold up the mobile phone. "Do I keep this one?"

She nods. Hands over a new SIM card. "For now, you can swap the SIM and keep the phone. We'll sort out something more permanent once we've got a home address to link it up to."

I look at the passport. My photo. The name's different again.

Joseph Hemingway

I look at her. One eyebrow raised. "Another new name?"

She nods. "You're Joseph Hemingway now."

I pick up the driving license and examine it, just to double-check, I guess.

"You're an artist and a writer," she says.

I smile. "You know me well."

She spins around. A little frustration creeping into her voice. "Not that it matters. VIRTUS will probably figure it out in another day."

I put most of the stuff back in the envelope. Keep the car document. I hold it up. "Any keys for this mysterious car?"

She shakes her head. "Yes, but no. Not yet. You need to stay away from anyone and everything. No contact with any human being except me. Is that clear?"

"And Holly?" I ask.

She shakes her head again. "Until we know how VIRTUS got their information, we need to play the cards pretty close to our chest."

I clench my fists. "How can I help you take down VIRTUS if I'm a prisoner within this tin can box?"

She sighs and nods at once. Both tiny movements. Not much effort. "The priority now is to keep you safe. Treat you like you're in witness protection."

I look at her. "What's your success rate in getting these witnesses to trial?"

She looks at the floor. "Pretty good."

That ain't a great answer. "What does pretty good mean? Eighty percent? Ninety?"

She shrugs. "I don't have any exact figures. We've just got to do the best we can."

I raise both eyebrows and look up at the wood-effect ceiling. "I guess I'll have to come out on the damn good end of pretty good."

She nods once. Heads for the door for some reason. "That's what I'm here for."

31. JUST CALLED TO SAY GOOD BUY

Enoch Flint's the loveable rogue. The guy with the bad rep who's not done half the things wrong people are claiming.

Joseph Hemingway? Well, he could still be anyone.

I'm trying to decide what kinda person he is when I overhear Demi on the phone in a spare room on my way back from the can. Maybe Flint and Hemingway have a little more in common than cabin fever.

"That's definitely the number that messaged Flint."

A pause while she hears something.

"Damn! Why are they always pre-paid and unregistered? Can't we for once catch a break?"

More listening.

"What sort of break?"

Can't tell what the guy on the other end is saying, but I know they're saying something.

"A shop near here? You got the address?"

She writes something down on note paper.

"Yeah, they're almost certain to have CCTV going back two weeks. Hopefully the quality of the video's good. With any luck, there weren't too many people around at half two on a Tuesday afternoon to muddy the waters."

I press myself against the wall as she leaves. Heads for the bathroom.

I notice two things. The piece of paper is still lying on that bedside cabinet, and her car keys are still on a counter top near the door.

She doesn't want me online. Wants me to lay low. There's only so much low-lying I can take. It's time I did something useful.

The bathroom door locks.

I make a move.

I pick up the piece of paper. I pick up her keys. I'm out the door and pulling out of the parking spot before she knows what's going on.

My head's telling me this is a bad idea.

My gut's telling me my head knows nothing.

I guess I'm going with the latter.

***

I breeze in past the group of youths, loitering near the entrance of the store. They're too loud and too boisterous to be sober. One of them falls to the floor while I'm watching, much to the hilarity of the rest of the group.

A middle-aged man walking into a newsagents means a whole lotta nothing to kids like that. They ain't gonna know me from Adam, let alone call anywhere and say that the believed-to-be-dead police officer's in front of them.

It's a tiny store. Got about enough room for one person to walk up and down each of two aisles. The walk wouldn't take long.

A wall of magazines is to my right. The cashier's desk to my left. Behind him all manner of tobacco products. A small fridge with some milk and a couple of soft drinks ahead of me. A few rows of cans of beer and some brightly coloured bottles of crazy alcoholic beverages sit above it.

Sat on the counter is a display of various makes of SIM card.

A man walks out from a backroom and stares at me. He's maybe of Indian origin. Some place where folks found a way out to the UK a generation ago. Maybe more. The new generation speak English to the same level as their parents and grandparents. Just enough to get by.

"You serve a guy a couple of weeks ago? Bought a SIM card. White guy. Sniffs a lot."

He looks at me like I've asked if he's seen the ghost of Elvis in here in the past few hours.

"It was a Tuesday. Two weeks ago. Two thirty in the afternoon. Ring any bells?"

He scowls a little. "Who's asking?"

"Police," I say.

"Where's your ID?"

I pat my pockets. I know I've not got a thing in them, but I've gotta make it look like I left it back at the station. "Don't seem to have it."

"Then I'm sorry, but I don't think I can help you."

I glance back towards the entrance. Look back at the guy making things difficult. "That group of kids out there. Were they in here earlier?"

He's got a blank look on his face.

"You maybe served them? They bought alcohol, didn't they?"

No reply.

"How old's the oldest? My guess is sixteen. You know what that means?"

He glances towards the door. Looks a little nervous.

"Means I get my friend, the licensing officer on the phone. How's that gonna work out for you?"

He shrugs. Tries to be coy, but it ain't working. "One of them showed me ID. Eighteen. Older than they look."

I nod. Smile back at him. I take a couple of steps towards the entrance. "I'll just go and check..."

He calls out to me. "Sir, there's no need." I walk up to him. He lowers his voice to a near-whisper. "We can keep this quiet. Now remind me, what shall we check the CCTV for?"

I nod. That's more like it.

***

I thought the CCTV would've been in that back room.

I ain't so lucky. I'm following the guy through a maze of corridors. Up a few steps. Round a corner. Down a few more.

Finally, I'm shown to a computer screen sitting on top of a big, black CCTV box. At least, I think it's black. Or it started out that colour. It's more of a murky grey, dust colour. I touch a spot in the corner. There's a perfect little dot of blackness where my finger just was. Could be black again if it was ever cleaned.

He's picked up a mouse that he's dragging on the edge of a table. Manages to input a PIN and get up the footage I wanted.

He shows me the controls by pointing at the screen. Hands over the mouse.

Doesn't seem to be necessary. The guy's right there, picking out a SIM card. Chucking it down on the counter. Paying cash.

Okay, so financial checks ain't gonna get us anywhere.

Doesn't matter too much. I know the guy.

Or at least, I know *of* him.

Met him a couple of times, in that hotel lobby.

My suspicions are spot on.

I hand the mouse back to the guy. Thank him. Tell him to hang on to that footage. I ain't got a USB drive, so a colleague's gonna come back for it.

I'm out the door and back in Demi's car.

I ain't long before I'm back at the caravan.

I'm gonna get an earful from Demi, but I've got something useful to come from my sneaking out.

All we've got to do now is put a name to that snivelling face.

32. TURNING UP THE HEAT ON THE FUZZ

Breaking the rules can take it out of a guy.

After Demi tries to tear a strip off, I've handed back the paper and the keys. She tells me she's gonna have to call it in if I do it again.

She didn't do it this time. Trying to save face, I guess.

I've retreated for a bit of shut-eye. Not a hell of a lot else to do with my early afternoon.

I wake up maybe a half hour later. Head to the kitchen for a drink to wake me up the rest of the way.

Demi's in front of the TV. She looks back at me like I've just called her fat.

"What's the problem?" I ask.

She steps back. Points at the TV.

A video of SITU station, shot from a distance. Some writing underneath.

ENOCH FLINT MISSING - MORE VICTIMS COME FORWARD

What do they put along that banner on the bottom when nothing happens? I suppose they always think of something.

She ups the volume. Turns out three women have claimed I've sexually abused them in some way. TV news ain't exactly sticklers for fact-checking like they used to be. You get more attention by chucking stuff out there. You apologise later, if needed. News organisations have a mantra. Dig up enough dirt to bury someone twice over, whether they're alive or dead.

First girl's barely out of her teens. Got that slightly rounded all-American-girl thing some folks go crazy for. Could almost be a young Britney Spears by the smile on that photo. She's got streaks of blonde in light brown hair, and she's speaking to some reporter we don't see in a ten second clip. Tears fill eyes that are a deep greenish blue, like the sea close to land, but not too close. Her lower lip's trembling as she tells of the time I cornered her down some back alley. Flashed my police badge, and then grabbed her in a few places before she ran off. All the story needs now is a Gruffalo to make it a full house of absurd. Never seen the woman before.

Second victim's crying that I raped her in some club toilets. She looks sixteen, but they say she's nineteen. Wavy hair, as light as golden blonde ever gets. Eyes too close together. Large nose. Oversized mouth. Something a little pretty about that face when it all comes together, but she ain't my type. That's also a hell of a long way from my style.

The women who'd been in my life could stand up. Be character witnesses. Trouble is, one's in the ground, one's nowhere to be seen, and another's in the company of a criminal enterprise. There have been others, but I doubt I made much of a lasting impression. They certainly didn't on me.

If the second girl looked young, the third could've been her younger sister. Only just eighteen. Similar blonde hair. Straighter. A cute nose. Grey eyes that have a hint of something sinister in them. Claims I blackmailed her online into sending nude pictures when she was underage. The accusations get worse. I wonder what's gonna happen if a fourth woman comes out of the woodwork. I'm not gonna dwell on that.

Back to the news anchor.

"These exclusive bombshell survivor stories are just the beginning. We're seeing a huge rise in people coming forward.

Examples of police brutality, sexual offences and abuse of power, among other things."

"See what VIRTUS are doing?" Demi asks, turning the box off.

I nod. "Flood the media with fake, paid stories, badmouth the police and burn a hole through the public's trust."

She gives me a sad nod. "There are parts of the country where trust in the police has been on a knife edge in recent years. You know how it is. One bad guy plays good long enough to get the uniform and tarnishes the rest."

I nod. "I happen to know that not every cop is a straight-shooter, which doesn't exactly help."

Another sad nod. The media might be barking up the wrong tree right now, but the right one's in the same park.

"There have got to be a lot of ugly truths hidden in police forces across the country," I say. "Better hope VIRTUS don't have their fingers in that many pies."

She sighs. Looks up at the ceiling. Looks out the window and walks towards it.

"How do you fight this?" I ask.

"You don't," she says. "Gotta let the tidal wave of pure garbage flow over us. Let it settle. Someone's gonna start a war, raise prices, tank the economy, kill the wrong person over the next few days. Attention will turn elsewhere."

She's still looking out that window.

"I hope you're right," I say. "If this deluge carries on, if the public start reacting, we're stuck in a hell of a hole."

We've got no words to encourage each other. Public opinion

beats everything in the moment. If the law get stuck in a hole, I'm not sure it's got the tools to dig its way out.

***

We sit down to watch the news again after we get a message from Holly.

She's charging round the station. It's like she's on fire and people have hidden the extinguishers.

Pretty much every Inspector and above's doing the same across the country.

Why?

The protests are starting. Those with beef against the flat feet have got their chance, and they ain't gonna waste it.

Hundreds are outside a police station in Croydon. A few more in Newcastle. A couple of thousand in Liverpool. Parts of Glasgow too.

"It's ramping up," I say. Turn to Demi. "Still think we can ride this out?"

She looks back at me. "To be honest, I have no idea."

I point at the TV. "This is after a couple of hours. What's it gonna be like after a day? Two days? How long before people have their heads full of more lies?"

Demi's got a sober look. "Gangs stir things up and their fans are going to join in."

"Fans of gangs?" I say, almost laughing at the suggestion.

She nods. Deadly serious. "They have their online presence. They brag about their achievements. They have followers and fans. Wouldn't take much to get them standing up against the police."

I nod. "I suppose it ain't a leap to chuck in there drug producers and sellers. Any criminal. Any ex-con. You get that lot shouting and hollering. The public ain't gonna take too much more convincing. Especially when the media's fuelling that fire."

"Next step is rioting in the streets," I say. "Mark my words. Police can get all their riot gear on, but they're in for a hell of a fight."

She wants to tell me it'll work itself out.

I wanna say I agree.

Either one of us could be the voice of reason.

Problem is, I don't see a way out of this now. Neither does anyone else working with an ID with a fancy police crest on it.

33. DON'T TAKE STUFF AT FACE VALUE

Sometimes, Security Services like a little bit of a chance to show off. Tell a handful of people they're pretty damn good at their job. That they have all the fancy tools to get the job done.

Trouble is, anyone who finds out ends up keeping quiet.

I'm on a video call with Alfie. A glasses-wearing, long-faced guy with a personality defect. The defect is that he ain't got one. A humourless, soulless man under a head of boring, thinning hair.

Alfie's on the left side of the screen. The other side's got their fancy ID app.

He's asking me about the man I've met. The one from the exchanges in the hotel. The one I've just seen on closed circuit video. The man with no current ID. No name to associate with him except VIRTUS.

Gotta try really hard to remember the details. I think about the gee, first thing that comes to mind is the sniffing. Then it's that head that looks a little too small for the body. Those details ain't gonna help a portrait artist.

Alfie's face disappears. The app's now full-screen. He starts out asking me to pick the closest head shape to the ones showing up in a gallery. He tells me if none of them match, to pick the closest. They can adjust it later.

I pick something a little square. Long, unkempt hair, receding at the front, but hidden by the remaining mop on top. Thick eyebrows. Sad eyes. A standard-sized nose that seems smaller at the nostrils than it should be. Large ears. Fat lips. A wide chin that hangs more to one side than the other.

He puts it all together. Looks a little more like a Lego character than the sniffing man. I start telling him where to pinch and pull, tuck or stretch. Before long, it's looking a little more human.

He keeps asking about each detail. Keeps asking me to close my eyes and picture the guy. Over and over we refine it. It ain't long before the guy could be standing right there.

"We've got to feed this into our system now. Got to wait while it runs a facial comparison. Various national security and law enforcement databases. It could take a while."

There are a few organisations in the UK that are pretty good at keeping secrets. Pretty good at storing information in the hope that it one day becomes useful. He didn't mention advanced face tracking on CCTV. Not a hint of GCHQ. I've got no doubt that photofit will at least have a fleeting association with them.

No clue how long a while's gonna be. One of those useless words. Depends on what you consider to be quick. If quick is thirty seconds, a while could be five minutes. If your idea of speedy is three hours, a while could be a day or more.

Can't say why no one along the way asked me to do this earlier. Maybe getting a sketch artist inside the police force ain't easy. A little like trying to sign Penn & Teller to do a magic show at your five-year-old's birthday party.

Still, we have ID procedures. No one was interested in this man. Like me, they maybe thought he was some lacky. Some unfortunate individual who got mixed up in the wrong crowd. No one, me included, thought the guy was anything more than background noise.

At least I've got something to wait for. Something to hang a little hope on. Since the time I got hooked for murder, things have turned bad quicker than a bad apple left out in the sun.

If things go well with this latest search, my luck could just turn around.

Thing is, when the needle on my own gauge of luck ever moves, it's further into the red by BAD LUCK. I think a little, every now and then, that it's maxed out. That things can't get any worse. Usually, I'm proven to be way wrong.

It would be nice, for once, for me to expect the worst. Be proven wrong in the best kinda way.

Life ain't kind to me in moments like this. I got a feeling it's not gonna start right now.

***

Any feeling that stuff's gonna start working out lasts exactly five minutes. Still, it was nice while it lasted.

I should stop watching the damn TV. I should disconnect the thing and throw it out the window. Burn every newspaper. Ignore the trash that's peddled to the masses under the guise of keeping the public informed.

The public need to know, they say. Codswallop.

The public have a right to know every detail of a celebrity's private life? Certainly not.

The public should be told about imminent threats? Do that every time, and come back and tell me how that goes. You tell the public about any possible impending disaster. Folks are gonna make it all come true with their response.

The latest stupid move is a breaking news story.

Another video's emerged. Posted online, this time. Found by

all the big networks. Looks like someone wanted it to be found.

"A disturbing video has shown up online that shows a police officer in a conflict with a protester."

They warn that some viewers may find the following scenes upsetting. Setting people up for a fall before they even hit play.

It starts. Some adult male. Maybe five-eleven, medium build. Near-shaven head. Sleeve tattoos. Standard police gear. No riot shield. No baton. Not even a helmet. Nothing more than the standard issue Kevlar vest. Seems to be down some back alley.

Gotta start asking questions about this from the offset. Who's gonna start videoing a police officer, on his own, doing nothing?

Some protester walks up. Some woman, maybe early twenties. Scruffy clothes. Brown hair to match. Got a university student vibe and some banner about not trusting the police.

The police officer shouts. Points at the banner.

The woman does nothing. Shakes her head. Points back at the police officer and shouts something.

Seems to rile the guy up. Yeah, believe it or not, we ain't robots. You push a person too far, any person, and they're gonna snap.

This one snapped hard.

He runs to her. Grabs the banner. Tries to tear it out of her hands.

She wrestles the thing out of his grasp. Turns and runs.

Out of apparently nowhere, the police officer pulls a gun. Aims it at her.

The screen goes black. The sound of a gun being fired.

Back to the studio.

Some ashen-faced woman's gotta wrap this up and move to their next segment, but she's not got a clue how to do it.

"We are still trying to verify the authenticity of this video. If this is real, then this could have severe consequences for police all around the UK."

I turn the box off. Hold myself back from embedding the remote in the screen. It's not gonna help anything.

I take a breath. Then another. Hands relax a little. The need to break the world apart seems to fade away.

I go back to the laptop. Doesn't take long to search for and find that video. It's everywhere. Views in the millions already.

I play it back. Demi wanders in from a back room.

"You heard about the video then?" she asks.

I nod. "Seen it on the news. Something off about it though."

I make the video full screen and I hit play.

I pause it after a second.

"You think that's strange?" I ask.

She looks at me, confused.

"No riot gear. Not a bit of it."

"Cutbacks?" she asks.

I shake my head. "No one's gonna hit a mob without any protection these days. They want the gear, they're gonna find it in a hurry, whatever their budget."

She says nothing.

"Then there's the fact they were being recorded in the first place."

She pulls up a chair and sits beside me. "What do you mean?"

"I mean, someone's got to be either doing something, or they're about to do something. No one's gonna waste their time, phone storage on some video of a cop doing nothing."

She nods. "I guess so, but maybe a lot of people are worried. They might record every officer they see. Thinking it's a protective measure."

I tilt my head sideways a little. Might be willing to concede the point there.

I let it play a little more. "Where's his radio?" I ask.

She looks closer. "There isn't one."

I look at her. "You ever hear of an officer doing this? Going anywhere violent or with upheaval and not take their radio?"

She shakes her head. "Never."

"No body-worn camera, either," I say. "If this is a real officer, they shouldn't be one."

We watch the events unfold again. He grabs the banner. She grabs it back again.

"Does it look like he just lets it go to you?" she asks.

I rewind. Watch that bit back. It sure does.

"Hold on," she says. She leans over the computer. Does something and the video quality just improved. "Just upped it to HD."

The woman lets got of the officer's arm and moves away. The added detail makes something else clear.

I point at the screen. Right at his arm. "You ever see a sleeve tattoo smudge like that?"

We rewind it, play it again a couple of times. Sure enough, it starts out looking normal. After a little scuffle, it's just a mess of lines and colours.

"Temporary tattoos," she says.

I nod. "A little sweat, and those things come off real easy."

The woman turns. Runs away. Doesn't get far.

The officer pulls a handgun. Raises it. Aims. Arms bent like he's held a gun before. Don't wanna lock the elbows when you fire. Gotta keep the arm a little loose to absorb some of the kickback.

"This guy firearms?" I ask.

She looks closer. Shakes her head. "Not with that gear on. Not with a pistol, either. Doesn't look right."

I nod. "That's because it's not."

He fires the shot. The woman hits the deck.

The video ends.

I turn to her. "You said you're pretty good at spotting a fake video," I say.

She nods.

"You think this is genuine?"

She shakes her head. "About as genuine as a teenager's apology."

I nod. "You need to get the word out that this is a fake."

She stands up. "What does it matter?"

I join her by getting to my feet. "Of course it matters!"

"You think police, MI5 or the government would say something? That this isn't real? You think people are gonna believe it?"

I raise my eyebrows and nod. She's got a point.

I sigh and spin around. Pace around the lounge. "So like everything else, we've got to ride this out? Let folks figure out it ain't real in their own time? There's gonna come a point when the storm doesn't pass. When we're stuck in the damn thing, and it's too late to fight our way free."

She gets out her phone. Goes to disappear to a bedroom again. "Got a call to make. There might be a couple of things we can do."

Police everywhere are gonna have to hope there's a way to counter these allegations.

There's enough mud being slung by the media to make the police look like Swamp Thing. If too much of it sticks for too long, confidence is lost.

When confidence is lost, you get a free-for-all.

We're too damn close to that scenario than I'd ever like to be.

34. DON'T DEBUG ME!

Folks from MI5 keep getting in touch. Still nothing from Holly. Nothing about Flick and Toby. Any day now, I'm expecting a severed finger in the post. Seems like their style.

Gotta hope they're still okay. That they've still got every limb and digit.

I'm a little surprised when Nahid Shamoon's on the other end of a computer video call. MI5 have their best people looking at the VIRTUS chat app. Seems their best people ain't as good as our lone analyst in SITU.

"I've been looking into the code behind the app," she says.

I know she's gonna lose me pretty quick if she goes all technical.

"I like to think I'm pretty good at spotting when I'm talking over people's heads. That being said, if I go too fast or too far, please let me know."

I nod. I'm glad we got that cleared up, right out of the gate.

"I started by looking into the person or company that submitted the app for inclusion in the app store."

So far, so good.

"Does Valiance Solutions mean anything to you?"

I shake my head.

"Me neither. A false company. No Companies House record. No hint of it online, anywhere. That in itself is strange. If you're a computer programming company, you'd want to get noticed. There's a name all over the code, too. Ted Valiance. No trace of anyone relevant online. I checked."

She's still talking my language. All good.

"And then, when I get into how the app works, it gets even stranger."

I wait for her to get on with it.

"Usually, an encrypted messaging app will send quite a lot of data back and forth when people use it. I've monitored this one, and hardly anything gets sent anywhere. Could be selective in what's sent. Maybe there's only one recipient. Could even be most of the data isn't sent anywhere, or it's not even encrypted at all."

"My bet's on the final possibility," I say, just so she's sure I'm still paying attention.

She nods. Smiles. "Also, messaging apps allow two people to initiate a conversation. This one only lets someone join once a specific place has agreed to it."

"Where is that place?"

A single raised eyebrow. "An IP address, which we can usually trace back. Sadly, this one's been bounced around the world in different ways, so I can't find where it started."

I nod. "So aside from the name Valiance Solutions, we're no further forward?"

She tilts her head to one side. "There's something else I'd like to try. I can attempt to exploit a weakness in the code. Make something that can attach itself to a conversation. Get it past the IP address problem. Have it report back with the details of where it ends up."

I nod. "Good idea. How long would that take?"

A shrug. "Could be a couple of days. Then we'd maybe need to try to get DI Chamberlain to chat with VIRTUS again. With any luck, we can get an exact location."

This certainly is good news. Much too good. "Is there a downside?" I ask.

A grave nod. "If they're clever, and they're monitoring the communication and network traffic. Chances are, they may spot a rat. If they do, we don't know how they might react."

I nod. I think we all know how they'd react. The way they've been threatening to react to everything for a while. Kill their two hostages.

"One last thing," she says. "The name VIRTUS."

I nod. "I know. Means something about power."

She shakes her head. "No, I know that already. What I was going to say is, we have a surname. Valiance, all over the code. Maybe it's a group name made up of the initials of its founding members?"

I hadn't considered that. We could find the V and still be missing the other five. Still, taking down one out of six is better than getting nowhere. Sixteen percent done is better than zero percent.

She thanks me for my time. Not like I was doing anything else anyway. I thank her in return and she leaves to get going on whatever she said she was going to do.

If Nahid is as good as I think she is, we might have finally got somewhere. We could find VIRTUS, or at least their main man in this area.

35. TURN OVER A NEW FLINT

Demi's rushing back into the lounge. Moving a little like someone tipped the caravan as she started walking.

"Right now? What channel?"

She slows down a little when she reaches the sofas, but she's still in a hurry to get to the horror box in the corner. Nothing good's come out of that TV so far. It looks like that run's set to continue. That is, unless her mother's got herself on some daft street-contacting show.

No such luck.

"This video was received moments ago, by an organisation calling themselves VIRTUS."

No further introduction.

Overhead video footage of a graveside funeral service. Looks like it was taken by a low-flying drone. A distorted voice starts speaking over the footage.

"You believed Enoch Flint to be dead. The police have told you this. They have confirmed previously that he has died."

This isn't going anywhere good.

"Our people have found that Enoch Flint is alive and well. The police have lied again. They will continue to do so."

Going from bad to worse. Where's this heading?

A shot of a generic police building.

"Police harbour liars and law-breakers. All the time they claim to be protecting and serving the British public. They are imposing harsh rules on people. Deceiving whenever they get the chance, to their own advantage."

I look at Demi. She looks back at me. Neither of us have any words.

A grainy, not-so-great photo of me shows up on the screen. I'm near a group of semi-drunk youths. Outside a newsagents.

"Enoch Flint is still alive. This was taken within the past few hours. He has murdered numerous people and ruined the lives of others. The police will not bring him to justice. In fact, they are protecting him."

How do they know all this? How have they found me and followed me? Are they still following me?

"Mr Flint, you have twenty four hours, starting now, to turn yourself over to us. You must face the justice that the police are failing to deliver. Present yourself at the Cookston town square. For every hour you do not cooperate, we will act. Details of your colleagues' misdeeds will be leaked to the media. Every wrongdoing will be out there for the world to see. Then the public will know exactly who claims to be protecting them."

I share a look of horror with Demi and then get back to the screen.

"In case you had any doubt..."

The final video clip is a bad one. How can they know?

It's an aerial shot of the very caravan I'm in. Captured by the same drone, most likely.

"This is the place where authorities are keeping Enoch Flint hidden. This is Kent Sands Caravan Park. If you'd like to exact your own revenge, this is the ideal place to start. We will pay a reward for his capture and delivery to us."

There we go. It got worse. A hell of a lot worse.

The TV turns off again.

"We've got to get you out of here," she says.

I run to the nearest window. People are already coming towards us. Angry. Wielding bats and hammers and anything else they can find that they could swing at me.

"We'd better hurry," I say. "The angry mob are already heading this way."

***

Movies and television shows love the absurd. Some nutcases have fed us with nonsense notions such as zombie apocalypse. Not gonna happen. Not according to science. Doesn't stop people talking about it, though. They still keep making new stuff, telling the same stories in the same old ways. Some folks take the whole idea like it's only a matter of time. They have a will in the specific event of a zombie event. They have zombie-proof bunkers. The whole bucket of chicken.

This caravan, right here, right now, could be as close as I ever get to a zombie-related event.

Hands are banging on windows. Fists on the door. An assortment of thuds against the thin, badly insulated metal walls. The mob outside are just a couple of death-rattles and shouts of 'brains' away from the real deal.

My mind's taken back to the most recent TV show where this scene would fit. Some of those extras in full make-up look better than some of the folks I arrested in my early cop days. The mob outside might look a little more respectable, if they weren't trying to take me out.

Demi's sitting on a sofa. Knees clamped together. One hand against the side of her head. The other holding a phone to her other ear. If I didn't know she was on the phone, I'd guess she was having some kinda nervous breakdown.

"What do you mean you can't?" she asks. Her eyes are widening.

A little listening.

"So you're saying there's nothing at all you can do for us? You put us up in this tin can and turn the other way when someone shows up with the tin opener."

She ain't even listening anymore. She's hung up the call. Looks at me like she's just watched her life savings go up in flames.

"We on our own?" I ask. The answer's obvious.

She nods. "They can't get to us. Roads are blocked with police protests."

I look out the window. "At least the mob can't drop me in the town square like some sacrificial lamb."

She shakes her head when I glance back. "They'll conduct the ceremony themselves if delivering you isn't an option."

I wanna point out the funny side. Ask if there's any mint sauce to go with the lamb. She ain't gonna appreciate it. Not right now.

She gets up. Paces around. "Half an hour since that video."

She's humming something. It's that damn cat jingle again. That commercial's gotta be the happy place she retreats to when the world goes to hell.

She stands on a sofa and peers out again. Tries to get a view of the group and put a number on them. "Twenty to thirty at a guess. They're moving around all the time."

I smile a little. "Almost like they don't know they're being counted. You think they'd line up neatly if we asked?"

She stares at me.

No time for humour, apparently.

She might have a point.

"You been in a real fight before?" I ask.

She looks at me. Nods a little.

"I mean a real, ugly, close-quarters kinda thing."

She looks at the ground. "Some back-seat battle stuff. Nothing like this."

I wait until she looks back at me. "First rule. If they can't get to us, let's not make their lives any easier."

She nods. Stands up with purpose. It's like she's forgotten that purpose as soon as her feet are holding her weight.

I look around. Open a cabinet or two. "Where do you keep the weapons in here?"

She closes her eyes. Scrunches up her whole face. "They're back at headquarters."

I stare at her. "You got anything on you at all?"

She shakes her head. "Weapons aren't standard issue. We're set up like the police. Got an armed unit who handle that stuff."

I laugh for a second. "An armed unit who can't get to us."

"It's a safe house," she says, "not an army barracks."

"It's whatever it becomes in the moment," I say. "Right now, it ain't a safe house. It ain't even a lock box. It's a big, metal prison cell."

"Do we stay here?" she asks. "Do we try to break free?"

I sit down. Shrug. "We've gotta think clearly through this. You think it makes sense to face that lot out there?"

She shakes her head.

I nod. "Good. We're at least on the same page."

She looks at me like there's a snake in my hair. "What if they break in?"

"We deal with it."

"How?"

I'm not gonna give her another shrug. Got to come up with something sensible. "We'll think of something."

She's got a decent disapproving look. I'll give her that.

I ain't got anything else to give.

One thing's for damn sure. It ain't a good time to start smelling smoke.

But we can both smell it. It's clear from the panic in our eyes.

***

Don't know how they got the fire started at the back of the caravan. Could be an open window. Seems fire safe curtains don't stay fire safe for too long. Not when they're shown nothing but a persistent lighter. Maybe they chucked in a few magazines, newspapers, books. They seem the book-burning type.

It ain't gonna go well, putting out a blazing fire in a place like this. The kit's not up to snuff. This lot ain't, anyway. A fire extinguisher that's as useful as peeing on the shoulder-high flames. I've seen sheets of paper bigger than the fire blanket.

With our heads down, we get away from the worst of the smoke. Back to the lounge.

"We're not gonna put this out," I say.

She shakes her head. Coughs. "I know."

She coughs again. So do I.

She looks at me. "What do we do now?"

"Only one way out," I say. I point at the door.

Some days you get a few decent choices lined up. Your day can be good or better, depending on what you do.

Today, we've got only bad options. Try to survive a growing, out of control fire, or take your chances with a swelling, angry mob.

"They got angry far too quickly," she says. She looks through the opaque glass of the door.

I nod. "Wouldn't surprise me if there are a couple out there, riling up others, on the VIRTUS payroll."

She shakes her head a little. "There's been growing resentment for the police in recent years. Too many dumb cops getting caught doing dumb things. Maybe you just tipped them over the edge."

Enough talk. It's heating up in here. The thug who started the fire, like almost always, maybe expected a smaller, slower fire. Instead, this thing's growing and roaring like some evil creature from a comic book.

I pick up a dining chair. Hold it near shoulder-height.

"What are you doing?" she asks with a shout.

"Coming up with a plan," I shout back.

Rule two: A good distraction's as good as a cheap shot.

I throw the chair at a window the opposite side to the door. It's stronger than it looks. The thing near bounces off it.

I pick it up. Step back. Charge at the window with the legs of the chair. Four hard points, turned sharper with speed, connect with the glass.

A crack appears. We're getting there.

I wind up one more time. Do the same.

The window shatters.

There ain't anyone around this side. They're all by the door.

The mob are on the move. They think we're escaping out the back.

The front door's clear.

She makes a break for it. Heads for her car.

I fling open a closet next to the door. A vacuum cleaner with a base, a hose and a long, metal pipe. I disconnect the flexible hose and the head. The pole's maybe four feet long. Hard. A good makeshift weapon.

One last look around. I don't see the laptop.

I head out the door. Demi's got it. She's cracking someone round the head with it.

It was a hard computer, made from a couple of pieces of precision-milled aluminium. Even that dents more than you'd think when it comes into contact with someone's skull.

Rule three: Use whatever you've got. Whatever it takes to win.

She's nearly at her driver door when the mob head back

around in a hurry.

"I'll hold them off," I say. "Get in the car. Get it started."

The vacuum pole is quite the tool for keeping people away. Light, strong, quick to swing at the heads, shoulders and arms of as many as are in the way.

I glance over my shoulder. She's in. The engine starts up.

I work my way to the passenger seat.

Some angry guy comes at me. Square head, broad shoulders and hands made for tough work. Grabs the pole. I can't wrestle the thing free. If he gets this thing off me, he's gonna have a good go at taking chunks outta me, as well as the car.

We've both got two hands on it. We're like two contestants in an old frontier American kids' game. Whether I push the thing towards him or pull it back again, he ain't letting his fingers slip.

I've gotta change tact.

I throw up a knee. Catch him in the groin. He stumbles a little but keeps hold.

I drop to the floor. Kick out at his legs. Get a boot near his stomach with my knee bent.

I heave the bar towards me while kicking out with my leg.

The guy flies over me like a late-reacting kid, flying over the handlebars of their bike.

Rule four: Use their size and weight against them where possible.

I snatch the pole back and fling it in a wild arc towards the crowd.

I wanna tell them they've got the wrong guy. That I haven't done any of the stuff people claim, but you can't reason with an angry crowd.

I've managed to get back to my feet near the passenger door.

Someone charges round the other side of the car. They're now running straight at me.

I raise the hollow pole at the right point and jab him right in the middle of his face. He hits the ground like an angry fist from a failed athlete.

Rule five: Don't play fair.

I'm in the seat. I get the door slammed shut.

They're surrounding the car. Punching at the windows. A couple of people are pulling at the windscreen wipers.

Demi doesn't need any more encouragement from me. She puts her foot down and gets us moving. People don't want to be run over. You head towards them, they're usually gonna move. If they don't it's a natural selection thing. Survival of the fittest means death of the stupidest.

The wipers snap off the car as she accelerates. A couple of people weren't gonna let go.

We're at the exit to the campsite.

The caravan's a burning, smoking mess in the mirror.

We've put rule six into action: As soon as you can, get out of Dodge.

36. PUZZLES, INTELLIGENCE AND THE RIGHT THING TO DO

Same things are true as always. You head to places where there ain't any people, you're not gonna get anyone in your way.

"Where are we going?" I ask.

Demi glances back with a blank look. Fixes her eyes back on the road. "No idea."

"We've been heading there for nearly forty minutes."

She stares me down out of the side of her eyes. "When I think we're a safe distance away, I'll call in. See what they can do to help us."

I look out my window. Gotta think of a few more questions. If I don't, the silence is gonna be filled. Demi's repeated nervous humming of that stupid cat jingle's most likely. She's only one eccentric trait away from being an Ally McBeal character.

Despite her eccentricities, I've gotta hope she's good at her job. That she knows how to pick up the pieces.

"When we get safe, then what?" I ask.

"We regroup. See how we take down VIRTUS from there."

"But we're nowhere" I say. "They're gonna keep tanking police reputation. Lies and secret truths in unequal measure. The entire country could end up under martial law."

There's a part sigh and a slight head shake. She doesn't seem to think it'll go that far.

I turn on the radio, if only to drown out the silence.

A news bulletin. Just what we need.

"Police around the country will not be thanking Enoch Flint for his recent deceit," says one guy. He's got a good, baritone voice. "Not after the raft of apparent secrets that have leaked in the past few minutes. Police around the country are refusing to comment on multiple allegations. These allegations include hiding evidence. Witness intimidation. In some cases, serious injury and sexual assaults."

"How much of that do you think is true?" she asks.

I look straight ahead. "Probably all of it. Putting on the uniform doesn't stop you from being human, good or bad."

"You don't think VIRTUS are exaggerating? Hamming things up to get more of a reaction?"

I shrug. "Soon, maybe. Not right now. They need people to believe the first things they leak. They've gotta be true. Wait a few minutes for officers to start resigning. Public apologies. Promises to fully investigate in the wake of allegations. Public trust in VIRTUS hits an all-time high. Public confidence in the police continues to nose-dive."

The guy on the radio keeps talking. "The promise from those behind the leak is that this will continue. The names and offences they've disclosed so far are just the tip of a very substantial iceberg."

"What happens when the entire country loses faith in the police?" she asks. "Who do people turn to when no one recognises their authority anymore?"

I look at her. Look out the window at the winding, never-ending road. "I guess we're about to find out."

***

Sometimes hiding places are hard to come by. Someone's counting to ten. They're on eight. You're out of ideas.

About the time I'm thinking this is one of those times, something changes.

We pull into a gravel road that stretches in a straight line for maybe a mile, beyond the trees in the distance.

We edge our way along. There's a building back there. A large one.

We reach the trees. The building in front of us is some huge, Edwardian mansion. Beige-grey sandstone. Big windows. High ceilings. Three floors, and another one hiding behind a bunch of Dorma windows up in the roof. A footprint that fills the windscreen when we're still fifty feet away. Might have more wings than a flock of pigeons.

"This another safe house?" I ask. I lean forward so I can see it better through the glass, without the car roof getting in the way. "If it is, why on earth did we use that stupid caravan?"

She shakes her head. "Not a safe house. You're not that lucky."

I laugh.

Lucky. She's got me mixed up with someone else.

Anyone else.

We park up near some fountain in the middle of the round end of a keyhole-shaped driveway. Huge, fancy wooden doors to the house seem to spring open. There's a suited man pushing each side. Each one tall, strong, wondering what's happened to their career.

We get in. The doors close behind us.

This place ain't what it looks like from the outside.

I was expecting ornate fixtures. Ridiculous cornicing. Fancy balustrades. Rugs that are worth more than the average pension. Shaped plaster ceilings. Maybe a mural or two.

Nothing like it. I've been transported from Edwardian to present day. Sleek stainless steel. Glass everywhere. Walls knocked through to make a giant, open space. Computer and TV screens everywhere.

"We're heading through to the briefing room," Demi says. There's an air of confidence about her. It's been missing since she was stood by her car, outside that caravan.

A section towards the back is divided from the rest by a wall of floor-to-high-ceiling glass panels. It's a hell of a ceiling to reach. Gotta be nearly three times my height. A long, glass table and a host of identical black office chairs inside.

The door closes behind me. The glass wall, which was clear as a Caribbean sea turns opaque. It's like a magic trick. Now you see us, now you don't. Seems they spent more on the glass than we spent on our house.

The TV at one end has the news on mute. Things are kicking off big-style around the UK. More revelations. More protests. More violence. A slew of police resignations. The army drafted in to maintain order. The bobbies that are left have their helmets and huge shields. All sorts of makeshift missiles are heading their way.

There's a TV at the other end. It's showing a map of one specific point somewhere in the bowels of central London. One squarish building, hemmed in by four narrow roads.

There's a man, tall, black, closer to bald than I've managed, standing up by the digital map. He's got the look of someone whose son blew his life savings at a roulette table. Eyebrows in the angry position. It's like they've been carved out of something and they ain't changing. Large, dark eyes. Straight, hard nose. The guy looks menacing before he says a word. Wondering if he's about to chew me up and spit me out.

Nothing like it.

Turns out, this is the guy's soft expression.

"Agent Brandon Hall," he says, introducing himself. "I take it you're Enoch Flint?"

Demi chirps up. Reminds me of the eager know-it-all school kid. "He just goes by Flint," she says.

He looks at her. Says nothing. Nods. Looks back at me.

"We've gathered our intel, and we've got a lead, from your place of work, of all places. The analyst there. She's done some good work of the messaging app. Internet records suggest it was made in the building on this map. Data's still being sent there regularly."

"What now?" I ask.

He waves a hand at the screen. As if by magic, it changes. Shows body-worn camera of the outside of the building.

Looks like every industrial site you've ever seen. A row of big garage-style doors for movement of goods at the bottom. Windows everywhere above. Most are still intact. Up where the offices are. Where some folks never got all dusty in the warehouse. They sit and do calculations and try to sell their product. A flat roof. Empty car park.

A rectangle on the wall near a main entrance is darker than the cheap brickwork around it. Used to have a company logo and maybe a welcome message. Now it's a reminder that in any line of work, you can go from boom to bust pretty damn quick.

"This is coming from a team we have about to go in. We can

watch it live."

It goes a little like those cop scenes that make the news. A team gather by the door. They pick up their small battering ram, or the "big red key" as it's sometimes called. They smash in the handle. Get inside. Shout a lot. Drag out those inside.

But this scene's a little different. The agents go charging in, shouting, sure enough.

Then, something that sounds like gunfire. One shot. Another. They keep going. Evenly spaced out. Maybe seven shots and then it's quiet.

The agents re-emerge from their hiding places. They've got to act quick. Whoever's shooting away might have stopped to reload.

Room by room, there are shouts of one word repeatedly. Clear.

They hit the room where all the noise was coming from. Has to be in here.

Nope.

They head through the doorway. A strange contraption's sitting on an otherwise empty table near the window. Like a gun on a tripod. It has a few levers to a couple of cogs. Linked to something that looks a little like a record player.

"No one's here," says the agent with the body-cam. "One handgun, firing on some kind of automatic timer."

They keep searching. Room by room, it's the same answer. Empty. No more random machines. No more of anything.

"Nothing else in there at all?" Agent Hall asks.

"Nothing, sir."

No people. No random server farm. Not even an old computer and a dial-up modem.

Not what these guys were expecting.

Agent Hall wasn't angry before. *Now* he's angry. I can just about tell the difference.

What do we do now?" Demi asks.

He glares at her. Says nothing for entirely too long.

Now we're all out of ideas.

***

"All our intel pointed here," Agent Hall says. "Every lead we had has just hit a dead-end. The public are tearing the country apart. We're officially nowhere near catching the group. They'll keep spewing this trash into the public domain."

They both look at me.

"Any ideas?" Agent Hall says.

I screw up my face a little. "Only one, but I don't think it's a good one."

He pulls out a chair and sits down. My thoughts weren't enough to make him do that. "Let me be the judge of that. We can see if there's anything we can do together to get this back on track."

Like the stuff on the TV behind me, there's a battle going on inside my head.

I've been set up by VIRTUS. Hung out to dry. They've got my family. I'm the guy with close links to these people. I'm the one who can help put a stop to them, because I've done it before.

But I'm all out of things to try. I'm an empty well. A dry river bed.

I'm tired. I need a good sleep. But life can't wait for me to catch up on a heap of Zs.

I wanna help. I want to find the big thing, get things moving again. I want to take VIRTUS down. I have to.

There's never been a need for me to solve a puzzle with so much riding on it.

Even without my family, the country's a mess. Riots. Looting. Destruction of cars and buildings. If I can't find a solution, we're all off to hell in a handbasket.

I've never given up on a puzzle. Never. The answer comes. Always does, eventually. Often when your body rests and your mind clears.

But that's not happening right now.

If I can solve this, come up with that perfect solution, VIRTUS won't be a problem anymore. No destroying of public confidence. No more loss of life.

But if I stay here, sheltered, hidden away, how bad's stuff gonna get out there? How many millions of people need this to be over pretty damn quick?

I've got no more thoughts than a very bad one. A terrible idea. One destined to do nothing but temporarily appease a few people.

I nod. Finally. Stare at him. "You got a helicopter?" I ask.

I'm now getting looks from two people like I've just asked for a giraffe playing a banjo whilst riding a unicycle.

Suspicion from Demi. "What are you thinking of doing?"

I look back at the TV screen showing the muted news broadcast. "The only thing there is left to do."

37. A PROBLEM KEPT IS A PROBLEM SQUARED

The guys who write the history books have been kind to conquering heroes. Of course they were gonna be. Else, they'd have had their head on a spike and the next guy would've come up with something more flattering.

The moment when an emperor returns home, flanked by his army. Glory abounds. Cheering crowds. Wealth and prosperity secured. What a leader. A hero.

My return to Cookston ain't heralded. No bands playing. No adoring crowd.

I didn't even get the helicopter. Busy on a training exercise, they said. I'm not important enough. They know it. I know it.

Right now, I'm only one thing.

Cookston's once thriving market's barely something worth mentioning these days. A handful of stalls, their faded, wide-striped fabric sides flapping in the wind. All offering cheap goods imported from China. No local wares anymore. If they had them, they'd be four times the price. The ten small stalls sit around the edge of the town square.

It ain't square. Not even a neat rectangle. Just an open space, vaguely squarish if you squint. Town hall on one side. Stone façade looked good a few decades ago. Now it's all covered in grime. More cracks every time I see it. Some stores occupy two of the sides. An overpriced American candy store among them. Also some fancy-looking bar that ain't as fancy as it looks. A couple of takeaway places. Some places that like to sell buckets and spades to those either poor enough or dumb enough to holiday here. An oversized pawn shop with bright colours and the promise of meagre offers for beloved tech.

The remaining side's filled with a monstrous, unsafe, deserted multi-story car park. All fenced off. Render's falling off the outside in chunks. You park your car on the top of that, it's like taking the wrong brick out when you're playing Jenga.

That's where they stop the van. It's the first thing I see when they slide open the back door. At least, it is once my eyes adjust. I guess someone had their reasons for getting me here in the dark rear section of a panel van. Not my idea of a good way to travel.

Still, it got me through the crowds. They're still not quite thick enough to block determined traffic.

From time to time, you're gonna see riots on TV. Folks shouting. Throwing things. Maybe even some looting. What you don't see is the other side of the camera. Most of the time, people put on a show for the cameras. Assemble where they're gonna be seen. The ignored side of the street might as well be a backdrop for some zombie apocalypse flick.

Riot cops know a thing or two about the larger crowds. Up front and centre are the folks with the big beef. The ones who wanna shout and scream until they get their way. Mixed in with them are the hooligans. They ain't got a cause, but they're gonna join in if they get a chance of cracking heads open like soft-boiled eggs. Behind are the second wave. The ones who watched or read about stuff online and wanted to join in. They're the ones who took the time to make the banners, usually. They wanna be seen and heard, but they've gotta keep their noses clean to keep their day jobs. Around and behind them, you've got the seemed-like-a-good-idea-at-the-time lot. The ones who get there. Hear the shouting. Wanna back out. Go home and hide under a duvet. They stay because it's something to stand up for. They stay because they don't wanna be called a coward by their friends somewhere in front of them.

The police assemble with their riot gear. If they can dent the confidence of the first wave, the rest's gonna start to fall apart like a thin pie crust. If the police can't stop the mob like a brick wall stops a running kid, stuff can get nasty.

There ain't much of a crowd in the square. A handful of people. The placard-types. The basement-dwelling kids who ain't got the money to get out of their parents' house. They blow their dough on clothes, shoes, phones and headphones, by the looks of it. A little more thrift and they'd get their own place a little sooner.

The angry bit of the crowd are somewhere else. On the move. Marching down the high street, maybe. There's a faint sound of mob. Also the slight hint of something burning on the breeze. The town square's got the leftovers, which suits me just fine.

The town's war memorial stands proud. Dead centre, surrounded by symmetrical patterns of glued-down gravel. Like most of them, it's some stone needle sticking up out of the ground. It's like no one had the imagination to make anything else. Could be that money was scarce and stone needles were come by easily. I don't know.

There's a metal, temporary fence blocking off the memorial and about ten feet in any direction. Got plans in place for their next Armistice day, coming up pretty quickly. Assuming the public calm down enough. Don't want an open-air war memorial service turning into a bloodbath.

I stand by one side of the fence. It's got the tensile strength of a used teabag. Can't lean on it. I'm facing the town hall. Wonder if the police have swept these buildings. Don't want some random sniper picking me off from a rooftop.

I shake my head. Not in this country. Sure, handguns can be

smuggled in. The big, heavy and bulky sniper rifles you need for a decent shot ain't so easy to hide.

A few police are wandering the square. Standard helmets and protective vests. Just here for assurance, now that the crowd's moved on.

For a whole lot of people angry with me, it takes longer than I'm expecting for someone to recognise me.

One guy looks my way. White, overweight, long hair. round, angry face. Wide eyes. He shouts something. Points. Yep, he knows who I am. Wouldn't have pegged him as being the type to watch the news and stay informed. Maybe he caught a story by accident on his last trip to his local pub.

Him and a couple of others make a beeline for me. My peripheral vision tells me a couple of the cops are also getting closer. When you've been wearing the uniform for long enough, you can smell trouble.

"What are you doing here?" one of them shouts.

"Get out of our town!" shouts another.

More of the crowd head my way.

"Murderer!" comes the cry from one woman in the midst, desperate to be heard.

I've gotta say something. "I'm here to turn myself over to VIRTUS!"

They're still coming towards me. Maybe they want their pound of flesh first.

The first guy's nearly within arm's reach. He's clenching his fists. Rolling his shoulders. Getting a kink out of his thick neck.

I've gotta let him throw the first punch.

Though I ain't sure why. Already getting strung up for murder, domestic abuse, rape and escaping custody. Hitting first ain't gonna add anything big to my rap sheet.

Screw it. Some big guy doesn't have to hit first for you to be acting in self-defence anyway. You feel threatened and in danger, you've got every right to strike first. I ain't Mr Miyagi. Not even Daniel LaRusso. I don't have to fight by any rules.

I duck to one side. Take a step. Grab the arm of the large guy when it's still moving. I shove a fist into his side. A shove with my shoulder sends him crashing through the barriers.

Some thin woman with glasses hoists a protest sign. Says something about wanting truth from the police. She wants to bring the thing crashing down on top of me, but she's not thought about wind resistance. The drag on that sign's significant, and it's not moving with the pace she imagined. I step closer. Grab her arms. I knee her in the stomach and push her back into the crowd.

That's enough to get the police stepping in. They wanna hold the crowd at bay. Get me arrested. Be the heroes.

There's maybe six officers fighting back close to twenty upset locals. None of them have got a hand free to put the arm on me.

Don't even know why I came here.

There's no one from VIRTUS. No one's gonna magically show up and release my family because I stepped outside.

Maybe I'm best making a run for it. Getting somewhere a little more sheltered. Wait until there's someone showing up who can negotiate the release of Flick and Toby.

I'm turning my head. Looking for options. Shallow doorways. Blocked off alley ways. Not a lot of great hiding places.

I turn to face the crowd again. The police are still just about holding them back.

But my attention's on the sharp pain in my neck. The cloth shoved over my nose and mouth.

My eyes dart around. I can only spot part of a police cap. A collar of a uniform.

Surely the police aren't resorting to tactics like this to cart me off.

Who knows? Maybe when they're dealing with the fugitive, they bring out all the stops.

Still, as I'm fading away to unconsciousness, I've got a couple of things to be grateful for.

First is that whoever wants me blacking out didn't whack me on the head.

Second is that the police ain't pulling out all the stops for me just yet. Any means necessary doesn't mean a sniper rifle.

38. BETTER THAN A POLICE CELL?

Okay, so not all prisons are terrible, as it turns out. This one ain't so bad.

Yeah, I might be locked in. Might not have any say in the food, but it could be worse.

I'm not chained to some scabby little chair in a forlorn warehouse. About to be tortured or electrocuted where no one can hear me scream.

This place has got the feel of an abandoned, luxury hotel with some modifications. The furniture is fixed to the floor. The bed, a chair, a table, bolted down in a rudimentary fashion. Brackets and bolts clearly visible. Maybe they're meant to be. Let people know this ain't a vacation spot now.

The door that got me in here's locked. A blacked-out peephole. There's a large, sliding door, also locked, leading out to a balcony I'll likely never reach. A huge, calm sky overhead.

I wouldn't have spent so long running from VIRTUS if I'd have known this was what they'd offer me.

Compared to this place, the 'safe house' caravan was a shack on the crater of an active volcano.

Thankfully, no one's nearby, whistling any annoying cat TV jingle. Always a plus.

Maybe initial appearances are deceptive. Maybe here, the white hot trouble spews out later. Could be in for a world of pain, but I don't know it yet.

The décor is some ugly combination of beige and brown. You can add whatever crazy patterns you like to the walls and the darker floor. They've certainly tried here. None of it makes those colours look any better. There are rusting brass colour vents low in the walls. A couple of smaller ones in the floor near the wall. Part of some ancient heating and cooling system.

A double bed's to the right as you walk in the room. To the left is a desk, missing a chair. It's got an old, boxy TV on it, though. Past the desk is the ensuite bathroom. Same ugly browns in the tiles, the can, the sink and the tub. Over near the window, the single chair and small, round table.

Maybe this place was bursting at the seams in 1984. Could be it was showing its age by 1992. Travel to other countries got cheaper. Other resorts got better. It's made somewhere like this a relic before the turn of the new century.

Some big fancy doors off some lavish lobby closed for the last time. This place still sits here. A reminder of failed investment. Dashed dreams. Great getaways were once had inside these now crumbling walls.

I can't get out to the balcony, but I can see most of the view.

Trees fill the horizon. They thin out as the eye travels downward. Patches of green grass emerge. Just as the grass starts to look like it's taking over, there's a strange cliff. Way down beneath it, below a wall of brown rock, is an almost perfect circle of murky, but blue water.

An old granite quarry, by the looks of it. Seems when the rock got cheaper, someone got folks to stop digging and blowing holes out here. Probably a decent spot for a date, back in the day. Sunshine. Serenity. Deep pool of water.

Like all these kindsa places, this one would've been fenced off years ago. Some kid jumped from the edge of that cliff. Hit something on the way down. Got himself drowned. Even though thousands of others hadn't so much as stubbed a toe, the place was too dangerous.

A new fence is put up. There's a security guard for a while.

But like it does, time dulls peoples' pain. Makes them forget. Causes them to question, to doubt what really happened. Justification and budget cuts led to a drop in patrols until no one bothered anymore. Holes in the perimeter fence you could maybe fit a truck through.

It ain't warm enough for the usual crowd this time of year. A few months ago, it was a little warmer. There'd be a new generation of kids. All sitting, laying around, jumping off, swimming. Someday something will go wrong again and people will remember to be upset about this place. Until then, it's a teenager's hangout. A view of this once-fancy hotel opposite.

I look around the room. Worn carpets and tired upholstery. Not a lot to look at.

But didn't VIRTUS want me dead? If they got me, why put me up here?

But look a little closer, and someone's updated something in this room.

There's a digital read-out. Glows red, next to a clock on the wall. Shows the number one. Nothing else.

Two wall-mounted cameras above it. Enough to cover anywhere in the room I can try to hide. Some round speaker built into the wall.

If they can speak to me, maybe I can speak back.

"Hello," I say.

Gotta say, it's as strange as a first prayer to some unknown god.

No reply.

"What's the number on the wall mean?"

Still nothing.

"How long should I expect to be trapped in here, until somebody kills me?"

A loud burst of static catches me by surprise. I take a step back, but I'm right in front of the bed. I fall back until I'm sitting, staring at that speaker.

More silence.

Then, a loud, distorted voice. "You will get your answers in time, and so will we."

"I don't know what you mean by that," I say. I let out a little laugh. "You think you can get secrets outta me? There'd have to be some in my head first."

"Mr Flint, we assure you that you will not find this situation amusing."

I shrug. "Whatever you think you can get me to say or do, you ain't gonna get there by torturing me. That's for damn sure."

Another crackle. "Turn on the television, Mr Flint."

I look around. No remote.

I walk up. Tap around the sides. Find one button. I press it and the thing lets out a high-pitch whine. Starts to warm up before it can show me a picture.

When it's up and running, it ain't a picture I wanna see.

39. NOT MUCH OF A SOLUTION

The swanky country manor house has a Jekyll and Hyde vibe. Outside one thing, inside another. It's got another visitor. This one's gonna keep showing up until Flint and his family are free.

DC Holly Chamberlain wasn't gonna be safe back at SITU HQ anyway. No one was. Those who can, are working from home. Everyone else is staying well clear of the public eye. Starting work at crazy times in the morning, just so some protestor doesn't spot them.

It's mad how much heat is being chucked on the thin blue line. The guys from the regular police in their riot gear aren't gonna be able to hold out against the crowds forever. What then?

Nahid Shamoon's with her. She's looking in every possible direction. She's got a jaw-dropped look on her face like a kid visiting Santa's workshop.

But the SITU folks aren't here for a guided tour. They're putting everything into finding Flint and his family.

They're taken to some meeting room at the back with some impressive, magic glass.

The same tall black officer is standing at the end of the room. The only one not sitting in one of the black chairs.

"Agent Brandon Hall," he says to his new audience. "What can you tell me from the work SITU have done?"

No introductions. Why waste the time?

Nahid pipes up. "I took a different approach. I went to

wholesale computer places. Searched their records. I found one. A local place. Provided a Valiance Solutions with eight high-powered computers about twenty years ago."

He looks at her. Stern look. Obviously. "You think one of these computers was used to design this secure messaging app that VIRTUS are using?"

She shrugs. "It's not likely, given their age. There's also a chance this is not related to anything at all."

He looks towards the opaque glass. Shakes his head a little. "We can't leave any stone unturned. We've got to see where it takes us."

Nahid's holding a piece of paper with an address printed on it. The billing address for those computers. "I already had someone scout this address out."

Agent Hall stares at her. An air of impatience about him right now.

She shakes her head. "The building's in an empty commercial development. The place is closed off."

Holly says her first words since sitting down. "We've not been able to find out who owns the building, or get any kind of paper trail we can follow."

Agent Hall walks to the door like he's late for something else. Flips a switch that changes the glass so it's crystal clear again. "I'll get a team together to check out the premises."

His hand's on the door handle.

"Agent Hall," Holly says, "what's being done about the stories VIRTUS keep leaking to the press?"

He opens the door. Points out at a floor of busy people. "Pretty much all these people out here are fact-checking. So far, we figure the stories are sixty percent false, or they're hugely embellished."

There must be some plan to let the news outlets know, but he's not about to go into it. Maybe they have ways of dealing with the national media. Methods they keep under wraps.

They can worry about damage control with the public at some point down the road.

Right now, they need to find whoever's behind Valiance Solutions. Somewhere along the resulting paper chain will be a link to Flint and his family.

But there's a look on Holly's face that says life ain't that simple. That she's been in this kinda situation before. Ducks don't get in neat little rows when you ask them to do it.

They're probably gonna hit a dead-end or two before they get anywhere.

They've just got to hope they've got the time to afford a couple of dead-ends.

***

Even the fence and the gate of this place has seen better days.

You've got the usual threatening signs about trespassing. Promises of prosecution if you put a toe beyond the gate. Truth is, no one cares. Someone did once, but nobody's got any clue who that might've been. All records held about the building and the buying of this site relate to people who are now pushing up daisies.

It's not difficult snapping the lock on the gate. It's been there a while. It's even left a rust outline on the gate behind it.

It's a gate suited to a scrap metal yard, or a car breakers. The sort of place where you half expect some big, angry rottweiler.

Some four-legged beast charging at you the moment you step inside.

If there *was* a dog, there isn't here anymore.

The car park's made up of a few huge slabs of concrete, laid down one next to the other. Weeds waist-high are growing through the gaps. There's space for maybe half a dozen cars. Not that any cars could get in.

Someone decided this entire site needed shutting off from the world. Commercial building and all. They put some big concrete barriers at the entrance, just off a roundabout. No one was gonna park at these offices. Nowhere outside the abandoned bowling alley or the run-down multi-screen cinema either. Another building looks like something's more likely to park inside it than outside. Could be that it was once a Pizza Hut.

Just like the lock on the gate, it doesn't take long to get around the single-bolt door lock. A glass door from maybe thirty, forty years ago. Door security's moved on a little since then.

An alarm sounds. The sharp, piercing wail that's supposed to alert folks outside. Might be just as likely to put off would-be thieves.

But these guys know how to disable an alarm pretty quickly. The shrill noise is snuffed out. It's been going long enough that half of the team could swear they can still hear it.

Valiance Solutions isn't on the list of companies near reception. Maybe their lease didn't last long enough for anyone to remember them.

The team split up and take different floors.

Ground floor's empty.

First floor's deserted with some office furniture scattered about the place.

Second floor's been sliced into a bunch of smaller office spaces.

One's got a sign on the door. Valiance Solutions.

Again, the lock's not a problem.

It's a small office. Got space for maybe four desks. So long as no one sitting at them's very big, anyway. Only one desk left. A pile of those once high-powered computers on the floor, over by the window. Five tower computers, three laptops.

Desk drawers are locked, but they're forced open. Nothing but a few pieces of useless paperwork. Some tax forms they never even got around to filling in.

Nothing left to do but to load those computers into a van. See what a forensics expert can get from them.

Seems whoever said they weren't in business long was right on the money. Maybe a few weeks. Seems their neighbours didn't do so well, either. Neither did the landlord.

Agent Hall keeps going on about how ideal this location would be. How criminal enterprises love these kinda spots these days. Says it enough that his team are wondering if he's gonna retire and start up for the other side.

Demi's looking through the sheets of paper. A couple of the agents get with loading the computers.

"One lead from here, at least," she says.

Agent Hall looks at her, a little puzzled.

She holds out a sheet of paper. "This half-filled in tax document. It's got a home address of a Ted Valiance. Could be worth a visit?"

He nods. It's not much of anything, but it could be something of something.

***

It's a new-looking pad, considering the age.

Built in the sixties, but you can only just tell.

Some old widow's maybe had her son use some of her savings to fix the place up. Maybe he's trying to improve her quality of life in their old family home. More likely, he's adding value to a property he'll have to sell in the not-too-distant future.

She swings the door open. Invites agents Hall and Wheeler to take a seat on a couch with a wide overly-flowery pattern.

"Sixteen years," she says. "That's how long he's been gone."

She looks at a picture of them both on the mantle. Must've been taken decades ago. They look young and happy.

"Nearly lost the house because of the business going under. It took its toll on both of us, but especially him."

These two have no need to ask this woman questions. Sit and listen. See where this goes.

"He put a lot into a computer company. It's where the money was at the time, but things got expensive really fast. Too many extra costs came out of nowhere."

The pictures on the walls tell their life story. Met when they were young. Married before they got much older. One son. He's got his own family now. Visits when he can. Might not be too often, given there's maybe two years between each of the family photos.

"Those poor people he took on, they didn't even get a first pay cheque. I tried to help out by working for free. Used to be a legal assistant before our son was born. Pretty quick, it got too much, and there were too many people doing what we were doing. Too much money going out, none coming in."

They nod, like they've got some clue about the private sector, despite having never really worked in it.

"You got any records at all from that time?" Demi asks.

She nods. "A briefcase of his. In a box in the loft if you wanted to go up there. I don't head up there anymore."

They turn to look at Agent Hall. He nods and gets to his feet. Finds the loft hatch. Pulls down the in-built ladder.

It doesn't take lot of searching through the freezing, dusty space. He finds an old briefcase in a box. Heads down with it. "The combination?" he asks.

She looks blank. No clue. Maybe she knew it once. She certainly doesn't remember it now.

"Never mind," he says. "Can we take this away and get into it back at the office?"

She nods. "I have no use for it now. Just another bit of junk I've been hoarding for years, according to my son."

They smile and nod. They're on their way to the door. Looks like it's the next thing that could be replaced.

"A beautiful home you have here," Demi says as they're leaving.

She smiles. Rolls her eyes. "Try telling my son that. He never seems to be happy with it. He doesn't even live within fifty miles of it."

She nods like she will.

The briefcase is flung onto the back seat of the car.

Hardly likely it'll contain a goldmine of information.

Another day spent jogging at a gentle place down some blind alleys.

But sooner or later they're gonna find something.

VIRTUS can't stay hidden away forever.

Demi's got her mind on Flint as they drive back.

Where did he go? Have they got him?

From his file, he's a difficult man to keep quiet and locked away for long.

40. HOW MUCH CAN YOU STAND WHEN YOU'RE SITTING DOWN?

I guess you've seen that grainy black and white footage of the moment man first walked on the moon. The ghosting as they moved. The static interference. Pretty good for the time. You think about the distance the signal had travelled through radio waves.

The feed shown on the TV reminds me a little of that. The difference is that this is from a source a hell of a lot closer.

It's a video of a room that looks exactly like mine. Bed, chair, window all in the same place. But it's not me sitting on the edge of the bed.

Two figures there. Blurry as hell, but I know who they are. Only two people on earth they're gonna be. On the left, Flick. On the right, the much shorter figure of Toby.

On the one hand, the last thing you ever want to see are loved ones being imprisoned. Still held against their will by VIRTUS. On the other, though, I've got to be thankful they're still alive. That rescue is still an outside possibility.

No sound. There are arms moving. Fingers pointing. Maybe words being said. I'm not gonna know what those words are.

There's a crackle over the speaker in the wall again.

"Mr Flint, I feel I need to explain a thing or two."

Seems pretty clear-cut to me, but I'll let him say what he's dying to say.

"First of all, yes, your partner and son are in the next room along from you. They are alive and in reasonable spirits. Their destiny is in your hands."

Whatever they're gonna get me to do is gonna be hell, but I've got to say yes. What choice do I have?

"You are all securely locked in your rooms. I've added some extra security measures. I have clever cameras that detect the number of people present in each room. There are pressure sensors under each entrance and exit. If the number in your room sinks below one, I will make something bad happen to both rooms. The same is true if the number for the next room goes up or down from two."

No dramatic rescue then. Not with these gadgets watching my every move.

"In case you doubt the veracity of any of this..."

I see the door to their room open. A tall man in dark clothing enters. Walks over to the bed. Has something in his hand. Can't tell what it is. Raises it above his head.

Then... nothing but static. The feed's cut out.

But there's a sound coming through the wall. A scream. No two ways about it. A woman in pain, crying out. Chilling. Goes on for a second. Then it only echoes in my ears.

The video on the TV resumes. The woman's hunched over on the edge of the bed. Head in her hands. Crying.

I get to my feet. I head for the wall. Throw my fists against it. "Flick!" I shout. "It'll be okay. I'll get you out!"

The speaker starts up again. I retreat to the bed and sit down.

"Mr Flint, you'll want to follow my every direction with exactness. This is the only way to prevent your family being hurt any further. Do you understand?"

I get up. Look right into one of the cameras. "How can I be of any use to you, being locked up in here?"

"We have uses for you. And in case you get any ideas of playing the hero, I have other ways to put a stop to you. I could instruct large men to throw you over the balcony. I could pump harmful or compliant gasses into the room."

No idea what a compliant gas is. I ain't gonna ask.

I sit on the edge of the bed. The feed on the TV goes again.

I stare at the static. Not much else to do here, by the looks of it.

It's maybe five minutes later when I hear a complaint through the wall.

The TV starts up again.

Flick's moved. She's in the chair near the window. Struggling, but unable to move. Tied down, but I can't see the restraints on this terrible quality video. Can't even make out her face.

There's a man standing in front of her. The table's got a case of some kind on it.

More crackles over my speaker. "We're considering the times you have failed to listen, Mr Flint. We feel you may need further demonstrations of our ability to cause pain."

The man's holding something on the TV. Could be a knife. Could be anything, in all fairness.

"It's amazing how simple, everyday objects can become weapons. The mundane can become tortuous in a different situation. You can see how a standard pair of pliers and a pack of sewing needles can make someone wish they weren't born."

"What is he gonna do?" I ask.

No answer.

The man steps towards Flick. Crouches down. He's doing something to one of her hands.

Another horrifying scream makes it through the wall.

I wanna cover my ears.

I wanna break through this wall and set her free.

I wanna find the people causing her pain and throw them off the balcony. Would have to smash them through the glass first. A challenge I'd gladly accept.

The voice on the speaker starts up again. "Fingernails are interesting things. They grow back in a matter of weeks, but they can hurt a lot when forcibly removed."

I clench one fist. Point with the other. Walk right up to the cameras. "I'll do what you want! Stop torturing her!"

"Mr Flint, you've said that before, and yet here we are. In a situation that could have so easily been avoided."

"There ain't many other options but to do what you want," I say. "You've seen to that."

I sit back down. A little out of breath, like I've been for a run. "I'll do what you say. I'll do whatever you want, as long as my family get released."

A crackle again. "Glad to hear it, Mr Flint. We need not do any further demonstrations."

Sounds good to me. I don't know how much more I could stand.

They can do whatever they like to me. I'll carry on, or I

won't.

But VIRTUS know how to get to people. They know which buttons to push.

Now I'm gonna have to sit around and wait to find out why they're pushing mine.

41. TIME TO MAKE A DEAL?

It's been a couple of hours since I last saw anything on that TV.

I haven't heard anything through the wall. Could be a good sign.

I've not long given up staring at that screen and laid on the bed when the door opens.

In walks a man holding a serving tray.

Same guy I keep seeing. The one with the nasal problem. He's been in the room for only a few seconds. Still has that problem, apparently.

The door's closed behind him before I even get up.

He walks over to the table. Puts the tray down.

There's a glass of orange juice. A freshly made ham sandwich on a plate with some potato chips on the side. This ain't exactly high-class room service, but it's not a high-class joint.

I ain't some high-roller with thousands to blow in their on-site casino. Not some bigwig in town for some big conference. Not even a politician at a party conference.

I'm a nobody. Anonymous food is about all I can expect.

I get up. Take a closer look. Plastic cup for the juice. Plastic plate for everything else. He ain't gonna give me something breakable. Nothing where shards can be used as weapons.

"Courtesy of VIRTUS," he says between sniffs. Said like it means something.

I nod. He backs away.

"When can I speak to someone to negotiate terms?" I ask.

I pick up the orange juice.

"Terms?" he says. A strange mixture of dumb and inquisitive on his face.

"Yeah, like securing the release of my family, now that they have me."

He purses his lips. Frowns.

"It's what they wanted in the first place, wasn't it? Lock me away? Stop me interfering with their next grand idea?"

A full scowl now. "What do you know about the latest grand idea?"

I look towards the window. "Not a hell of a lot."

He sniffs again. Then coughs. "What else can you offer an organisation like this?"

"I can still be useful. I can work for them."

He laughs. "I think we're past that point, aren't we? You're not a police officer anymore, are you?"

I shake my head.

"You're not even an upstanding citizen."

Another head shake.

"You're on the run for, what was it, murder?"

I nod. "Technically, but-"

"You have vast amounts of money we don't know about?"

I shake my head again.

"Okay, then you must have some important information for us. Something vital to the success of VIRTUS."

I shake my head again.

This has got to be the worst starting point for a negotiation ever.

He turns to leave. Looks back over his shoulder. "I'll have a word with the bosses. See if there's anything they think you can offer."

I nod like he's done me some huge favour.

I watch him leave.

I could've rushed him at the door. Grabbed it. Fought my way free.

For all I know, there's some armed guy outside. If not, some goon in Flick's room, just waiting for the kill command when I do something stupid.

No, all I can do is sit in my prison and wait.

Keep watching that TV, just in case it shows me anything of the people next door.

The people I'd give anything to free.

But as we've just discussed, I don't have much of anything for anyone.

***

A clock on a wall of a place like this is a good thing, and a very bad thing. Not too much can be both of those at the same time.

It's good for the brain to see how much time's going by. It preserves your sanity, somehow. You know when someone leaves and comes back, it's fifteen or twenty minutes. When someone says they'll be back in five minutes, you can time it.

Trouble is, you can count the minutes, the hours and eventually the days you're stuck here. The clock lets you know about every second that ticks by. Every one that's gone is a chance wasted. There are opportunities out there in the world somewhere. Not in here. Each slight movement tells you that your life's ebbing away. Little by little. Your heart's beating, but for how long?

It's almost exactly seventeen and a half minutes before he's back again. Timed precisely by that damn clock.

"They've given me very specific things to say," he says, before he sniffs again. Looks down at a slip of paper. "We are not negotiating. We state how things are, and the consequences when people step out of line. If you want your family to be freed, your best chance is to do exactly what we ask."

He looks up at me. Sniffs again.

I look him right in the eyes. "What have they got on you?"

He frowns. Looks away. "What do you mean?"

"VIRTUS. They have a certain way of recruiting. How did they get you onboard?"

He looks around, but not at me. Shakes his head. "I don't think that's relevant. I don't think I should tell you."

"Well, which is it? Is your story not relevant or top secret?"

He finally looks back at me. "Both, I guess."

"You don't seem too sure."

He looks at his feet. Nods. "I am sure. Very sure."

"Sure enough that they'll keep a promise they've made to you if you keep working for them?"

He leans in closer. "These people are not to be messed with.

You need to do what they say."

I smile. Turn and walk toward the balcony doors I can't open. "I've got this far without listening to them."

He nods. Sniffs. Sad look on his face. "So have your family."

He turns around. Goes to leave. "They also said to watch the TV for another lesson."

He's out the door.

He's left a slip of paper and a pen next to the TV.

The television springs into life again. Same kinda fuzzy picture. Same room. Same hostages. Same places as before. Toby on the bed, Flick in the chair.

There's another click from the speaker. "There are many ways to inflict pain. Often with injuries that heal with no visible scarring whatsoever. You are about to witness one. It involves the pushing of needles into the sensitive part of the finger. Just below the fingernails. I'm sure you'll be able to tell from the sound next door whether this is effective. Maybe you'll reconsider trying to undermine us with ideas of negotiation."

A large man enters the frame on the TV. Walks towards Flick. Crouches down in front of her. Picks up something and messes with her hands.

Another scream I can only hear through the walls. It's like they're getting louder. Easier to hear.

The speaker crackles again. "Shall we say we're finished with negotiations, Mr Flint? Failing that, should we move on to methods that leave very definite wounds?"

I turn from the TV. Rub my eyes. Let out a sigh. "I'll do whatever you want. I'll leave you to decide what happens then."

"Very good," comes the voice over the speaker. "Someone will be in the room with you shortly for the next step."

I've gotta hope that next step doesn't involve bringing any tools with them. Even so, I'd rather they use them on me than on the people next door.

42. THE CAMERA LOVES ME. NOT SURE ABOUT THE EDITOR

I'm sitting on the edge of the bed when he walks into the room again, the sniffer.

If I meet the head honchos, I'm gonna suggest they find a lacky without such an annoying set of airways.

He's holding a couple of cameras on small adjustable tripods. He sets them up on the table. One pointing at the chair, the other at a space in front of it.

He goes again. Comes back with another chair. Puts it down facing the other one, in range of that second camera.

He sits in the chair he just brought in. Points at the fixed-down one opposite. "Take a seat, Mr Flint," he says. Another damn sniff.

A request, but also a command. I get up. Sit down in that seat. My only motivation is to not hear another scream from Flick through that wall.

Gotta say, I'd do anything for my family. Right now, that's a problem. I've got no option but to submit to these people. They've got the leverage. I've got nothing. Flick has her work. What do I bring to the table? Danger and difficulties. If I've got to give up my freedom to save them, I'd do it lickety-split. They're gonna live a longer, happier life without me.

I shuffle around a little. It ain't gonna make the seat any more comfortable. Even so, seems like I'm gonna be in it a while.

"This is disgraced police detective Enoch Flint," he says. Tries to put on a voice like he's some television news reporter.

"I'm here on behalf of my employer to ask a few questions and see if you can set the record straight."

He's without doubt flipped a switch in his head. He's flapping his gums like he's a twin of the last guy and he's been hiding in an attic somewhere.

"First of all, what can you tell us about DS Tobias Hutchins?"

I shrug. "A friend. A trainer in my early days in blue. A good investigator. A damn fine police officer and human being."

"How did you feel when you heard that he had died?" he asks. There's a look on his face like he's really interested in the answer. It's got a fake, someone's-at-the-door-asking-for-donations vibe. Still, it's more convincing than some.

"It was a shock, obviously. I hadn't seen him for years. Didn't know what he was working on. I guess I wonder how I could've helped him."

"You think your help might've stopped him from being killed? What do you remember about the way he died?"

"He got too close to something. Didn't tell me. Next I heard, he'd been cut up into pieces and put into holidaymaker's luggage. Terrible, the way he went, and such a horrible experience for all those who had their travel plans ruined. I'm sure you'd think he deserved what he got. I found out while investigating. There was a fear that anyone could be next."

He glances at the camera pointing at him. Still recording. He nods.

"What can you tell me about DC Jasper Sommer? Did you get on?"

I shake my head. "Not at first. Not for a while, really. I

didn't like the guy for the longest time. He was just so different to me. I started to wonder how he became a detective."

He nods. Lets me carry on.

"Then something changed. I warmed to him a little. We worked together pretty well. I trusted him, and then I found out he was on the take. It hurt me. Hurt my pride. Made me question my own ability to understand people."

"So you regret getting him killed?"

I shake my head. "No, I didn't get him killed. He put us in a difficult spot. None of us were getting out alive. At the last moment, he dove in front of me. Took the bullet meant for me. I just watched him bleed out in front of me. I spent a while wondering if I killed him. If I was the one that somehow twisted the situation so that another person around me ended up dead, and I came out okay."

"So when Mia Miriam Belcher also went the way of the other two, you must've felt responsible? You must've wondered if everyone around you was going to die?"

I nod. "I feel like everyone around me is cursed. Doomed to die. Certain to get in the way when death comes looking for me. I feel a little like I'm killing people, one by one, and that's all that's keeping me alive. I have to keep telling myself that they didn't die because of me. Some gave their lives so I could survive. Doesn't seem like a fair trade to me. Every day, I'd happily give up my own life to get them back."

He nods. That fake sympathetic look again. "How did she die?"

"She stole a hell of a lot of stuff. Threatened to shoot me and others. I had to chase her down and stop her. During the chase, they crashed. She had gone against my trust and paid the price.

But she did it to herself. It ain't like I smashed her head on something."

"You didn't want the glory of solving the Heathrow Heist by yourself?"

I laugh. "What glory? I didn't want recognition. I didn't want people to call me any kind of a hero. Not my kinda thing at all. I live to keep people safe. That's all I've ever wanted."

He nods. Fake solemnity now. "Now, you went from there straight to the Orkney Islands?"

I shake my head. "I was given some time off. In truth, I was ready to pack the whole police thing in. But the same cases found me, whether I was getting paid or not. I was hired to find a woman up there."

"Yet you stayed when she'd been found dead?"

I nod. "I was determined to find her killer. Didn't matter that her brother didn't want me there. Turned out there was a serial killer, and I had to help the police find them."

"You stayed several nights with a prostitute, and investigated during the day? Seems like a good enough deal for hanging around?"

I shake my head. "It wasn't like that. She offered me her sofa to sleep on. I had promised to help her and some others to be free. I couldn't do that by leaving."

"You ended up chasing Graham Craigie, a local Elder in the Church of Scotland. All the way up a tower. Then he mysteriously fell off?"

"I know how this all looks. Death follows me everywhere. I find trouble wherever I end up. But Graham Craigie was the killer, without a doubt."

"But he can't be questioned, can he?"

I shake my head. "He slipped and fell from that tower. You can try to say I killed him. I wanted him dead, I won't lie. But he slipped. He wasn't pushed over the edge."

"You saved the Mayor, but another officer died, didn't he?"

I nod again. "DC Stephen Sutherland. I couldn't have saved him, but it feels like I killed him, just like I killed the others." I shake my head. "I mean, their deaths are because of me. Not directly. I've not taken anyone's life. But all those people would be alive if I wasn't around."

"One last thing," he says. "Eve Flint. Did you abuse her? Did you kill her?"

I shake my head. "There was a time I loved that woman. When she loved me too. Sadly, things changed. No one can say I resented her. That I wanted her out of the way. I've been accused of hurting her before, but the truth came out. She nearly died because of me. She got shot when Jasper died. I ended up saving her and getting her to hospital."

"And you had an affair with another woman?"

I nod. "I'm not proud of it. Ended up with a child. I had to let go of a doomed marriage and give this new family a chance. I don't know where Evie went. She's not in some hole in the ground. She's moved on from me. I don't blame her. That might've saved her life. But that's not because of any abuse. I did not ever get angry at her. Never hurt her in any way. Not physically. I have never stopped her leaving he house or meeting friends. The woman who claimed to be her friend, I've never heard of her. I ain't free of guilt. I ain't some knight in shining armour. The more time I spend on this rock we call home, the more I feel people around me are gonna get hurt or die. Seems like a curse I carry round with me. I'm not happier with these people gone. If anything, the more people that die around me, the more miserable my life becomes."

"Any word on the homeless man who died?"

"Leo Ryan was not killed by me. I had seen him the day before. It's true, he broke into my home. I was angry. Who wouldn't be? But I had no desire for him to die. I found my way free from police custody, but I turned myself in when demands were made, to protect others. Please don't think all police officers are like me. They are generally a good bunch of people. They are human beings. They make mistakes. They also pay for those mistakes, just like I do, every day."

He thanks me for my candour. Ends the interview. Packs away the cameras. It ain't long before he, the equipment and the chair are all gone.

I'm left alone in the room.

Gotta wonder what they're gonna do with the video of that interview.

One thing's for sure, I can't see it working out in my favour.

***

"Mr Flint, I've allowed you to watch the television in your room."

It's the distorted voice over the speaker again.

I get up. Take a couple of steps. Turn the thing on.

Some exclusive about Enoch Flint, escaped murderer. Picked up by one of the TV networks. Maybe all of them.

Makes me wince.

I'm gonna pull some facial expressions as I watch. Some will be a hell of a lot worse.

It's gonna be a long few minutes.

***

The staff of MI5 and SITU watch on, helpless as every TV shows the same interview.

Someone's conducting a sit-down interview. A blurred-out face and a distorted voice. He's sitting across from Enoch Flint.

"This is disgraced police detective Enoch Flint," it starts. "I'm here on behalf of my employer to ask a few questions and see if you can set the record straight."

He jumps right into the questions

"First of all, what can you tell us about DS Tobias Hutchins?"

Flint shrugs. "A trainer in my early days in blue."

"How did you feel when you heard that he had died?" he asks.

"I hadn't seen him for years. Didn't know what he was working on. I wondered how I could kill him."

Folks are glancing at each other. Did he really just say that?

"What do you remember about the way he died?"

"He got too close to something. I cut him up into pieces and put him into holidaymaker's luggage. I think he deserved what he got. Anyone could be next."

DC Chamberlain's looking on horrified. Someone's been messing with his words. Some creative editing. But it looks so genuine.

"What can you tell me about DC Jasper Sommer? Did you

get on?"

A shake of the head. "No. I didn't like the guy. He was just so different to me. I started to wonder how he became a detective."

A nod, and then Flint carries on.

"We worked together pretty well. I found out he was on the take. It hurt me. Hurt my pride."

"So you regret getting him killed?"

Flint shakes his head. "No. He put us in a difficult spot. I just watched him bleed out in front of me. I killed him. I twisted the situation so that another person around me ended up dead, and I came out okay."

"So when Mia Miriam Belcher also went the way of the other two, you were responsible? Everyone around you was going to die?"

Flint nods. "Everyone around me is cursed. Doomed to die. I'm killing people, one by one, and that's all that's keeping me alive. They die because of me."

He nods. "How did she die?"

"She stole a hell of a lot of stuff. Threatened to shoot me and others. I had to chase her down and stop her. She paid the price. I smashed her head on something."

"You wanted the glory of solving the Heathrow Heist by yourself?"

Flint smiles. "I want recognition. I want people to call me a hero. That's all I've ever wanted."

He nods. "Now, you went from there straight to the Orkney Islands?"

Flint nods. "I was hired to find a woman up there."

"Yet you stayed when she'd been found dead?"

Flint nods. "I was her killer. Her brother didn't want me there. Turned out there was a serial killer, and I had to help the police find them."

"You stayed several nights with a prostitute, and investigated during the day? Seems like a good enough deal for hanging around?"

Another shake of the head. "I liked that. I had promised to help her and some others to be free. I couldn't do that."

"You ended up chasing Graham Craigie, a local Elder in the Church of Scotland. All the way up a tower. He mysteriously fell off?"

"Death follows me everywhere. I was the killer, without a doubt."

"He can't be questioned, can he?"

Flint shakes his head. "I killed him. I wanted him dead, I won't lie. He was pushed over the edge."

"You saved the Mayor, but another officer died, didn't he?"

Flint nods again. "DC Stephen Sutherland. I killed him, just like I killed the others." He shakes his head. "All those people would be alive if I wasn't around."

"One last thing," he says. "Eve Flint. Did you abuse her? Did you kill her?"

Flint nods. "There was a time I loved that woman. Sadly, things changed. I resented her. I wanted her out of the way. I've hurt her before. The truth came out. She nearly died because of me. I ended up getting her to hospital."

"And you had an affair with another woman?"

I nod. "I'm proud of it. Ended up with a child. Evie's in some hole in the ground. Because of my abuse. I'd get angry at her. Hurt her. Physically. I have stopped her leaving the house. Meeting friends. The woman who claimed to be her friend, I've heard of her."

It cuts to the blurred-out man nodding.

"I ain't some knight in shining armour. The more time I spend on this rock we call home, the more people are gonna die. A curse I carry round with me. I'm happier with these people gone. More people will die around me."

"Any word on the homeless man who died?"

"Leo Ryan was killed by me. I had seen him the day before. It's true, he broke into my home. I was angry. Who wouldn't be? I had a desire for him to die. I found my way. All police officers are like me. They make mistakes, just like I do."

The interview ends all-of-a-sudden.

No one in the room can do anything but stare at each other dumbfounded.

What had they forced Flint into doing?

Was any of this even slightly genuine?

In this world of deepfakes, who knew anymore?

What did it matter?

A whole heap of viewers are already walking out their doors. They were on the edge of adding to the swelling numbers of protestors and rioters. They're all gonna join in now.

"I think the police as we know it is finished," agent Hall says. "We need to prepare for martial law, and most likely, constant chaos."

43. LOCATION, LOCATION, VOCATION

Agent Hall's coming alive. Now that he's had a moment to collect his thoughts. Now that he's starting to realise he can maybe stop the sky from falling in.

He points to a row of desks. Or to the folks sitting at them. "You lot, get on the blower to the news outlets. Get their original contact from VIRTUS, sending them the video. Get the closest to the original as you can get. If they bang on about protecting their sources, tell them this is about national security."

Points at the next row. "You can focus on finding ways to discredit this video. Look into the raw data. Analysis of micro-expressions, anything."

Points at another row. "You people. Release any information we've got to the media. Anything that proves Enoch Flint innocent of any of those deaths."

He raises his voice. "The rest of you, we're doing anything we can to find VIRTUS. Start with Valiance Solutions. Any employees we can find. Any data at all from those computers."

He stands on a nearby desk after a moment of struggle. "Everyone, it's vital we find VIRTUS and Flint now, more than ever. For the sake of this country, we cannot fail. Nobody leaves until we find our man."

***

Seems the folks in charge think I've spent enough time watching the world fall apart. News broadcasts paint a dim picture.

The string of lies and absurdities from the edit make my

blood boil. They've already been played like they're factual a few times.

They've switched back to the terrible quality video of the next room.

I get up. Walk to the part of the wall where I heard Flick scream.

I beat my fists against it. Make as much of a racket as I can. "Flick! Toby! Can you hear me?"

I back off. Look at the television. No response at all. Not even a turn of the head.

I look around for something to jab into the walls. Everything big's bolted down.

But there's a small drawer in the desk. Does it come out completely?

I yank the thing hard. It stays put. I jiggle it around. Shove it. Move it in every possible direction while it's pulled out as far as it'll go.

The drawer comes away from the unit.

It's solid wood construction. Looks like a reasonable carpenter put some effort in. The thing's solid. No flex. No bend.

I charge at the wall. Swing the drawer until it collides with it. A sharper thud.

Back to the TV. Still nothing.

I swing the thing at the wall again. I'm gonna leave a sizeable dent pretty soon.

Another loud noise. Another sound that someone the other side of that wall couldn't ignore. Yet a complete lack of reaction.

My stupid, tired brain throws up a suggestion. Maybe it's sound-proofed.

I shake my head. Okay, but what about the fact that I could hear Flick? Does sound-proofing work one way and not the other? Pretty sure it doesn't.

I drop the drawer. Stand back in full view of the cameras.

"Hey!" I shout and wave my arms. "Why are you doing this? When are you gonna let the others go?"

I bang on the wall underneath the speaker again.

Nothing.

Not even an acknowledgement of my questions.

I pick up that small drawer again. I smash it into the wall again and again. Once more. The thing cracks. One final time and it breaks into close to a dozen pieces of splintered wood.

I turn over my left hand. There's a small shard of wood sticking in it. I pull the huge splinter free. I let out a little yelp. What's with the brain only noticing pain when you've seen it with your own eyes? Gotta wonder what would happen if you'd never seen it.

I head to the bathroom to wash he wound. See what I can do to treat it. The cut's a little deep, but not too wide. I flex my fingers. Everything moves, even if it hurts a little more than before.

I get a small hand-towel. Soak it in the sink with cold water and wrap it around my hand.

I head back. Sit on the bed. Flick and Toby are still sitting there. No idea I'm even here, apparently.

I get up close to the TV screen. The picture's pixelated. The grain looks artificial. Like someone's taken a decent quality feed and messed around with it. With today's tech, it's quite likely you can add a bunch of visual filters to a live video stream. I've never tried it.

But why make the quality worse? They trying to add to the drama of this whole thing somehow?

There's gotta be some method behind the madness of the way VIRTUS are operating.

I'm gonna keep hitting things. Shouting. Making a nuisance of myself. Sooner or later, someone's gonna get fed up. They're gonna want me to be church-mouse-quiet.

They can want it. Doesn't mean they're gonna get it.

They wanted answers. They got them. They messed around with them and used them against me.

Time to see what I can do in return.

I stare at the TV. Unchanged. I stare at the speaker and the cameras on the wall.

Still nothing but silence.

Come on, VIRTUS. Your move.

***

"Now we're getting somewhere!" Demi Wheeler declares.

She's been following the video tech guys around.

One of their geeks is pointing at his screen. He's talking to anyone who'll listen about the frequency of key frames in a video file. How the ones in this file are all over the place. Not consistent. That alone suggests a myriad of cuts and edits. Then there are the changes in micro-expressions on Flint's face halfway through sentences. Add that together, you're at least halfway to discrediting the video.

"Good work," Demi says. "We'll get the word out to the news companies. The video's been altered and cannot be relied upon."

The geek scoffs. "I'm sure they'll listen to any government source right now. Of course a Home Office funded person's gonna say this."

She pauses. Thinks. "I need to find an independent expert to discredit this. I'll be back."

She's off like a scared cat from an out-take of that stupid commercial.

Agent Hall's walking around nearby. He's hassling all kindsa folks to see what they've come up with.

"I've been analysing the reflections. Any details in the background of the video," says another geek. Shakes his head. "Not got a solid lead on a location from that."

Agent Hall stands up a little straighter. "Anyone got any good news for me?"

The forensics guys in the corner give him a wave. He hurries over.

"We've got details of some of the employees of Valiance Solutions."

Agent Hall almost smiles. Almost. "Get me a list and any details you can. We'll see how far we can take this. One of those people might lead us to Flint."

A bit of digging around. A few moments to assemble a team of people. They might have some possible locations for VIRTUS inside a couple of hours.

44. ANYONE GOT A SMOKESCREEN?

Takes a certain kinda situation for a sane, grown man to shout at a wall.

At least, that's when they've still got most of their marbles.

I've been stuck in this room a little too long. If that ain't cause to get a little crazy, then shoot me.

I ain't far off the point where I'd do anything to get outta here.

But I'm shouting stuff in full view of the cameras. Whatever mics they've got are hearing me loud and clear.

"You think I haven't figured out what's going on?"

"The poor quality video of the room next door. You think that's fooling me?"

Silence.

"I bang on the wall..." I thump it a few times. "Nothing! You think you've got me fooled?"

Still nothing.

"Did you forget that I've figured out how you've worked before? Surely I can do it again."

Still nothing. Not even a crackle.

"You don't wanna know what I really know? You don't think I know about Valiance Solutions?"

Surely that's gonna get their attention.

I point to the window. "Plus, there's an army of people out there, figuring out that app. How it works. Where it sends its data. They're gonna be getting close to finding you."

Still no reply.

"Are you gonna admit to the link with Valiance Solutions, or should I take a wild guess?"

Nothing.

I nod. "Okay, let's try this on for size. Valiance and VIRTUS both start with the same letter. Not a coincidence. Is the guy I've seen the V in VIRTUS?"

Still no answer.

"By the way, if you've got more than one person on the books, now would be a good time to let me know. I've only seen the same snivelling guy at every single place and time I've interacted with VIRTUS. Are you the sole employee in this country?"

Still nothing.

"Or is the deceit even more ridiculous? You're gonna look more powerful, more menacing when you're an organisation. You talk about being a lone wolf, you lose a little credibility. I know a few of the tricks. They're not hard to figure out. Fake accounts. Virtual Private Networks. Getting an Artificial Intelligence chatbot's not hard these days. You can get all that just from following the news."

Surely someone's gonna chime in. Tell him to shut up any time.

But no. Still a wall of silence and apathy.

"Using apps that bounce your location around. Server hopping. spoofing some other address. I bet you've raised your money with ransomware and hacking. Built up some funds. Pretending to be a whole consortium with deep pockets. Most of what you've done so far has been on the cheap. Admit it."

A crackle. Finally, some sign someone's listening to my spitballing.

"Mr Flint, whatever you think you know, you couldn't be further from the truth."

I shake my head. "Oh, I don't think that's true at all. If I was so far off base, why would you decide to speak up? Why would you need to tell me I'm wrong?"

I point at the speaker. "No, I'm on to something. You don't like it. Might be onto a whole bunch of things."

They've gone quiet again.

"Like that weak video footage. So grainy and fuzzy. Could be anyone in that footage, couldn't it? Funny how they don't respond at all when I bang on the wall. Yet I can hear their screams."

They've gone quiet. Maybe he's coming to shut me up.

"What if I said it ain't even them in the footage? Wouldn't be too hard to hire a couple of actors. Record a few scenes. Play them back when I'm not being your little sheepdog. Throw in some screams from an audio library. Am I close?"

Quiet as a mute church mouse.

"I'm not gonna sit here quietly anymore. I'm gonna raise hell, because you can't prove to me you have Flick and Toby. You haven't convinced me they're next door! You're nothing but smoke and mirrors. Dust in the sunshine. Moonlight in someone's palm. You're a whole lot of layers of deceit, covering a big, wide open space of nothing at all!"

No sign of the guy owning up to anything.

"How about you come in here? Convince me that you're not the only one here, other than me? You come in here. Talk to me. I'll get this magic voice in the wall to answer my questions. Then I might go somewhere closer to believing."

Something's moving outside the door. Could be someone coming. Could be nothing.

"I've gotta know why you're doing this. What's your endgame? There's got to be one. Have you made some bad investments? You needed to do something to turn things round? You been stockpiling weapons and ammunition, but no one's fighting? You got a finger in some pies about arms trading? The police discredited, the military need more kit to keep the peace. You got shares in the companies making it? You've done your best to convince people that you're this powerful group. This mighty collection of like-minded people. What if it's all just some greedy man's attempt at screwing the world to make a buck?"

I'm doing what I can do to rile the guy up. Get him storming in through the door.

But that's not how a guy like that responds. He's not gonna come and challenge me to a fist fight. He'll have other ways of working. Some other buttons to push to keep me quiet.

I look around the room.

There's a new sound. Not one I've heard since I've been here.

The wimp's pressed one of those buttons.

45. GIMME A CHANCE TO VENT

They got the details of those employees. Wasn't hard.

Trawls of social media turn up a hell of a lot these days. Passports, driving licenses, details of recent utility bills. It ain't tricky to track someone down when you know where to look.

Now, they're looking for a link between any of those folks and the criminal enterprise. Any small crossover could be enough to justify heavy-handed tactics.

Most of the people look squeaky clean. Not so much as a parking ticket. They work good jobs. Have families. Do the stuff normal people do.

That doesn't mean someone's living clean. Even mob bosses have families. Not just the metaphorical, gun-toting guys they call family. Tax cheaters can have a mortgage and a dog. Drug dealers can look a lot like a typical nine-to-fiver with a little discretion. Often, the only way to find the bad eggs is to suspect the whole box of being a little off.

Still, they got a few pairs of people. They're heading out in different directions to speak to these former employees. They're under strict instructions. Anything that feels a little wrong, call it in.

The last name on the not-so-long list is Lewis Preston. Looks young now, with a thick shag-carpet-like mop of hair hanging onto every part of that scalp. Facial features look like they were bought in bulk and stuck on in a hurry. A vague shadow of a moustache he's never let grow. It's threatened to make an appearance any time since puberty hit. Looks a little like a self-conscious, hairy mushroom cloud.

Lewis must've been young when they started out. Maybe he went to work for them instead of heading to university. Maybe he walked in the door straight after he got some computer science degree. Either way, he wouldn't have looked any older than sixteen back then. Barely looks twenty now.

It ain't long before the report comes back from the agents assigned to his digs. No answer. No signs of anyone there.

"Any easy way inside?" Agent Hall asks.

"Not that we've found," comes the reply over the speaker phone.

"Hang around a little while," he says. "Let's see what the others turn up."

One by one, the others call in. Nothing unusual. Nothing to set the Spidey-sense tingling.

Just this one guy, alone, and no signs of life.

"Got it!" Demi runs over with a piece of paper in-hand.

Agent Hall snatches it from her. "Got what, exactly?"

"They've found where the encrypted data's being sent. We got an IP address and we-"

"I don't care about the technical details," Agent Hall says, cutting her off. "Tell me what I'm looking at."

She smiles. Her eyes widen. "They've double-checked the results. Data's being sent to a fixed line internet connection in the home of..."

She peers over Agent Hall's shoulder to read the name. She's forgotten it already. "Lewis Preston."

He nods. "Same address."

He calls the agents back. "You've got just cause for getting into that home. Any means necessary. It's a matter of national security."

He likes wielding that phrase like he's flashing around a Samurai sword. How many times a day does he say it?

Anyway, the agents head back to the property. They've got a damn good reason for breaking the door in.

Time to see what's on the other side.

**

I can picture the sniffing guy now. He's sitting at some massive control panel. Dials, buttons and flashing lights all over the place. He's trying to figure out whether to send in the hounds. Maybe open the floor underneath me so I can fall to my death. Some other, maniacal deadly trap from which I'd need to escape.

But this is my life. It ain't a Bond movie from the seventies. He's not sat there, bald head, stroking a cat in his lap. Not waiting in a swivel chair for me to break free, so he can say he's expecting me.

There's a noticeable hiss. It's coming from the air vents. Some vaporised chemical's being pumped in. Again, not like the movies. No smoke filling the air. Just an invisible toxic gas that's making me feel like my head's about to detach and float off into the sky.

A frantic look around the room. I've got nothing to shove in front of the vents.

Nothing except the towel wrapped around my hand.

I press myself closer to the wall. The cameras won't see all of me.

I force out a few coughs.

"What are you doing?" I say in a deliberately weakened voice.

I press the wet towel to my mouth. Okay, it ain't exactly a gas mask, but it's gonna help me breathe a little longer.

My head's swimming, but at least it's doing the breaststroke back to me.

I lift the towel long enough to let out a couple more loud coughs.

I've got an idea forming. A way of getting outta this room. Chances are it's not gonna work, but it's worth a shot.

I grab the pen that was left on the edge of the desk. A couple of splinters from the shattered wooden drawer. I stick them in my waist band. Uncomfortable, but they're not hurting me.

Some clunky noises coming from the vents now. A louder hiss. Something that looks a lot more like smoke's starting to fill the room. What do ya know? Maybe the movies had it right after all.

I cough for the camera again. Disappear to the bathroom. The air's cleaner there. I get the other hand towel. I soak it the same. Put them in front of my face, making a few layers.

Harder to breath, but the air that makes it through is more breathable.

"STOP!" I shout out in a croaky voice. "I can't breathe!"

I walk just into view of the camera.

I hit the deck hard for effect.

He's trying to knock me out. He's gonna move me, or torture me, or chuck me off the balcony.

I'm gonna play dead until he thinks he's winning.

If things go to plan, if Flick and Toby are really next door, I could be outta here, with them, in no more than five minutes.

But my plans don't ever go the way I hope. Not so far, anyway.

46. GOTTA KNOW WHEN TO PLAY DEAD

There are a couple of screams coming through the wall again.

Not much difference between the two, if any.

Something fake in those, now that I think about it.

Some vain attempt to get a rise outta me. Make sure I'm out like a light.

Laying on the floor ain't a bad move. Most of the smoke and fumes are rising with the warmth in the room. It ain't one hundred percent clear, but twenty's better than zero.

The hissing's stopped. Whatever was being pumped in has taken the rest of the day off.

Pretty sure I'm not getting picked up by the camera. Even so, I'm keeping myself still in case they've got some other way to keep eyes on me.

The wet towels are working pretty damn well to keep me breathing. Again, it ain't perfect. Still feeling like my head's just done a spin cycle in a washing machine. Like my arms and legs have been stretched out like elastic man's limbs. Like they've only just snapped back into position. Maybe you need to breathe in a lot of this stuff for it to do you any damage.

But I'm awake. I'm aware of what's going on around me.

I've got a way of taking my captor down.

I'm lying with my legs towards the door. Head towards the window. But my head's tucked in a little. I can look straight across and see the door.

A little sliver of light's creeping underneath the bottom.

As I'm watching, it gets a little wider.

Wider still. The door's almost fully open.

Footsteps. Gotta be heavy shoes to be heard on this carpet.

He walks over. Stops by my side.

He nudges me with a boot.

I lie there and take it.

He nudges me a little harder. "Mr Flint?" he says before he sniffs again.

I heard about this fish on the sea floor that lies still. Even lets enemies take little nibbles at it before it strikes. That's me. Right here. Right now.

He sticks the boot in harder. A kick to the ribs. Not hard enough to break anything, but hard enough to knock the wind outta someone. The mechanics of the body suggest you'd let out a breath whether conscious or not. But if you're conscious, you feel the pain and it comes out as a groan.

Gotta keep silent.

He crouches down. Stares at me for a moment. He's got some kinda mask on.

Got my eyes mostly closed. Squinting just enough to see shapes. In the gloomy setting, it's gotta be enough to fool him.

He leans over. Gives me a shake.

I let everything hang loose. My right arm flops backwards.

He lets out a satisfied grunt.

Now's my chance.

I get the tension back in my right arm and swing it for all I'm worth.

My hand's a fist by the time it collides with some part of him.

I'm spinning on my hip.

I swing out my legs and take the guy down with a sweeper kick.

Now I'm crouching over him.

I get a couple more fists in. Midsection and face. He gets over the shock and starts making some attempt to block.

It's a fool's errand. Too much of him's exposed for him to cover much with his arms.

He's a computer-type. The sort to use tech to get ahead. He ain't the super-muscly kind. There's a pretty good chance he's never had a real fight his entire life. But this ain't one he can talk or sniff his way out of.

I stand up. Get a few kicks in. Knock him down until he's nearly where I was laying.

I rip off his mask. Put it on myself. Let's see how he likes the fumes that haven't cleared yet.

I reach into my waist band. Pick out the plastic disposable pen. Snap it in half. Got a couple of nice sharp shards of plastic now.

He's getting up again. Trying to come for me.

I jab him in the leg with one of the pieces of plastic.

I get him in his side with another.

He sinks down.

The injuries and the fumes are getting too much for him.

I ain't gonna run the risk of him coming back at me. I pick

him up. Drag him over towards the table. I let his head hit the chair on the way over. I lift him a little higher than the table and I let gravity smack his head into it a couple of times.

He drops to one knee. Blood pouring from his nose and a cut on his cheek. He's trying to see me through both eyes, but he's only gonna manage one. The left's swollen up like I've jabbed a bicycle pump in there and just kept on pushing on it.

He's swinging his arms out like a wild drunkard.

I take a step back. A step towards the open door. He can't reach me.

He lunges for me. Falls to the floor.

He's groaning. Trying to get up again. Not quite out yet.

I lay the boot in once. Hit his head. Hard and heavy. See how he likes it.

He collapses. He'll get up some time, but not for a while. Maybe not without a lotta help.

I hurry over. Pad his pockets.

There's a set of keys. A phone. I take them. Pick up as much of the broken wood as I can see. Head for the door.

A quiet groan's all I hear as I near the other side of the room. He's awake again. Wasn't out for long. All he's doing with his consciousness is complaining. I ain't hanging around to hear it.

I'm heading out the door and locking him inside.

Let's see how he likes that too.

Maybe he's got some way out. Could've built some escape route in that I hadn't found.

Could be that I'm about to hit an army of VIRTUS

employees I didn't know existed.

But this is a chance to get out. Turn the tide.

I ain't gonna waste it by hanging around and seeing who comes after me.

***

You wanna find someone? You wanna know what they've been doing?

There's one key rule in doing both. Follow the money.

Money talks. It really does. Tells us all kindsa things.

The folks who commit your everyday crimes have still gotta have somewhere to sleep. Food to eat. Gotta have a source of income. You find it, it tells you about them. Any state benefits? They looking for work? Working for some cash-in-hand type?

You get up to the ones like our friend. The guy who may or may not be all of VIRTUS. You know they've got money somewhere.

Lewis Preston's got a standard current account. Someone at MI5 has been studying it like he's cramming for a test. A salary coming in. That's interesting. From Valiance Solutions. How can he be getting paid from a company that went bust decades ago?

Follow that trail. See how far it takes you.

Some other weird stuff going on.

More incomings than outgoings.

Every few weeks, a refund is applied in the region of five hundred. No purchases, just refunds.

They're gonna be easy to figure out.

She gets in touch with each retailer.

Sure enough, at each, a computer's been bought with cash. Been refunded direct to his account. The big stores only refund using the original payment method. He's using small-time places who don't live and die by such rules.

He's played it safe with all but one. Used some other payment card. A credit card.

It doesn't take long to get the details. Soon afterwards, the balance sheet. One purchase. Paid off in full. Not from his current account.

Some unusual foreign bank. It's gonna take some time to persuade them to let go of customer details and transactions.

But things are moving. Little by little, they're finding the mistakes. The ones that are gonna bury him.

Those little errors just might lead them to Enoch Flint.

With any luck, Lewis Preston's gonna pay dearly for the things he's done.

That's assuming Enoch Flint doesn't get to him first. Take out another key suspect before they can answer for their crimes.

47. NOTHING OUTSIDE BUT A WHOLE LOT MORE INSIDE

You spend some time stuck in one room, you're gonna start thinking about the rest of the building. Does the rest of it look similar? Are other people trapped like me?

You have this idea that outside that door's a hotel-style corridor. A row of doors. Maybe a maid's trolley somewhere.

But stepping outside that room's like stepping into another dimension.

Yeah, there's a hallway out here. Grey concrete floor. Walls made up of a whole lotta semi-permanent panels. Not a hotel-style elegance. Even a hotel from forty, fifty years ago.

The corridor goes on forever in both directions. Doors off to the left and right. Maybe thirty of them in total.

I head to the room next to mine. The door's a plain, hollow internal wooden door from decades ago. No lock. No signs it's got anything inside but a mop, a bucket and some cleaning supplies.

I turn the handle and swing the thing open.

It ain't a room like mine. Same size. A window at the end looking out. This one's got a tiled floor. An armchair. A sofa. Pictures hung on the walls. A sideboard with flowers in a vase, on top of a lace covering. The place is dolled up like a grandma's lounge.

What's it doing here, wherever *here* is?

I didn't see it at first. Behind the sofa's a massive, free-standing speaker. It's almost pressing, speaker-end against the wall. Some cable's running from the side. It disappears through a hole in the floor. I guess that explains the source of the screams.

Then it hits me.

I ain't saving Flick and Toby. They're not even here. They never were.

There was something strange about the whole setup. Somewhere inside me, I'd allowed myself to hope. Get ready for the possibility that I'd not be leaving this strange place on my own.

I get out of that room. I need to carry on. Check everywhere. Make sure I'm the only one here.

I hit the next room. It's maybe five times the size. A load of desks and chairs. cartoon-like pictures stuck to boards around the walls. A blackboard at one end. A vinyl floor with a white and black tiled effect. A school classroom.

This place is getting stranger by the minute.

Next, a dining room to match the style of the old lady's bungalow living room. Dark wooden table. Fancy, hand-carved chairs made from the same dark wood. A fruit bowl in the middle. A large family portrait on the wall. Covers part of the tasteful, flowering patterned wallpaper.

I was hoping that the farther I got, the more this place would make sense. No such luck.

I was drugged when I got here. Means all I know's what my brain told me. Turns out, my brain made up a whole bunch of lies, just to try and make sense of it all.

Nothing about this place is what it seems. None of it.

But I ain't got time to explore each room. Most have closed

doors and lights turned off.

I poke my head into rooms that could be all kindsa things. Kids' playrooms. A gymnasium. A weight-lifting room. A changing room. Another lounge. A nondescript office.

All empty. All have got the same amount of weird to them.

Room by room, I'm calling out for Flick and Toby. Door by door, I'm disappointed.

Still, at least I haven't been shot by an army of henchmen hiding in a break room somewhere.

I find a staircase. White-washed walls. Blue railings.

I head down a floor. Another corridor. Many more doors. I open them one by one.

Dressing rooms. Chairs. Mirrors with lights around them. Some have minibars.

Starts to dawn on me what kinda place this is.

Maybe it just took this long for my head to clear.

Could be one of the side-effects of that gas is that, if you survive, you're pretty stupid for a while.

I pull the guy's phone from my pocket. Turn it on. The thing's locked, but I can make an emergency call. Should be all that I need to do.

This is gonna confuse the hell outta someone in a control room.

Let's see how long it takes for them to get my call to the right place.

Maybe someone, somewhere can tell me where I am.

As things stand, I've not got a clue.

***

A call comes through. They've all got better things to do than to stop to speak to someone. Seems that way, anyway.

Demi picks it up.

Some woman from a control room.

"I've been trying for nearly ten minutes to find where to direct this call," she says. "It's an Enoch Flint on the line. He says he needs to speak to you."

There's a click. She's off the line. She's not wasting any more time.

"Flint?" Demi says.

There's a heavy sigh.

"I was wondering if I'd ever get through to anyone!"

"Where are you?" she asks.

"I was hoping you could tell me. Any tricks for finding my location?"

"Hold on," she says. "I'll find one of the tech guys and see what we can do."

She puts the phone on the desk and rushes around. Someone has to be free for this.

Some tall guy. He's maybe as tall as her when he's sitting down. Short black hair. Serious, long face. He looks at her.

She gives him the lowdown.

He nods. "We can help. Transfer the call to me, and in less than five minutes we should have a location."

"Five minutes?" she says.

He glares at her. "You expect it to take seconds? It doesn't work like that. We've got hoops we've got to jump through. Authorisations to get."

She nods. "Thank you. Let me know when you have something."

She's back at her desk in a few seconds.

"Flint? I'm transferring you. We should be able to find your location. Hold on."

***

I've never met the guy on the phone. Never laid eyes on him.

But I know the type.

A face that makes everything look dull and uninteresting.

But a deadpan expression too soulless for decent stand-up comedy.

"You don't' know the number?" he asks.

I can feel him glaring at me, even though he's who-knows-how-far away. The guy's got a gift.

"I already told you. I picked up this phone. It ain't mine. Not got any idea what the number is."

He lets out a laboured breath. "Never mind. I have it now from a caller ID system. What can you tell me about where you are? Anything to narrow this down before we start?"

"Seems a little crazy, but it's a disused television or movie studio. Near some kinda abandoned quarry."

He thanks me like that information's worth something. I know too well that he's rolling his eyes at me.

I'm down on the ground floor of the building now.

A giant, open plan space is laid out before me. High ceiling. A fake city backdrop with panels and plants in front of it. A cliché of the late night talk show set.

Spin around a little, you've got a green screen and a bland, wooden panelled area with a long desk. Three chairs behind it. A news studio.

Long, thick cables are strewn around the cavernous concrete space. Scratches and grooves in the concrete floor everywhere.

I'm wandering around. Still trying to find a door. Any way to get outside. Maybe there's some clue out there that'll tell me where I am.

With all that I've seen as I've searched, I've not seen another person. There's no army with this guy. Not even a single bodyguard. Just one man, keeping another one locked away. Nothing but lies and more lies from him.

But he's gonna learn what lies get him. He's stuck in that room now. Trapped in a prison of his own making.

Feel like it's some kinda metaphor for my life. Just not sure how it all lines up.

"You still there?" the guy's voice is loud in my ear.

With all the wandering, I've almost forgotten about the phone call.

"Still here. Any progress?"

"I have authorisation. Just waiting for the actual information on your whereabouts."

"I'm trying to find a way outside," I say. "See if there's something that'll tell me where I am."

He replies with an okay. That doesn't mean he's the least bit interested.

Something digs a little into my leg when I take the next step.

The keys.

I pull them from my pocket.

A car key. Of course there would be.

Gotta find the right exit. Gotta figure out where the car is.

I can get myself somewhere.

There's a door leading off to a kinda prefab section. A handful of offices look like they've been glued onto the inside of the mammoth concrete structure. Looks like a box in the wrong place.

Where there are offices, there must be a front entrance.

I head through the built-on section. A couple of offices off to the right. One bigger room off to the left. Straight ahead, a reception desk and a waiting area.

The front door ain't what I'm expecting.

You think you might find some glass door. Help out the receptionist with who's coming.

If you don't see that, you might find a revolving door, like some of those fancy hotels. Nothing like that either.

A huge steel door. Gotta be at least twice as old as I am. Bolted shut. It ain't budging when I put my shoulder to it.

No way to unlock it. No standard keyhole.

Nothing but a keypad stuck to the wall. Seems weird that they'd lock folks in.

Unless someone's changed the door a little. Added this fancy lock.

I take a closer look. There's a patch that's been filled in. Maybe welded shut. Seems some sheet of metals' been stuck over and pained to match.

The guy who made the modifications could be the same guy stuck upstairs. At the very least, he's had someone else put this on. He's gonna know the code.

Seems I ain't gonna find my way outta here without some help from the man I've locked up.

That's not all. I've got to remember who I am, and what's going on.

I'm a guy on the run.

I can't just swan outta here, get in the car and drive some place I know.

I'm also hunting for a partner and child, and I've not got a clue where I'm going.

Before I find a way out and dust outta here, I've gotta find the man's base. The place he set something up to watch me. Listen. Speak through the walls. Set up that fake scream.

I head back upstairs. Back to the room next door to my little prison.

I look at that wire again, disappearing into the floor.

If I can picture the layout of this building in my mind, I could follow that cable. It might lead me where I wanna go.

Out into the corridor.

Down the stairs.

If I'm right, it's maybe halfway down this dressing room corridor.

I check a room. Nothing. Next one. Still nothing.

Third try's a charm, so I'm told.

It ain't right now.

Turns out, I get the right place on the fifth time of trying.

A cable hanging down. It splits as it comes out of the ceiling into three. One section's plugged into some big, black box. A large computer.

A desk has a mouse, a keyboard and a good-sized screen.

The second cable's disappearing into a tiny TV screen to the left of the computer.

The third's connected to a free-standing microphone. Got a big, red button built in, front and centre. It's sitting right in front of the TV screen.

I sit down in the seat.

I've got a fairly awful picture on the TV. The guy's still lying on the floor.

There's a login screen on the computer.

"Are you still there?" a voice comes from the phone.

The agent's still on the other end. My mind's been on other things.

"I've got the details of your location. You're a fair way north of London. An abandoned regional TV studio. Consolidated with another one in London twelve years ago."

"You sending anyone to come and get me?" I ask.

"I'll have to let people know where you are. If you happen to get free before then, obviously we're not gonna be able to take you into custody."

I frown. "Are you saying what I think you're saying?"

"I'm just telling you the facts. But you've got to get out of that building first. You got a way out?"

"Not at the moment," I say.

"Can't say I'm surprised. It's an old World War II building. Thick concrete walls. Tiny, reinforced windows. Some kind of command centre. Repurposed after the war for television."

"A little more like a prison than I'd hoped," I say. "But I think I can persuade my captor to help my find a way out. He's currently sitting in the room he'd kept me in. He was kind enough to allow us to trade places."

I'm off the phone and pressing the big red button on the microphone.

"Are you awake?" I ask.

I hear a couple of curse words through the television.

I guess that's a yes.

48. NO PIN INTENDED

He's getting to his feet now. Unsteady. Blood-stained clothes.

He looks a little more helpless. Lost. Pathetic.

Like I've trapped someone who's too young to be stuck in there. He looks younger now. Not high school, but maybe university student age.

"Why don't we start with your name?" I ask.

He sits down on the edge of the bed. Turns his head. Spits something out onto the floor. Maybe some blood. "Why would I tell you anything?"

"I'm just trying to have a civilised conversation."

He shakes his head. "There's nothing civilised about this," he says. He's still sniffing.

"You can't tell me anything I'm not gonna find out through other means."

He's quiet for a moment. Maybe trying to think up a fake name. Trouble is, when you start doing that, nothing that comes to mind feels convincing enough.

"Lewis," he says. A low voice. A defeated tone.

"Thank you. Now, Lewis, I need to get out of here. How do you suggest I do that?"

He laughs. "You need *me* to get out of the building."

I lean forward a little. "Couldn't you tell me the code for the door?"

Another shake of the head. "It's a biometric control. Two-factor. The PIN is only one part."

"What else do I need?"

"My fingerprint."

Okay, not too bad. That's easily obtained without having to drag him with me.

"And before you get any ideas," he says, "it's got to be a *living* finger. Cutting off a digit and pressing it to the plate won't work. You can't cut a bit of a person, pluck out anything and expect it to work. Not like in those terrible movies where they do it."

"If I bring you with me," I ask, "Would you enter the PIN and put your finger on the panel?"

He laughs. "You expect to just walk free? What are you going to do? Where are you going to go? You're a wanted man."

"I can use you to clear my name."

He laughs even louder. "I'm not going to tell anyone anything. Not giving them access to my phone or computer.

"Where are you keeping Flick and Toby?" I ask.

He shakes his head. A sinister smile visible through the grainy image. "Sorry. I have no idea who you're talking about."

I look at his phone. It's asking for a fingerprint to unlock. There's gonna be something on here. Some kinda evidence. Some sign of where my family might be.

I get up and head for the door. Turn left and up the stairs.

A few seconds later I'm outside the room. There's a key on his keychain that looks like it'll fit. Sure enough, the door opens.

He charges at me. He's holding a splinter of wood like a knife, high in the air. It ain't how you come at someone who knows how to fight.

I step forward. The door swings closed behind me. I get up close and personal. He can't bring the hand down with the makeshift weapon.

I throw a hard punch at his face.

He hits the floor like a bad day's trading on the NYSE.

I get the shard of wood from next to him. I pick up the remaining bits. Nothing left for him to try to stick me with.

I grab his wrists and drag him closer to the bed.

I turn on the phone. Press the forefinger of his right hand against the fingerprint symbol on the phone. The thing unlocks on the second attempt.

I only know enough about these things to get by. I'm swiping around, opening apps, checking for anything useful.

The bank app is fingerprint protected. I reach down and use his finger without his permission again.

A whole chunk of money going in and out of a current account in the name of Lewis Preston. Doesn't tell me where it's going.

A secret folder. I use a finger for a third time. He groans a little.

I've got to be ready to knock him out again. Most of the time, folks only black out for a few seconds. Gotta be prepared.

Nothing but a few naked pictures of some bird in that part of his phone. Wouldn't surprise me if they're for some kinda blackmail.

I open the mapping app. Gonna check recent locations. Searches. That kinda thing.

But I don't get that far.

A sharp pain's come out of nowhere. Back of my left ankle.

Damn, it hurts.

I look down. Lewis is biting down hard on my left Achilles tendon.

I try to kick him. Hit him. Do something to dislodge that steel-like jaw of his.

Can't seem to shake him loose.

I try to stand up Tear my left foot away.

I scream out as the pain gets worse. One more hard yank of the foot and I'm free of him.

I turn around and give my right shoe leather a taste of his midriff.

He coughs. Sniffs. Coughs again. Wheezes a little.

"You're really not gonna help me?" I ask.

I take a couple of steps away from him. Towards the large windows and the balcony. My left ankle hurts like hell. Can hardly put my weight on it.

He shifts until he's on his hands and knees.

I want something outta the guy. I guess I should be polite and let him get up.

Problem is, he ain't getting to his feet to concede defeat.

Before he's upright, he's running at me.

I duck into the chair, fixed to the floor. The way he charges at me, I can reach down, grab his legs, pivot so I can throw him over my shoulder with his own momentum.

I launch him behind me like he's barely there.

He crashes through the glass door. Comes to a sudden, bleeding stop on the balcony.

I look at him. Barely moving.

I look at the door. Single-paned glass. Easy to break with some effort. Could've maybe been a way out when I was stuck in here earlier.

I stand up. Look over the severely injured man who keeps trying to hurt me. He's got small cuts all over his face and hands. He's getting up again. Doesn't know when he's lost.

I limp backwards a couple of steps. I wanna stay as far from that balcony as I can. There's gotta be a decent drop the other side of it.

Lewis is starting to slip on the balcony floor on his own blood. He reaches out. Steadies himself on the door frame, but shoves his hand against another shard of glass.

He lets out a cry of pain. Hunches a little. Maybe lets out a couple of feeling-sorry-for-himself tears.

He shakes the sorrow out of his head. Stands up straight. Glares at me.

It's a menacing expression when mixed with the blood dripping down his face.

I gotta say, the kid's tougher than he looked. Maybe not strong, but tough.

He walks back through the glass and goes to climb over the chair.

I run at him. Pretty much launch myself at his centre mass.

He flies backwards. I fall, stomach first, into the chair.

Takes me a few seconds to be able to fill my lungs again.

I get up.

No menacing guy charging at me. Not even staring at me.

There's only two bloodied hands, holding onto the railing from the wrong side. The grip in his left's slipping. His right tenses and he loosens and reattaches the left. Does the same for the right a moment later. It's gotta be tough holding on with injured hands. They're spilling out a pretty capable lubricant.

He ain't got the upper body strength to get himself up and over again.

I hobble over. Peer over the edge.

A straight drop into the quarry pit. A pool of water, could be deep or shallow, at the bottom. If he falls, he's got a good chance of hitting the sides on the way down.

I see the face of Lewis. Panicked. Pleading.

In a moment, the face is different. Stephen Sutherland's staring up at me. Wanting me to save him.

But it ain't him. He's long gone. My stupid guilt-ridden brain's not gonna let me forget it.

I reach to grab him by a wrist. He pulls his arm away. "No!" his shout's in a strained voice. "I don't want you saving me! I can't owe you anything!"

I go for his arm again. "We can both get outta here."

"No!" He closes his eyes and shakes his head.

I reach for the other wrist. He claws at me with his free

hand. He can't get a grip on the railing with it anymore.

"Let me help you!" I shout. "We can figure everything else out later."

"No!"

I reach for him again. He's wriggling, doing whatever he can to make this as difficult as possible for me. I grab his shirt.

I start to pull towards me. My feet slip a little, but I get my grip again.

"You're not getting out of here," he says. "No matter what you do, *someone* will come after you. Your family too. Watch your back, Enoch Flint!"

I wanna say he's wrong. That this can end like a Hollywood movie. He'll help me get free. He'll lead me to my family. I can help him cut some sort of deal. Bring down the rest of VIRTUS. Or if he's the lone wolf I think he might be, to hand over the reins.

I've lifted him a good couple of feet. He can get a decent hold on the railing now.

But he's not doing it. He's letting me do all the work. I can't lift him up and over by myself.

"You need to grab on to something!" I shout down.

No reply. Not a verbal one, anyway.

He grabs onto my arms with his. About time he did something.

He lifts himself up until his head's level with my hands.

The shirt's starting to rip. We're running out of time.

Just as I think he's gonna do something helpful, he ain't that helpful anymore.

He bites down hard on my hands.

Those stupid steel-like jaws are cutting into my flesh, my tendons. The pain's shooting through my nervous system.

I try to resist the reflex action where my hands get themselves out of the way of the pain. I try, but I fail.

My hand spasms open. The other one's not got enough of a grip. The shirt falls away.

He lets go of my arms.

He's free-falling.

The face has changed again. Stephen Sutherland, the innocent DC. Lost him last time out. He's again staring back at me, pleading, but knowing I can do nothing for him.

I turn and move away from the balcony.

I can't watch that face fall away and die a second time.

Whatever comes of him now, I can't help him.

He can't help me, either. Those fingers are joining his stupid jaws at the bottom of that quarry.

49. GET IN, GET IN, GET OUT

My easy ticket outta here just disappeared down a huge hole.

All I've got is an unlocked phone and a lotta nothing.

I limp back inside.

Gotta wonder why the guy would let himself fall to his death instead of living and helping me. I guess he must've had his reasons.

Maybe he ain't the head of this snake. Maybe VIRTUS goes further. He could've been their UK rep. Could've faced all kindsa heat if he let me go. Maybe he would've traded a watery grave for a shallow one.

Either way, I'm limping back to that computer. Try a few random passwords. What's the harm?

Takes me maybe four times longer to get back. I unlock the door. Close it behind me.

Head down the corridor with all the grace of a dog that's been run over.

A flight of stairs going down's easier than going up would've been. Gotta be grateful for that, at least.

Still takes me two attempts to find the right room again.

The computer screen's glowing. Begging me to find a way in and review all its lovely files.

I sit down. Take his phone outta my pocket and put it on the edge of the desk.

A message pops up on the computer screen.

Something about a proximity setting. How having his phone

nearby's the same as putting in a password.

I click OK. The thing unlocks. Security beaten, like it's a magician's padlock.

I throw my hands up in triumph. I beat the stupid computer.

First thing I do is open settings and change sleep settings. It's one of the little things I've learned how to do. Gotta stop every new computer from turning off every thirty seconds. That gets pretty irritating. I set it to go to sleep after about an hour. Might give the law the chance to come and take a look.

There's a folder with my name against it. Videos. Documents. Photographs. All sorts of information. Could be enough to clear me. I'll let someone else figure that out.

My mission's to find out where he's been hiding my family.

The next thing I find's a whole long list of bank statements. A current account in the name of Lewis Preston. A lotta incomings and outgoings. Some serious sums of money, always in the tens of thousands, moving back and forth every few days. Can't see where it's come from or where it's going to.

Some weird circle at the bottom's his web browser. It's still open on online banking for that same account. It's got a balance of three hundred grand. Would be nice to find a new home for that much cash.

I stop with the computer. I hunt through a couple of desk drawers.

A USB thumb drive. An IT geek looked like he was in pain last time I called it a memory stick. You wanna see a computer nerd squirm? Use the wrong technical words on purpose. Even if they keep a straight face, there'll be a vein bulging somewhere around their neck.

It's got a label and a word in marker pen.

CRYPTO

I stick it in my pocket, in case it's worth something, someday. When I can find someone who can tell me what it's got on it.

Even heading back to the computer, I've got no leads on where Flick and Toby might be.

Gonna start resigning to the idea I'm never gonna see them again. They could already be dead. Could've been dead for days.

Still, the computer's done with spilling Lewis's secrets. His phone had nothing useful, either.

I stick the phone back in my pocket and I head down the stairs.

That big steel door's gotta be my exit route.

I turn right. Find a desk. Flip it over. Wrestle with it until a leg's come free.

I return to the door.

With a few steps run-up, I launch the desk leg at the number panel.

The thing explodes with a spark and some smoke.

Broken plastic flies around more than I'd have thought.

Two wires at the back of that thing. Enough to provide power. Nothing else.

Did this panel do nothing?

Is it even possible to get out of this door?

Did he seal us both in? Some nut with welding equipment can be a dangerous thing.

I hit the area where the door should meet some kinda frame. I keep hitting it.

Nothing but tiny pieces of concrete flying off.

I take a closer look at the edges of the door. No daylight coming in. Either it's a really good seal around the door, or this thing hasn't been openable for years.

I've wasted enough time on this.

I need to find another way out.

I grab the keys again. The car key remotely unlocks something. If I press that and listen hard, I could figure out how he got himself in and out of this building.

I press it.

Nothing.

I wander around as close to the outside wall as I can get.

Another press.

Nothing.

I keep going. Twenty, thirty steps and then another go.

It's gotta be at least the tenth time of trying when there's a beep.

I frown a little. Couldn't hear it that clearly through such thick concrete walls.

Tucked away are boxes and bits built onto the inside of this cavernous structure.

I press the button again. The sound's coming from inside a box room to my left.

There's a frosted window next to a cheap wooden door.

The door's no match for my foot. It swings like it's trying to fly away south for the winter, but it's caught on something.

Through the doorway, there it is. Americans would call it an SUV. Folks here might call it a four-by-four. Not sure what the number sixteen's got to do with cars. I'd never asked. It's large. It's a sparkling, emerald green thing. Looks the kinda vehicle you might wanna hide away from people.

The other side of it's a roller door. The size of a standard domestic garage door.

I'm looking around for buttons. Something that's gonna make it open.

Still finding a whole lotta nothing.

The bunch of keys are missing a remote opener.

I get in the car and search around. No garage door opener here, either.

Gotta remind myself the police are on their way. I ain't got time to find a clean way out of here. If I wanna save my family, I can't be caught up. Can't end up in police custody. Waiting for someone to put a thousand pieces together.

I get in the car and I search for a place to shove the key. There isn't one.

There's a start/stop button next to the steering column. I press it and the thing comes to life. Lights up like the bridge of a starship.

I put it in first and I slam my foot on the accelerator pedal.

The thing flies forward. Comes to an abrupt stop.

I lurch forward a little. Sit back. Slam the thing into reverse.

I head backwards until the wall behind me's a distant

memory. Gives me a good run-up for smashing my way out.

I shove it in first again. I floor it.

Tyres complain against the concrete floor.

The car hits the garage door. The thing bends and flies in a few directions.

The car keeps going.

That ain't always a good thing.

There's a chain-link fence ahead of me.

The other side of that? A hell of a drop into the quarry.

Gotta bring this thing to a quick stop, or I'm joining Lewis at the bottom.

50. A PROBLEM TO ADDRESS

The phone in my pocket starts ringing.

Can't answer now. I'm about to fall to my death. Leave a message and I'll likely never get back to you.

My foot's hard on the brakes. The couple of tons of car keep sliding forward on a gravel-type surface.

Of all the ways I could've gone out of this world, I didn't predict this one.

Death's been after me for years. Trouble is, every time he gets to me, his scythe needs a sharpen.

This time, the fence does a better job than I'm expecting. Not a perfect job, but better than it could've been.

The car smashes about halfway through. The tension in the hundreds of wires of steel absorb some of the impact. Sends it back like it's trying to be a vertical trampoline.

I'm sent back towards the building. I'm pressing pedals. I'm moving the steering wheel. Nothing's doing anything just yet.

After a hair-raising few seconds, the vehicle's stopped. I'm facing something that looks like an access road. I've no clue how I've managed it, but I'm free of the building, and still very much alive.

My heart's thundering so loud it drowns out the phone.

I close my eyes. Take a couple of slow, deep breaths.

The phone starts ringing again. I answer it.

"You found a way out of the building yet?" It's Holly Chamberlain.

"Yeah, I have now. Any clues where I should be going?"

"Away from there's a start. You've only got a couple more minutes before some people show up. They're gonna want to arrest everyone in the building. You haven't got the time."

"Preaching to the choir," I say.

I put my foot down. I get out of dodge like I'm fleeing an active lava flow.

I put the phone on speaker. I turn the sound all the way up. Throw it on the passenger seat. "You still hear me?" I shout.

"Yeah, Flint," she says.

I get a couple of tiny roads behind me before she speaks again.

"The guy who's been holding you. He's called Lewis Preston. He's running VIRTUS operations in the UK, as far as we can tell."

I nod. "I figured that much out. Any known addresses?"

"One," she says. "We already tried it. No one there."

"You've gotta help me here, Holly. I've got to find my family. This guy was the only one who knew where they were."

"Wait, *was* the only one? Where is he?"

"He kinda fell into the quarry pit. Quite a drop, by the looks of it. I tried to help him, but some folks don't wanna be saved."

Silence for a moment. Maybe my best bet for finding Flick and Toby was MI5 interrogation.

"We've got people digging up more data all the time," she says. "They're sure to find something."

"What else have you found out?" I ask.

"Scams aplenty over the years. All over the world. He's even conned money out of heads of state and leaders of countries. Promises election victories. Extremist uprisings on command. Rises in sales for some dodgy businesses. The spread of misinformation to benefit whoever the client is."

"He ever deliver on any of those promises?"

"Not by the looks of it. He's just taken the money and run."

"Then maybe VIRTUS is just another scam," I say.

"You might be right."

"He got any family?" I ask.

"Parents died a few years ago, according to the file. People are still looking into it."

I turn at the end of a small road. I join a larger one. Maybe a hundred yards after turning right, a glance in my rear-view tells me I got out just in time. Cop cans are heading down that small road like there's a free ice cream stand at the end of it.

All I've got to do right now is keep on driving.

Sooner or later, MI5 are gonna find where my family are hiding.

Just got to avoid capture long enough to show up when they do.

***

"Can't we have him cleared yet?" DI Chamberlain asks.

A shake of the head from Agent Hall. "Not until the evidence clears him. The agents on scene are finding promising things on that computer, but it's gonna take a while."

She sighs. Shakes her head. It's like talking to a tall, dark, handsome brick wall.

She starts doing the rounds again. Desk to desk. What do they know? Can it help Flint?

The first few have financial details. They're not gonna help much.

Someone's looking into the parents. Sure enough, they died a few years back. No doubt there.

Someone's looking for Preston's car. Thing is, Flint's probably in it. Someone should reassign them to something more useful.

Another team's been busy picking apart that video. Discrediting it. Getting some data solutions companies no one's ever heard of to go public about it. They're getting somewhere, but it ain't helping Flint in the short-term.

She's reached the end of the desks. Nowhere further forward. How can that be?

She turns around. Heads back again.

The family history agent's waving his arm in the air. She heads on over.

"I think I've got something," she says. She's a thin, pretty little thing. Dark hair. Not the type people would associate with such nerdy work. But times are changing. Gotta expect folks who look like anything to do pretty much anything.

"His father, John Preston's house." She brings up a photo.

Holly nods. "Yes, so what?"

"According to the records, it's still being rented by him. The same lease agreement's been kept up all these years."

She brings up a document. Two signatures. Both deceased.

"Who's paying the bills?" she asks.

The girl shrugs. "I'm about to find out. I have a pretty good idea who it might be."

She thanks the girl and hurries away from the group.

She's back on the phone to Flint. This could be the missing piece of the puzzle. It could just be where Flint's luck starts to turn.

51. IT'S HARD BEING KEPT APARTMENT

Sure, it's a fancy apartment block. But could you say it's worth a million? That's what I'm told.

Back in the day, this place was on the edge of London. Forgotten. Forlorn.

But something's got this place cleaned up and respectable. Redo some cladding on the outside. Refurbish the apartments. Make the entrance look like some kinda hotel lobby. The place is sparkling. Maybe that what folks pay the money for these days.

John Preston didn't pay much for it. He bought it back when the area wasn't worth more than the change in your pocket. You could say he was a visionary guy. Knew the area was going places. Else, he was lucky.

This place was bought when the second highest floor was a disadvantage. John Preston still thought it was right for him. So many stairs when the elevators ain't working. The way this place would've been, that was gonna be most of the time.

The argument with the chain link fence hasn't helped Lewis's car. No doubt the thing's seen better days. It ain't too bad, but a whole loada scratches and dents on the bodywork draw attention in the capital. Not the kind of car where you'd throw your keys to the valet and ask them to be careful parking it up.

I ditch it a couple of streets away. I keep the keys, even though I don't want to. Nice to have the option of a quick getaway if things head south.

I head on in through revolving doors. The kind that start

moving all by themselves when you step inside. Fancy.

I get out the other side. I'm greeted by a high ceiling. Crystal light fittings. Pink granite tiled floor with an unnatural level of shine.

No seats to take a load off. No soft music playing. No bar off to the side. Maybe they're all on the to do list. Stuff that can be done when they wanna jack up the apartment prices a little more.

I head across the pool of granite. I do my best to hide the limp. My best's nowhere near good enough.

There's a concierge desk near two brass elevators. Back in the day, the guy behind it would've been called a caretaker. They stuck a suit on him. Gave him next to no more training. Called him something fancier. Whatever works.

I resist the urge to go up to him. Ask how much for caviar and a call girl. He might be in a suit, but he's still gonna be better at dealing with a blocked toilet.

I take one of the elevators. The doors open. Mirrors on every side. Clean and clear. A brass hand rail around three sides. A thick, dark red carpet underfoot. Dark walnut panelling. I look at the control panel. I hit the button for floor twenty.

Above it, I'm being warned this thing's built for no more than eight people. Those eight people would have to really like each other to squeeze in so close. If it wasn't for the fancy décor in here, they could maybe fit in a ninth.

The doors slide open with elegant smoothness.

Ahead, a hallway shared by six apartments on this floor.

I need 2004. An odd-looking number. Gives the wrong idea of the amount of people living here.

Part of me thinks there should've been an armed guard outside the door. I'm pretty delighted to be wrong.

None of the keys work.

Makes me wonder what he did with the key for this place. Who'd he give it to? Why?

Is there someone keeping the hostages company? Keeping them quiet?

I put my right hand over the peephole and knock with my left.

I stand back. The doors look a little fancy, but a good kick's still gonna put one in.

Turns out, I don't need to.

It unlocks. Starts to open.

They put one of those tiny safety chains on. They can peer out, but nothing bigger than a hand's getting in.

There's an eye peering at me. It grows a little wider.

The door starts to close again.

Now's time for the big boot.

I step back. Take one, two steps towards the door. Raise my right leg. I stomp on that door with all the anger burning away inside me.

The chain snaps. The guy behind the door staggers backwards.

I'm in.

He swings a wide fist at me when I step into the apartment hallway. I dodge it and use his momentum against him. Plant a quick couple of punches to the ribs.

The fight scenes on TV are a little different to real life. You see carefully choreographed punches. Kung Fu kicks. The works. Nice, neat stuff. Real fights have more biting, hair pulling, scratching of skin and eyeballs, kicks to the groin. There are no rules in fights like this. All that counts is the person who's standing at the end of it.

I stick a knee to his groin. He's pretty much my height. The kind who goes to the gym but has never quite got the muscle they wanted out of it. Lean. Fast. A little weak.

He hunches over a little. I yank his hair with one hand. Punch him in the face with the other.

He's taken about all the punishment he can take. He's gonna fall to the floor if I let go.

I oblige.

I ain't looking as he slides down the wall.

I'm moving forward, checking room after room.

Bathroom clear.

Kitchen too.

Bedroom one is empty.

Bedroom two as well.

Library? They've got a room for that? A little snooty. Anyway. Clear of people too.

I'm running out of rooms.

Dining area, nothing.

Lounge... two people. Blindfolded. Gagged. Zip ties around their wrists. One's a lot smaller than the other.

I hurry over. Tear off the blindfolds. Take away the gags.

Flick and Toby are still alive. They're a little shocked to see me. Happy as well, I guess.

But we don't have time for the happy-ending hugs and tears. We've gotta get out. Get clear of here.

I lead them out the door and down the hall.

In a minute or two, we'll be free of this place. All safe. All finished.

But then a fist hits the left side of my face hard enough to spoil my happy ending.

52. GOTTA STAY SHARP, FLINT

Turns out, the lean guy can throw a punch.

Feels like he was winding that one up for two days before he let fly.

I hit the floor.

Flick and Toby back away.

He moves a little closer.

He lifts a foot. Gonna lay a boot into me. But he's too slow with his legs.

I spin around and do a sweeping kick to the knee of his standing leg.

Something snaps.

He hits the floor. Cries out something that might make sense to someone.

We run for the elevator. Problem is, two of them, serving over one hundred apartments, means a hell of a wait.

But we can wait.

It should take a guy like that a minute or two to even think about standing up.

It would take a tough guy another minute to decide to pretty much hop on out to take me on again.

I look at the panels above them two lifts. One's on the thirteenth floor. The other's on the seventh. Either could make it up here first.

The number thirteen's counting down. Twelve. Eleven.

They're heading for the ground. That ain't gonna be here first.

The number seven goes up as far as twelve. Stops for an age. Starts going down again.

I sure as hell hope one of these things hurries up. I ain't got the legs for the stairs. Not with my ankle the way it is.

We've already been waiting here way too long.

A door opens behind us.

Sure enough, the lean, wannabe tough guy with a fist like a mallet is standing there. Well, he's leaning against the door frame.

His left leg's a mess. Not even close to being straight.

"You should get that looked at," I say, pointing.

He doesn't look impressed.

He's pressing against the wall. Almost hopping on his one good leg.

He's edging closer.

I look at the elevator situation. Eleventh floor and climbing. Twelfth. Thirteenth. Fourteenth.

This is ours. We've had our turn waiting. We're getting in this box whether the guy likes it or not.

But he's edging closer. He's got some momentum going now. He's in a rhythm. Don't know what he thinks he's gonna do when he reaches us.

The elevator reaches us. Squeaks a little as it slows.

The doors slide open with a shrill sound that could be the gates of hell swinging open.

He's getting closer as we hurry inside. Press ourselves against the far wall. I'm closest the button panel.

I'm doing the press-the-button-many-times thing. It's never hurried up an elevator and it never will. Doesn't stop me, though.

He does a kinda hopping jump and makes it just the other side of the doors before he falls over.

He's using his left arm to push himself up and drag himself along the floor.

His right arm is searching for something in a pocket.

He pulls out a flick knife. Blade's gotta be close to four inches long.

He puts his right foot to the floor and drags himself up using the outer frame of the elevator.

He's gonna be inside any second.

The doors start to close.

He sticks a hand in the way.

They keep closing for longer than they should.

All this fancy work in doing up the place, someone's not changed the safety bumpers.

They spring backward with a clang and the doors stop. Then they open again.

He tries to jump for me, knife out ready.

He only just makes it to our side of the sliding doors.

I step forward and push him. Both hands against his chest.

He falls backwards, but the knife blade slices into my arm.

One thing you've gotta know about fighting a guy with a

knife. Whatever you do, you've got a pretty good chance of getting stabbed or cut somewhere. You've gotta decide. Where can you take it? How can you make the best of it?

He falls backward.

The doors start to close again, but they're stopped by a trailing foot. They clamp his foot for a moment before letting go. They open again.

He turns himself around. A pathetic, whimpering mess of a person on the floor. Shoves out the hand with the knife. He's barely made it as far as the doors.

They start to close again.

This time, they close on his fingers.

Any second, they're gonna react and the doors are gonna spring open again.

This time, they don't. The door seems to think having fingers stuck inside is just fine and dandy.

The guy's screaming again.

We start moving down.

The sound of fingers snapping echoes around the small space.

He's still up there. But as the numbers count down. His bloody fingers, and the knife, are still our side of the sliding doors.

Flick's covering Toby's eyes. No doubt he's already seen too much to be scarred by all this.

Flick's also crying. Stifling a scream. Doing what she can to keep it together.

We get all the way to the ground floor without anyone else trying to get on. A good job, really, They wouldn't have liked what they saw.

I pick up the knife. Better to be protected by something than by nothing.

We head out the doors. Make a run for the exit.

We clear the revolving door.

I hand Flick the keys.

"The car's round the corner. Big, green thing. You'll see it when you hit the unlock button." My leg gives way for a moment. The left ankle's complaining. "I'll be right behind you, but you can get the car started while I make my way over."

She nods. Takes the keys. Takes maybe three or four steps.

Then it happens.

Someone to my left comes up. I don't see him until he's on top of me. Hits me. Calls me a low-life. Calls me murdering scum.

I wanna shout out, "Any chance you've seen me on the news?" but the voice has gone.

He smashes my hand against the ground. Something skids out.

The knife.

A second or two later, there's a dreadful, piercing pain in my stomach. Another in my side.

There are screams. Probably from Flick and Toby.

There's a guy running away and almost being hit by a car.

There's a guy on the floor, bleeding out. Wishing life

could've gone just a little different.

The other rule about knife fights springs to mind too late.

Most folks who take a knife into a fight get stabbed by their own weapon.

Now I'm lying here, another bloody statistic.

"Go!" I shout at Flick. "Get outta here! I'll find you!"

"Flint!" she screams. "No! I can't leave you!"

"The police are coming," I say in a weaker voice than I might have thought. "They'll get me the help I need."

She doesn't move. She stands there, looking on in horror.

Maybe it's even worse than it feels.

"Go!" I shout again. "Get Toby out of here!"

She looks down at him like she forgot he was there. She grabs his hand and they run off in the direction of the car.

I watch them go as long as I can.

I can't be certain I'll ever see them again.

53. ONLY WAY TO LIVE UP TO EXPECTATIONS IS TO DIE A HERO

Inspector Holly Chamberlain's been many things in her police career.

Child minder hasn't been one of them. Not until today.

She looking after Toby Parsons. The kid's the closest she'll ever get to Flint again.

There are similarities. Some features she recognises. He's got the hairline. The smile.

What kinda kid's he gonna grow up to be? He gonna be the type to cause the police daily problems? The sort that never put a toe out of line?

Living the rest of his life without a father's got to be tough. He's already spent enough time without one. But kids are resilient. She's been told that a few times. But how resilient? Surely absent parents invite problems. There's a hole to be filled, and they're gonna find something to fill it. Too many have done it with strangers online. Drug dealers. Anyone who acts all patriarchal before they take advantage.

It might not be long before Flick returns.

A burned-out house is no place for a kid. He's better off in the hotel room. Their temporary home until they can sort their life out.

She's checking the place out. Hunting through the remains. Looking for any keepsakes from their old life. Reminders of a nearly happy time they had together.

She gets the call she's been expecting. Finally. All clear.

Flick returns. Just as she hangs up the phone.

"That was work," Holly says. "Flint has officially been exonerated. Cleared of all the charges against him."

She looks at the floor. Shakes her head. "Fat lot of good it does now, though."

"It makes a difference though. He died a serving police officer. That means something to you and to Toby."

"Means a little more money?" Flick asks. "Who gives a damn about the money?"

Holly nods. Finds something else to look at. Anything's gonna do.

"It's not just the money," she says after an awkward silence. "He'll be remembered. Honoured every year on his birthday. I've arranged it. A minute's silence."

Flick just shakes her head. "It's not gonna bring him back."

Holly shakes her head too. "No, it won't. It's a big loss. For you, certainly, but he's a big loss to me too." She hadn't expected she'd get so close to tears. Doesn't happen often. "I grew to care for him. I mean, he was a complete pain in the backside to manage."

Flick laughs through the tears. "Don't I know it?!"

They sit on the edge of a bed. Smiles and tears keep trading places.

They share stories about Flint. How he drove them nuts. How he made up for it again. How, all round, he was a decent guy.

If nothing else, they're digging up some pretty decent stuff. Could be a good memorial service.

Holly pauses. Looks back at Toby. She can only think one thing.

Damn you, Flint. Why did you have to die?

54. ONCE MORE FLINT, FOR ME

Flint's office came out of the fire okay, all things considered. Sure, the roof caved in, but some stuff in the desk drawers, in that beaten up filing cabinet somehow survived. No passport, though, No birth certificate. Maybe that vanished years ago.

The stuff Flick found in the house is added to a box of things he'd left behind at work. She's not got a clue what to do with any of it. Probably nothing. It'll sit in some corner until she's got the heart to go through it.

Photos of the two of them. Another framed photo of all three.

A trip to the seaside, just a few miles down the road. That was a good day. The cone of chips they shared. The ice cream. The building of the craziest, biggest sandcastle. Letting Toby bury him up to his neck in sand.

He was always up to his neck in something.

She shakes her head.

But he always found a way out of it.

So many tokens of commiseration from his colleagues. Like her, they somehow thought he was immune. That the bullets, the knives, every weapon would keep sailing on by and miss Flint. Except he wasn't unbreakable. Not really.

Some would call it luck. So many brushes with death. So many survived. But it wasn't good luck. Certainly not. All it meant is each case brought another barrel-load of guilt for him to cart around.

Still, he's gone the way of his old mentor. Same place as his former partner. Maybe he can hang out with them, in the great wherever. Joke around. Chew the fat about police stuff again. Talk about all the stuff that once seemed so important.

But what's important now?

This mystery organisation he was chasing seems to have dropped off the earth. No sign of his ex-wife, still. Maybe she's living happily with someone else. She could be living unhappily. It would make little difference to her.

The house next to the park was the dream. Growing old together. Watching their son go through every stage of life. Watch him grow up to be the kind of man Flint would be proud of.

That's her job now. All on her own. Again.

The house is a symbol of life with Flint. You try to build something nice from the bits and pieces of your life. You make progress. You're moving in the right direction. Then something comes along and burns it all to the ground.

They got a nice picture of Flint for the memorial. So many people had nice things to say about him. Too bad they couldn't have said them when he was alive. When he was accused. When he was being hunted.

She shrugs. Might not have made a difference in the end.

The man she loved was always close to death. One day or another, he was gonna get too close. But at least his death meant something. He gave himself up for them. Died setting them free. If he'd done nothing else to show his love for the two of them, that would've been enough.

She's holding the order of service. Flint's smiling back at her. Only at her.

"Come on, Flint," she says to herself with a tear in her eye. "You've come back from the dead before. You've beaten the odds. Do it one more time, for me."

She puts the order of service back on the small table in the hotel room.

It won't be long before they get to build a new life.

It just ain't the life she wanted.

Not anymore.

***

A man grips tightly at the armrests of the plane as it touches down.

He's never been keen on flying.

No matter how much he does it, somehow it never gets easier.

Not that anything's easy right now.

Not when you've got to leave your life behind and start again.

It ain't easy getting those closest to you to think you're dead. It takes some serious cash, and some medical people willing to be bought.

Doesn't take away the hurt, though. That's gonna stay. Lying to the people you love most in the world. But it's necessary. They're always gonna have a target on their back as long as he's doing what he does.

Thankfully, the VIRTUS money he transferred was more than enough.

He ain't sure what they buried in that cemetery, but it sure as hell wasn't Enoch Flint.

That's me, stepping off a plane at LAX. Only hand luggage. No chance of anyone sneaking anything in there. Drugs. Explosives. Body parts.

There's still about half a million left in the kitty after the new ID documents.

Not enough to buy a house out here. Prices even in the rough areas are crazy money.

Might be enough to set up for myself, though. Find out a little about my mother's side of the family. Her parents. Some siblings. Aunts and uncles. It's decades since I heard from them.

Would be nice to find some family out here somewhere.

Anyhow, this town's had its share of private detectives. The pushing-their-nose-in kind. Always there when there's anything worth investigating.

Maybe there's room for one more.

Simon Whitfield

FLINT WILL RETURN SOON AS HE ATTEMPTS TO SOLVE AN IMPOSSIBLE MURDER IN LOS ANGELES.

ABOUT THE AUTHOR

Simon Whitfield has previously written under the pseudonym Will Thurston. This is his sixth novel.

Simon works in an office in a less-than-perfect building with a sea view, when he's not working and writing in his home office (which is actually a renovated caravan). He lives in Suffolk with his wife and two adopted children (and a dog), and longs for the day he can write full-time. He may eventually have his own website and social media stuff, in his own name.

Blog and social media details are below, along with an email address for feedback from readers.

Website: https://simonwhitfield.uk/

Twitter: @willbthurston

Instagram: whitfield_author

Facebook: www.facebook.com/simonwhitfieldauthor

BOOKS BY WILL THURSTON

THE REPLACEMENT PHENOMENON

Jake Hingham gets his wish to rewind time to save his brutally murdered little family. When time continues to unwind he seeks to find out why, and to trace the events that led to the death of his wife and two boys.

THE TALENT SCOUT

Brian Townley must save his brainchild, the Talent Scout, from falling into the wrong hands. A device that can detect natural abilities in anyone's DNA could be used for good or evil. Will he survive the fight against organised crime to protect his research and his prototype?

THE DOLL COLLECTOR

When PI Dan Castle gets a message that his teenage daughter has been captured, he embarks on a rescue mission in which he hopes to find and bring the Doll Collector to justice. His chase through the disturbing underworld of child abuse could save more lives than one, but can he save his own daughter before it's too late?

DEATH BY CHAPTERS

Sam agrees to be the protagonist in Larry Llewellyn's next gruesome novel. She knows the character will die, but has the man's killing spree merely been confined to the printed page? Horrible truths suggest otherwise, and now she must find a way to stay alive.

ENOCH FLINT INVESTIGATIONS

1. **The Departure Lounge (2023)** – Flint investigates a murder which becomes apparent when body parts show up in holidaymakers' luggage all over the world, but is there something bigger about to go down?

2. **The Dark Isles (2024)** – Flint is hired to find a missing person, but uncovers a series of murders that are designed to push the island community to its limits. Can he find and stop the killer before they strike again?

3. **Breaks Like Flint (2024)** – Flint must succumb to the whims of a secret organisation to find his family. Can he track them down, against huge odds, before it's too late to save them?

4. **Dead Ahead (Due 2025)** – Flint is called in to investigate a murder that happens in slow-moving traffic. How does someone get shot when there's no one else in the car, and the windows are undamaged? What will it lead to?

Printed in Great Britain
by Amazon